# PRAISE FOR THE NOVELS OF KATE MOORE

"Kate Moore is a writer to treasure."
—Sabrina Jeffries, *New York Times* bestselling author

"A beautifully crafted love story that will melt your heart completely....
Moore writes with a lyric beauty that will leave no heart untouched."
—*Romantic Times*

"A desperate heroine, a determined hero, and a villain fixated on
vengeance interact beautifully in this intricate story of wicked schemes,
lies, and double-dealing, blissfully relieved with passion and lighthearted
humor. VERDICT: Moore has hit her stride with this marvelously rewarding
conclusion to her "Sons of Sin" trilogy. Fans will hope for more of Moore's
sinful delights to come."
—*Library Journal* (STARRED REVIEW)

"In addition to a fast-paced, exciting plot, Moore infuses the story with
snappy banter and a large dollop of speculation and lore...and she skillfully
whets readers' appetites for the final tale.
—*Booklist*

"Like Lorraine Heath, Moore draws on the Dickensian aspects of
London to enhance a story already filled with realistic characters and
pulse-pounding adventure. Moore is a talent to remember."
—*RT Book Reviews*

"Very enjoyable."
—*San Francisco Book Review*

# The Husband Hunter's Guide to London

## Kate Moore

**LYRICAL PRESS**
Kensington Publishing Corp.
www.kensingtonbooks.com

Lyrical Press books are published by
Kensington Publishing Corp. 119 West 40th Street New York, NY 10018

All Kensington titles, imprints, and distributed lines are available at special quantity discounts for bulk purchases for sales promotion, premiums, fund-raising, and educational or institutional use.

To the extent that the image or images on the cover of this book depict a person or persons, such person or persons are merely models, and are not intended to portray any character or characters featured in the book.

Special book excerpts or customized printings can also be created to fit specific needs. For details, write or phone the office of the Kensington Special Sales Manager:
Kensington Publishing Corp.
119 West 40th Street
New York, NY 10018
Attn. Special Sales Department. Phone: 1-800-221-2647.

First Electronic Edition:
eISBN-13: 978-1-5161-0174-0
eISBN-10: 1-5161-0174-X

First Print Edition:
ISBN-13: 978-1-5161-0175-7
ISBN-10: 1-5161-0175-8

Printed in the United States of America

*For Sebastián and Elizabeth Jane—*
*the family's next generation of story lovers and storytellers.*
*You fill our days with the world re-imagined.*

# ACKNOWLEDGMENTS

*The Husband Hunter's Guide to London* has been great fun to write. I read many chapters aloud to the Mill Valley Library Drop-In Writers Group, and I'm grateful to my fellow writers for their feedback. My agent and editor offered their usual invaluable insight and commentary, and my husband kept me laughing and supplied with lattes. As always, Jane Austen inspires me to write about young women facing the expectation that they must and will marry no matter their own views on the subject. Austen's heroines have no "guide" to help them, so I wrote one in the spirit of their time and place, and put it in the hands of a heroine who finds London "foreign" after years of living abroad. To understand my heroine's experience, I consulted works by travelers of the Silk Road over the centuries. Spies like the hero and the heroine's father were very much a part of the time period when England and Russia were engaged in "The Great Game," to see which nation would control the land routes across Asia to India. Finally, I must acknowledge my parents, whose way of communicating past the censors in World War II led to my plot. Seventy-five years later, my mother still has the map they used. Any errors are my own.

*Every unmarried gentlewoman who comes to London for the Season must accept that finding a husband is the business of her life. Neither her family nor society offers any other honorable provision for her future. Therefore, until she forms an attachment with a man of respectable family, decent habits, and comfortable income, a sensible woman will make use of every available means to put herself in the way of eligible parties and will devote her time and her energies to determining who among them is both suitable for the purpose and susceptible to her charms. To waste even a single evening in idle flirtation or to pin one's hopes on unreasonable expectations is to risk no less a thing of lasting value than her own happiness. The purpose of this slim volume, then, is to guide the Husband Hunter through the perilous waters of the Season to the calm shores of wedded life.*

—*The Husband Hunter's Guide to London*

# Chapter One

Jane Fawkener looked up from the little blue book in her hands at the two solemn gentlemen seated opposite her in the office of her father's bank. The book's title in ornate gilt script must be a joke, a cruel joke. Surely, she had not journeyed a quarter of the way around the globe for news of her father only to receive the little blue volume.

She found it difficult to breathe, some pressure squeezing her chest, not just the unfamiliar stays. She had come to the bank straight from the Foreign Office where Lord Chartwell, the official in charge of the near East, had shared with her a letter her father had written to his cousin Teddy Walhouse. Chartwell had no letter for her. She had known better than to expect one from her father through such a compromised channel, but from her father's bankers, his most private and secure means of communication, she had expected a letter of her own. Not a book, and certainly not this book.

She turned the worn little volume over in her hands. "Marry? My father wants me to marry?" She tried to keep her voice steady.

Both men nodded with grave and awkward sympathy. She was unaccustomed to pale English faces, but she did not detect in either man any of the signs of duplicity or avarice her father had trained her to recognize, nor any of the indifference with which Lord Chartwell had met her inquiries earlier.

George Hammersley, the older gentleman, had blunt, sober features and black hair peppered with gray, while his son Frank had a youthful, open face in which the same features were softened and refined, but contracted by just a pinch of pain in the expression. The younger man leaned heavily on a cane whenever he stood.

She wondered what they made of her. She did not recognize herself in her borrowed mourning clothes. Before her ship docked, a pair of well-intentioned lady missionaries who had been in Greece to bring translations of the Bible to the warring factions there, had taken her aside and helped her to dress for her arrival in London. Today she wore her first stays, laced tight under three layers of petticoats, and a heavy black gown of a dull, stiff fabric. Her usual clothes, her loose pants and bright tunics, lay folded in her trunk.

George Hammersley cleared his throat. "Miss Fawkener, an entail of this sort is very common in England to keep an estate within a family, but your father's will does authorize us to provide two hundred pounds for your use until such time as you…marry."

Jane regarded the book in her hands. It could not be all that remained of her father. She could understand why he had not written to her through the Foreign Office, but she could not fathom why he had not sent her a direct message through his bankers. With what composure she could muster, she refrained from flinging the little book on the glowing fire in the grate. It surely deserved all the curses of Arabia.

*May you crumble into dust finer than the smallest grains of sand in the desert, may weary asses and camels grind you underfoot, and may the four winds blow the specks of you to the ends of the earth.*

Silently, she sent the curse into the fire-warmed air of the office, and wished it up the chimney flue and out into the sky. Her father was missing somewhere along the vast mysterious network of trade and intrigue from the Mediterranean to the Himalayas. The British Foreign Office, which had swooped her up from her father's house in Halab and hustled her onto a ship in Koron Harbor, now refused to help her discover his fate. Instead they promised to bestow upon her father a knighthood and a piece of shining silver that meant nothing. He would be *Sir* George Fawkener, *deceased*. Lord Chartwell had turned from her to the paperwork on his desk as if he had already forgotten the existence of her father and expected her to do the same.

But it was impossible to forget one had a father, that he had taught her Greek and Arabic and taken her with him everywhere, that he had been endlessly funny and energetic and reckless and brave, that he'd had crinkles around his clever blue eyes, did magic tricks with his big hands, and filled his pockets with almonds and pistachios.

She had been delayed at the dock while some customs matter was resolved, and while someone apparently searched her trunk. Her father's previous letters remained in her possession, but she recognized from the alteration in the ribbon with which they were tied, that the bundle had been opened. Someone in London was spying on her.

In those circumstances she had felt an unreasonable burst of hope a few moments earlier when the Hammersley's produced a brown-paper package from her father. Whatever he sent through them had escaped the scrutiny of his enemies. But all hope of a personal message from him had died when she unwrapped the little book. Her father had washed his hands of her. Her head felt like mush while her heart felt squeezed in her chest. She stared down at the little book lying on the voluminous folds of her black skirts.

A moment of dizziness overcame her. She was not at sea, not bobbing and dipping in an unsettled way over vast gray waters, but in the grip of an odd uneasiness that had started the moment she stepped off the ship.

The cursed book remained clutched in her hand. She was far from any desert where camels might trample it underfoot. She flipped it open, looking for a message, a word in her father's looping scrawl, but there was no inscription, no hint of his intention. There was, however, a map, folded inside the front cover, along the interior edge of the book's binding. She opened its folds, a map of London in watercolor pale greens, pinks, and browns with the great blue ribbon of the river, the Thames, snaking through it.

She straightened her spine. The map meant there was more to his message than the unexpected advice to marry. His bankers might believe him dead. The Foreign Office might believe it, but Jane refused to believe he was dead without confirmation. After all, he had only gone on one of the trips he had been making for the British government for nine years. He'd always come back before. She just had to figure out what he meant by leaving her the little guide. It had to be one of her father's games, a game she could learn to play.

She closed the book. When she looked up, the motion again triggered that feeling that she was at sea with her chair pitching under her like a rowboat in rough swells.

Frank Hammersley watched her face. "Miss Fawkener, the Foreign Office is sending a protocol officer to take charge of you, but as we are a little ahead of our time, may I bring you a restorative? A glass of wine, perhaps?"

She lifted a hand to refuse the wine, wishing she could refuse the Foreign Office functionary as well. A flock of questions stirred in her head, but the two earnest gentlemen across from her did not look the least bit ready to answer them. They both jumped at a light knock on the office door.

A striking young woman, with a merry face framed by glossy black ringlets, and figure that announced her to be with child, stopped abruptly midstride, looking abashed for interrupting.

"Oh, I beg your pardon. I didn't realize you two were with a client."

"Come in, Violet, my dear." The elder Mr. Hammersley hurried to her side as if she might escape. "You may be able to help us if Miss Fawkener is willing to share her circumstances with you. Miss, Fawkener, my daughter, Lady Violet Blackstone."

Smiling, Lady Violet turned to Jane and offered her hand. "Hello. Have these two bankers offended you, Miss Fawkener?"

Jane shook her head cautiously. "Not at all. It's merely that…"

Frank Hammersley chimed in, leaning on his cane. "It's merely that the subject of marriage came up, and two males found themselves of no help in the matter."

Lady Violet turned a bright, curious gaze on Jane. "Oh dear, how awkward for you. If you would feel more at ease talking with me, we could retire to my office. I have a friend with me at present. We were about to take tea, if you'd care to join us."

"You have an office here?" Jane could not help her surprise.

Lady Violet's eyes brightened. "I do, the privilege of being a banker's daughter. Shall we go? I'll call for some tea, or would you prefer wine?"

"Tea, thank you." She did not ask for coffee. The English did not drink it as she would at home from a copper pot hot off the fire with a rich sweet foam on top of the tiny cup.

"When you are refreshed, you may share as much as you like with me. I will treat anything you say in the strictest confidence, of course."

Frank Hammersley offered Jane his hand, and she rose, still clutching the book. "My sister will take good care of you, Miss Fawkener, and we'll look out for your visitor from the Foreign Office."

Jane thanked him and took her leave of the two gentlemen. She followed Lady Violet to another office, less grand and austere than the first, but with a businesslike desk in spite of some feminine touches. Seated on a small sofa was an elegant lady a few years older than Lady Violet, who introduced her friend as Her Grace the Duchess of Huntingdon.

The lady with the bright green eyes and Titian hair laughed. "Violet likes to announce my title, but believe me, I'm just her copper 'Penny' when we are having a heart-to-heart talk."

Lady Violet and Jane settled in pretty blue and white chinoiserie wing chairs, opposite the sofa, and Jane let the friends talk until tea arrived. Lady Violet made a face at a pair of round, flowered pots. "I'm afraid I'm only permitted herbal tea these days, Miss Fawkener, but you and Penny may have some of this lovely bohea."

With a steaming cup in her hands and under the influence of her new companions' easy manners, Jane found herself explaining her dependence on certain funds, which she could only obtain, according to her father's will, by marrying. She did not mention the Foreign Office's interference in her affairs. At the word *entail* both ladies shook their heads.

"And you find that you are not conveniently in love with some eligible gentleman?" The Duchess shook her head. "I'm afraid that puts you at the mercy of the London marriage mart." She spoke with a sympathetic frankness that warmed Jane as much as the tea.

"I admit I don't know the first thing about getting on in London, let alone finding a husband here. But surely a woman doesn't find a husband with a guidebook?" She hefted the little book in her hand.

Lady Violet raised one dark brow. "I suspect that many a miss would consume that volume quite eagerly. You've no enthusiasm for the hunt?"

"Only to know how fast it may be done," Jane confessed. Her throat ached in spite of the comforting tea. She needed money to search for her father, but marrying to gain money would mean accepting that her father was truly gone.

Lady Violet put down her tea. "All you have from your father is this guidebook? May I see it?"

Jane passed the book to her.

A tiny crease appeared on Lady Violet's brow as she opened the book and read its title page. Her eyes flashed with interest as if she were trying to solve a puzzle. "I wonder what your father was thinking, Miss Fawkener? Presumably, from your knowledge of his character, you can see some hint of his intention. We must assume that he has your best interest at heart, but even to acquire certain funds, a hasty marriage hardly seems the sort of thing a wise father would advise."

"But fathers rule, don't they?" Her grace commented with a wistful laugh. "In my experience a dead father's will has a powerful influence on a living daughter's life." She looked embarrassed at the strength of her opinion and turned to their hostess. "Violet, I really must take my leave and let you get to the bottom of this dear girl's situation with all the privacy you need. But"—she turned to Jane, her eyes alight now with mirth—"I can offer one service I know to be of value to the husband hunter—an invitation to one of my Thursday evening gatherings. You may depend on me in this matter, Miss Fawkener."

Lady Violet saw her friend out. Jane heard their parting laughter and it struck her that the lady missionaries on board ship, who had lent her the proper clothes to wear, had not laughed. At the time Jane had not recognized the lack, but now she realized how strange it had been not to laugh.

Lady Violet returned and settled in the blue chair, refreshing both their cups of tea. "My friend, Penny, has a great deal of influence in the fashionable world, and I think you'll find her sincere in her offer."

Of one thing Jane was sure. If her father wanted her to have the book, and if he had used his bankers rather than the Foreign Office to get the book into her hands, she needed to find its hidden meaning. Once her world stopped rocking unreasonably, she would study the cursed book again.

After a moment of silent contemplation, Lady Violet spoke. "Miss Fawkener, whatever you decide, your confidences are safe with me, but tell me, what are your immediate plans?"

"I've been advised to take rooms at Mivart's Hotel."

"You do not go to your family then?" Lady Violet did not conceal her surprise.

"None opened their doors." It was one of the difficulties of Jane's situation. She had no *wasta* as her neighbors in Halab would call it, no person in a position of influence to support her cause. The English consul in Halab had simply turned her over to the Foreign Office, and no one there wished to do a thing for her father.

Lady Violet made a sympathetic murmur. "Mivart's costs can be quite steep. You'll need additional funds. Have you any?"

"You think my two hundred pounds will not permit a hotel stay of any length?"

Violet looked grave for the first time in their conversation. "It might get you through months of frugal living in London, but it will last less than a fortnight at Mivart's. The hotel will charge you for each bag a footman carries, the number of coals on your fire, and who knows what else."

"I see." Jane set down her tea. The hotel would consume the money she needed to launch the search for her father.

"Do not despair." Violet reached out and gave Jane's hand a squeeze. "As your bankers, we would be remiss if we did not help you reduce your expenses. You must have time in which to decide the future partner of your life. We also have the resources to...how shall I say it...investigate any gentleman not fully known to your family. Now, what may I do for you straightaway? I'm afraid you've been taken here and there, subjected to our government's high-handedness, when what you most need is time to restore your powers."

An aching lump rose in Jane's throat at the unexpected kindness. "Thank you. I'd like to go to the hotel, if I may."

"Of course." Lady Violet stood. "You may wait to thank me, for I must warn you I can be of no very great help should you wish to pursue a match as *The Husband Hunter's Guide* recommends. In the eyes of polite society, as a *banker's* daughter, I've trespassed on exalted territory in marrying Lord Blackstone, a peer. I've only escaped total censure because Blackstone himself was considered too scandalous and too impoverished for a noble bride."

Jane watched her companion. The lady's eyes sparkled happily. "Of course, I suspect that sometimes, the least eligible gentlemen make the most remarkable husbands."

*The man you want to marry wishes to become a husband in time. That is to say, he, like the famous sinners of the past, wishes to repent of the follies and excesses of his youth, after he has fully enjoyed them and not before. The title "husband" has such a settled air of gravity and responsibility about it that young men do not rush to acquire it with the same eagerness with which they seek to become captains or majors in the army, commanders in the navy, or nonpareils of the sporting set. Therefore, you must consider the length of time a gentleman has been on the town and seek to learn from his acquaintance or his reputation whether he has acquired the dashing titles he once sought and is now disposed to seek the very title you alone can confer.*

—The Husband Hunter's Guide to London

# Chapter Two

Edmund Dalby, Viscount Hazelwood, stirred as a particularly heavy dray rumbled past, shaking the carriage from which he watched the white portico of Hammersley's Bank. He had chosen to remain in the carriage across the pavement from the bank to await his quarry in relative warmth. London was currently experiencing Arctic temperatures, and he saw no sense in congealing into a block of ice before the appointed time. Jane Fawkener had entered the bank not thirty minutes earlier. No one appeared to be following her, except himself.

Outside the carriage, clouds roiled overhead in a dull pewter sky. The pavements glistened from a brief downpour, more ice than rain. A penetrating wind came up off the river, and blew the sooty smoke of chimney pots away in long black plumes. Rows of pillars and columns glared self-importantly at one another across the narrow street in the heart of London's banking district, competing in dignity, oblivious to the more modest commerce of hawkers on the pavement.

Hazelwood contemplated his new and unexpected assignment—playing nursemaid and guardian to Jane Fawkener. It would be his last assignment for the spies. Nearly a year earlier, he'd been recruited by Samuel Goldsworthy, a shaggy giant of a man with the solidity of a craggy red bluff of rock jutting out of a mossy bank.

Years after the long war with Bonaparte, England was now engaged in an unspoken conflict with Russia for influence over the vast territory from the Crimea to Afghanistan. At the moment, it was a war of spies rather than soldiers, and the inscrutable Goldsworthy was the Foreign Office's chief recruiter of gentleman spies.

Hazelwood couldn't say why he'd taken Goldsworthy's offer in that moment, why he'd turned his back on the path to ruin he'd been cheerfully pursuing since his father, the Earl of Vange, had disinherited him in his twenty-fifth year, but he hadn't regretted it.

One day Hazelwood had been playing *vingt-et-un* in a dismal sponging house to earn his keep, and the next, he'd been lounging in the elegant coffee room of Goldsworthy's Pantheon Club accepting the attentions of its very competent staff. The terms of the agreement meant that he lived in Goldsworthy's club with his fellow spies, Lord Blackstone and Captain Clare, and that in return for a year and day of service as a government spy, all his debts would be paid.

Hazelwood liked the club, with its good coffee, clean sheets, and excellent tailor. He liked his fellow spies, Blackstone and Clare. They'd had some blood-rousing adventures together in spite of the different spheres of London society to which each had been assigned. Blackstone, with his title and scandalous reputation as a womanizer, had been assigned to the ballrooms and bedrooms of the West End. Clare, with his hero's honors from Waterloo, roamed the public houses where old soldiers gathered to air their discontents. As for himself, his reputation for idle dissipation, had fitted him for work in the pleasure houses and gaming hells where young men squandered their fortunes and opened themselves to the temptations of foreign agents, like the wily Russian Count Malikov.

Hazelwood had seen little daylight in the months he'd been working for the government, but spying suited him, and he liked being sober. The ruse, of course, was that he was a regular tosspot, a four-bottle man. Kirby, the club's tailor, had contrived a series of claret-stained cravats, and waistcoats reeking of brandy that kept the objects of his scrutiny from noting his attention. In the eleven months he'd been a spy, no one seeing him in a brothel or a gaming hell had credited him with a brain unfuddled enough to take note of meetings, exchanges, or stray bits of conversation. As a result, he had intercepted a number of foreign office papers before they passed from English hands into Russian ones.

At midnight Goldsworthy had summoned him from a gaming hell where he'd been observing the downward slide of a young lordling whose brother's ties to the Foreign Office meant that the man was a potential target of Malikov and his followers.

Now Hazelwood wished for cotton stuffing for his ears. The din of working day London, of horses, wheels on stone, and hawkers shouting their wares was only slightly muffled in the carriage's interior. As he waited, his mind restlessly turned over the few facts he knew about the girl and her missing father.

Goldsworthy had handed him a year-old letter from George Fawkener to his cousin Teddy Walhouse, asking the cousin to look out for the girl if he did not return from his mission. And the man had in fact disappeared. The government had collected the girl from foreign parts and returned her to London, but the family had not taken her in as expected.

Goldsworthy, as usual, was sparing of the details of the father's fate, but he had told Hazelwood about the girl's insistence, against the odds, that her father was alive and that the government should be looking for him. Apparently, the Russians were quite interested in what the girl knew about her father's travels. Any papers in her possession were up for grabs.

Hazelwood understood what Goldsworthy wasn't saying. The government had a problem. Some chit of girl knew more than she should about government secrets. The Foreign Office had told her a convenient lie about her missing father, and she had turned the tables on them. She might even know what her father had been up to. Hazelwood's job was clear—keep the girl from falling into the enemy's hands.

He had formed no plan as yet for winning her confidence. He was to introduce himself as the protocol officer assigned to her case to see her through the investiture ceremony in which the king would bestow a posthumous knighthood on her father. It went without saying that she should not suspect him of spying. Though how he would get much out of her through a discussion of a brief public ritual, he did not know. Even a half-wit could learn to kneel on a red velvet cushion and back away from His Royal Highness on cue.

A sharp rap on the carriage door brought his thoughts back to the present. The youth he'd employed to keep an eye out for his quarry opened the door and announced, "Look alive, Guv, the lady in black's come out of the bank."

Hazelwood grabbed his hat and slipped from the carriage to the pavement. Letting the girl go about London unprotected was not the plan. The Hammersleys knew he was expected, so what was going on? He told the driver to walk the horses, and set off across the pavement, dodging vehicles, and keeping his eye on the party standing at the columned entrance to the bank.

There was no mistaking old George Hammersley or his son, Frank, and daughter, Violet, now the wife of Hazelwood's friend and fellow spy, Blackstone. The unfamiliar figure in the group was a woman in severe and matronly mourning dress with one hand resting on the elder Hammersley's arm. Hazelwood observed her as she stood poised at the top of the bank steps. An ugly brown bonnet with a deep coal scuttle poke hid her face, and the overlarge black gown with its skirts dragging on the wet stones concealed most of her shape. Not a beauty, apparently.

The little group paused as Hazelwood reached the bottom of the wide steps. Clearly, the Hammersley's didn't realize the danger to which they were exposing the girl. Hazelwood glanced up, intending to catch Violet's gaze, when the lady in black swayed as if the ground under her had shifted. She started to crumple, and sliding from her companion's grasp, pitched forward into the air.

Instinctively, Hazelwood stepped forward. *Well then, Miss Fawkener, aren't you the lucky one! Instead of falling into the enemy's arms, just fall into mine.*

Down she came with a flutter of skirts, like a shot bird with slack wings. With a grunt, Hazelwood staggered back as he bore the impact of her unconscious form. His hat tumbled from his head, and he found himself clasping to his chest the first fully clothed female body he'd held in his arms in more than a year. The clothes had deceived him. The girl was light and limp as a straw effigy, and encased in what felt to be a set of stays akin to medieval armor.

No wonder she had passed out.

Her head lolled back over his arm, and the bonnet fell from her face, hanging by its black ribbons from her white throat. He looked down at the curve of a smooth cheek, straight dark lashes, and thick glossy hair, as dark as winter fields. Her heavy hair had been gathered at her nape, not been teased into frothy curls about her face as was the fashion. She had a strong face in profile, a high forehead and a long, straight nose with a slight bump in the middle that saved it from cold perfection. He loosened the girl's bonnet strings and shifted her in his hold, getting an arm under her knees.

"Where may I take her?" he asked Violet.

"My office. At once. I'm afraid she's had a shocking day."

"And she's laced as tight as the Exchequer's purse," Hazelwood muttered. He wondered, not for the first time, how women managed such ordinary activities as breathing with their lungs squeezed like a cheese in a press.

At Violet's command, doors opened and bank employees scurried.

In her office, Hazelwood set the unconscious girl on a low blue couch and rolled her to one side facing him. As he felt for the girl's pulse under her chin, he could hear Violet sending her brother and father away and ordering a restorative.

"Have you something sharp? Scissors?" he asked, reaching out.

Immediately, Violet slapped a bone-handled paper knife into his open palm. Hazelwood stuck the point of it inside the row of covered buttons up the girl's spine and popped them open. As he'd expected, she was trussed like a goose.

He slit through the knots of petticoats and stay laces at her waist and again applied the knife to the spiral of ties that held her plain muslin corset in place. When he pulled apart the sides of corset, the creased folds of her chemise stuck to the skin of her back. Whoever had helped the girl to dress apparently had all the fashion sense of a medieval torturer.

He rolled the girl onto her back and pulled the top half of the stiff black dress off her shoulders and down her arms. Her corset was remarkably ugly, almost as ugly as the gown, and he couldn't help but pull it away, too, exposing white shoulders and the rounded tops of her breasts, watching for rise and fall of her chest. He took one of her small hands in his and pulled off the glove, thinking to chafe her hand and perhaps restore her to consciousness that way. Her other hand clutched a small blue volume. Even in a swoon she had not relaxed her grip on the little book. He could not see the title, but he guessed its importance from her hold on the thing.

He warmed her free hand between his palms. His job was going to be easier than he'd thought. She was in his debt. He had merely to explain that he had been about to enter the bank for their appointment when she fainted. He was only too glad to be of assistance in the moment, and of course, ready to be of further assistance in the weeks ahead.

She did not stir. Her pale cheeks gave no sign of a blush. He did not recall seeing such perfect stillness in a female before. The unmarried girls he remembered from before his fall from grace had never been still. Their curls bounced, their eyelashes fluttered, and their bosoms rose intriguingly in a constant motion that drew the eye—at least it had always drawn his eye.

Jane Fawkener slept like a princess under a spell, and in her face Hazelwood saw not plainness but dignity, an untainted dignity that made him feel the weight of his dissolute years. He wondered briefly how the fairy-tale prince leaning over the sleeping beauty had dared to wake her with a kiss. Hazelwood had not been tempted to kiss a female, let alone a chaste maiden, in a very long time. But princes were a different lot altogether from wastrels like himself. It was their privilege to kiss a princess and claim her.

A quiet hand touched his shoulder, and he turned to look up at Violet.

"Hazelwood," she spoke softly, "how fortuitous for Miss Fawkener that you appeared on the scene."

"Not at all. I'm the protocol officer assigned to her."

Violet's dark brows knit in a little frown. "Ah, so this spontaneous gallantry is government-backed."

"Entirely." He smiled grimly. He had a job to do. He should be looking at the book in Jane Fawkener's hand, not at her face. "Why is she clutching a book, Violet?"

"It's a gift from her father."

With one hand Hazelwood pushed the slim volume up through the girl's fingers until he could read the title. *The Husband Hunter's Guide to London.* He straightened. The title brought him back from the realm of fantasy. The girl possessed no secret papers, no map of her father's journey, and she was not a princess after all, but a more common variety of female intent on marrying to advantage.

His jaw tightened, he knew the type and had once been their quarry. He glanced at Violet for an explanation. She merely shrugged. Her expression said she would not betray another woman.

"Miss Fawkener might not wish to wake with an unfamiliar protocol officer staring down at her in a state of undress. I suggest you leave us, and let me and my female assistants help her dress before you spring that bit of information on her."

"Right." He looked down at the sleeping maiden. He could not reconcile the solemn face with the light-minded pursuits of a London flirt. He should step back and let her awaken with a woman at her side, but he found himself reluctant to let go of the small hand before he received a sign of returning life. He uncurled the slack fingers in his and rested his thumb in her palm.

Violet spoke again. "You never know, my friend, with a sudden waking, the lady might fall in love with the first man she sees."

"Now that would be fatal for the aspiring husband hunter," he said briskly. "I'll let your father and brother know that she's under your care, but promise me you'll find her something decent to wear and burn this gown. And, Violet, I'd prefer to introduce myself, if I may."

Violet gave him a shrewd glance. "As you wish."

He nodded. He took the small hand and laid it gently on the sofa, and the girl exhaled a long, shaky breath. Her eyes fluttered open, and for brief moment a dark gleam of sharp intelligence met his gaze. The hand with the book clutched it tighter.

Her lips moved to form a "Thank you." Then with a flutter of those straight lashes, light as a leaf settling, the eyes closed again.

Hazelwood stood. It was nothing to disturb his peace, after all, a mere glance, nothing that should get in the way of his assignment. It was just that those eyes had been unexpectedly keen, not dazed at all, and he'd been caught gazing at her like a man starving for a kiss from a sleeping princess.

*One advantage I may claim for this little volume is that
it has been authored by a woman. You will have read in the
published lectures, sermons, tracts, and histories of mankind
entire catalogues of the follies and frailties of woman. The
world of letters apparently judges women to be the weaker sex
in intellect and character, as well as in body. Nonsense. Those
volumes were written by men. You may toss all the books ever
written by men on the subject of love or marriage into the
Thames, and they will not stem the tide, nor will those volumes
diminish by a single slur the real character and strength of a
woman.*

—The Husband Hunter's Guide to London

# Chapter Three

When Hazelwood next met Jane Fawkener, he was in command of himself again. There was nothing, after all, in a dazed girl's glance to trouble an experienced man about town. He took a minute to observe and approve the changes that Violet's help had wrought. Upright and clothed in a gown of burnished brown silk with pale color in her cheeks like the pink of morning clouds, the girl looked unexceptional, that is until she met his gaze, her eyes alive with that alert consciousness that looked far too perceptive for a man's comfort.

He sketched a quick bow to both ladies. "Miss Fawkener, permit me to introduce myself. I'm Hazelwood, your protocol officer, at your disposal to help you as you prepare for your father's investiture."

For a moment she didn't speak. She merely studied him with that shrewd assessing gaze. He felt her take note of the way his hair curled in a fashionable cut, the way his white linen cravat fell in an artful arrangement, the sheen of his gray silk waistcoat, and the high gloss of his boots. She seemed unaware of her own appearance as she assessed his. He knew what any Londoner would make of the blue coat and gray trousers the club's tailor had crafted for him, but Jane Fawkener had the look of a woman never taken in by flashy merchandise or a shiny bauble.

"Thank you for the offer of assistance, but I won't be needing a protocol officer." Her hands remained folded in her lap around the little blue volume.

Hazelwood glanced at Violet whose raised brows and lively eyes revealed her amusement at his situation.

"I will leave you two to settle your differences. Miss Fawkener, you have my full support whatever you decide to do." She smiled at them both and took her leave.

* * * *

Jane studied the government's protocol officer. There was nothing about him to suggest a mere...functionary. She guessed him to be thirty or so. He was taller and broader in the shoulders than she'd expected and carelessly handsome. His dark hair had deep fiery lights. He had straight brows, a strong blunt jaw, and a full mouth with a sensuous symmetry. There was far too much assurance in his laughing green eyes. She let her gaze drop. There was too much of him in general. She was unused to English dress. He wore no loose *salvar* pants, no robe or tunic. Instead the gray wool of his trousers clung to his legs, and his coat was cut in a way that concealed nothing of his maleness.

When she looked up again into his face and met his green gaze fixed on her, he returned her frank scrutiny in equal measure.

She took a moment to steady her hands in her lap and summon her wits. Her instinct said he was her adversary as much as any ruthless bandit bristling with weaponry, or any rapacious official whose palm must be pressed repeatedly with an astonishing amount of coin. She told herself that she had nothing to fear from him. He was not a devious khan who could snap his fingers and lock her up in a cave or order her limbs chopped off. Perhaps it had been unwise to faint in his arms, but she was on her guard now. Her muscles tensed, and her spine stiffened.

"Miss Fawkener," he began again, a note of patience in his low voice. He took a step closer. It was not a big step. There was still a distance between them, but his nearness warmed her like drawing near to a fire in the hearth on a cold night. His glance shifted as he apparently weighed a strategy of sitting next to or across from her. He chose the confrontational strategy of sitting across from her, on the couch where she'd lain earlier, and she looked away from the spot. "As you've not been in England for some time, allow me to assist you in these early days. I will answer any questions you have about the investiture ceremony itself and about London society in general."

"Thank you. I'm sure you mean well, Mr. Hazelwood—" She wasn't sure at all, but her father would advise trying a bit of honey before vinegar.

"—just Hazelwood."

She blinked at the correction, puzzled at the absence of the "mister." He did not enlighten her. His name, plain and unadorned, invited intimacy. A slight shiver passed over her. "Advising me in this matter would be a waste of your time and mine, as I do not intend to participate in a ceremony that does no honor to my father."

One of his brows arched upward. "The king might find it awkward to withdraw your father's nomination."

"The king will do whatever the king is inclined to do, I'm sure, but he will do so without my presence."

He made no reply, gave no indication that her refusal to participate in the sham ceremony had any effect on him. If anything he appeared amused by her declaration. He leaned back, his arms extended along the curved edge of the upholstery. She had a feeling that he had taken possession of the couch.

"If you wish to thank me for my small service in catching you earlier as you fell toward the rather unforgiving London pavement, now would be the perfect opportunity."

She straightened her shoulders. His change of topic was no less provoking than his earlier remarks. She could not recall fainting, ever. He pointed out her moment of weakness to gain the upper hand. She wanted to set him straight on that matter. He should not imagine her some sort of delicate bloom needing protection.

"I don't faint, you know. As a rule."

"But, as a rule, you don't wear stays tighter than an Elizabethan thumbscrew."

"How did you know… Oh…" Certain details of their previous encounter came back to her, and heat rose in her cheeks. She quelled the feeling. Blushing was another thing a woman of sense did not do. Clearly, he thought no more of taking charge of her clothing than he thought of taking over a couch. "My borrowed garments were lent me by some very godly women, so I'm sure they were no test of your virtue."

Like him, she wore English dress and no veil. She could not look out at him from behind the mesh screen of a *chadri*, her feelings hidden. He was deliberately trying to provoke her, testing for weaknesses, as any bandit would.

"You may not faint again, Miss Fawkener, but London society can trip the unwary in unexpected ways."

She lifted her chin. It was something her father might have said. One could dress almost any part, but a gesture, a turn of phrase, a missed conversational cue, or even the way she chose to take a seat could mark her as the outsider she was. She had not trained to be an English gentlewoman, yet she must look and act the part to prove that her father lived. "I will find trustworthy people to advise me."

"You have already found one in Lady Violet. Let me be another. I am at your disposal at no expense through the investiture ceremony."

There was just that note of sympathy in his voice that brought a lump to her throat as if he were intent on helping her. Then she shook her head. "As I told you…Hazelwood, I have no intention of participating in a ceremony that so wholly ignores the truth of my father's situation."

"It is *your* situation that concerns me. Do you wish me to take you to your family?"

Once again he came at her with the unexpected. Her father's family had no intention of taking her in. Her gaze dropped to his lap, which was a mistake, the stretch of fabric against muscle, one more sign of immodest English dress. Her hands tightened on the book she held.

"I wish to thank you and send you on your way."

"Ah, we are at an impasse, then. I'm afraid I'm not permitted to leave your side, Miss Fawkener, until the king himself drapes the bejeweled order of Saint Michael and Saint George around your fair neck and lets you back away from the royal presence, or until you pick a husband to take over in my stead. So, let us come to some agreement. Do you wish to become a husband hunter?"

He smiled that green-eyed smile at her. He seemed perfectly cordial. He carried no weapon that she could see. He had not come to their meeting with scimitar-wielding strongmen at his side, but she was not fooled. Though he asked her what she wished, he gave the orders.

She realized that clutching the little book in her lap signaled the importance she attached to it. That would never do. He had seen the book and no doubt read its title. The smart move would be to smile like a proper idiot, a swooning woman grasping a book, as if by magic the slim volume could produce a gentleman's proposal. Maybe playing along was her best strategy. With a sudden insight, she saw the book as the perfect disguise of her intentions. Perhaps that was her father's message. He was telling her to play a part, as he so often had on his journeys.

She met her adversary's gaze. "Do women *hunt* husbands in England?"

A flash of amusement lit his eyes. "Oh, they do. In all the parks, theatres, and ballrooms of London."

"Then, I shall, too."

With her announcement, his manner changed abruptly. His easy smile died. Stupidly, she missed that smile at once. She should not care that this stranger found her a source of amusement or contempt. If husband hunting deceived the government into believing she had abandoned her quest to rescue her father, she would do it. In time the government's spies would grow careless or be withdrawn all together. First, she had to deceive the man in front of her.

He stood and held out a hand to help her rise. She guessed that he was being polite. No man in Halab would offer his hand in public to a woman, but she was not in Halab, and it was likely that Hazelwood had never heard the saying, "Better to stab yourself in the hand than to touch a woman's hand." She hesitated only the briefest instant. She had to unlearn the habits of the past nine years. Her disguise depended on showing comfort with English ways. She took the hand he offered, and let him help her to her feet. Once again dizziness threatened, but his grasp held her steady.

She looked up and met his gaze. Shocking as it was to look so directly into a man's eyes, she sensed that she must show resistance, not submission, to gain any advantage with such a man.

"If it were merely a matter of the king himself, I'd put my blunt on you, Miss Fawkener," he said cordially. "But kings have ministers and minions, secretaries and chancellors, all of whom have a vested interest in bestowing the Order of Saint Michael and Saint George upon your father. You have no idea of the forces of government arrayed against you."

She recognized his words for the warning he intended. She didn't know why, but the government wanted her father to remain a dead hero.

\* \* \* \*

Hazelwood clearly meant every word he'd said about sticking by her side. He escorted her in the English manner from Lady Violet's office to a black coach crouched on the pavement below the bank steps. Taking a gentleman's arm was an unfamiliar act of public intimacy. It set them apart from others but bound them together. Hazelwood's nearness, his height, his distinctly masculine way of moving, and the strength of his arm, impressed themselves upon her senses. She feigned a degree of comfort she was far from feeling. Outside the bank, London washed over her again, a surging wave of noise and movement, pushed by a powerful cold wind, and stinking of brine and dung. It made her cling more tightly to his arm.

Hazelwood pulled her closer against his side. "Is your boat still rocking?"

She nodded. It was easier to admit that she had not yet shaken off the effects of the long sea voyage.

"Let's get you to your hotel then." He nudged her down the steps toward the black coach. In Halab she most often traveled by donkey. It was hard to imagine that the coach before her would hold a man of Hazelwood's height, let alone the two of them. A young man in a dun-colored coat and black top hat held the door open. A narrow iron step hung down.

She gripped Hazelwood's hand more tightly when she set her foot to the lowered stair. She ducked into the carriage, which tilted and righted itself again under her weight. She settled in the far corner of the front-facing leather seat and closed her eyes against the motion.

Hazelwood followed her in, setting the carriage dipping again. With one hand he pushed her sprawling skirts aside as he took the seat beside her. The stiff fabric brushed against her legs, and she realized she'd betrayed her ignorance of English ways by not subduing her unruly skirts. Hazelwood wore a fawn-colored wool coat with shoulder capes that brushed against her. Their garments touched with no respect for the strict propriety of Halab.

"Open your eyes when we get moving. The dizziness will pass," he said.

She nodded, keeping her hands folded around the book in her lap. She wanted to be alone to open it and study that map.

"When were you last in London?" he asked.

"Nearly ten years ago."

"And where have you been since?" He knocked on the carriage roof, and the driver set the vehicle in motion. Immediately she felt better, as if her head and body were no longer at odds with each other.

"In Halab. Do you know it?" She opened her eyes.

"Only as a dot on a map. There was an earthquake, wasn't there?"

"Four years ago."

"You'll find London strange, in contrast, I suspect." He leaned back against the seat and stretched out his legs, at ease.

"I do." She straightened and turned away, but really there was nowhere to look in the confines of the carriage that did not include him. She had not expected him to see London through her eyes. Her father would advise her to study him as she would any adversary.

"May I?" Hazelwood indicated the little book in her lap.

She glanced at him. His mouth was drawn in a line of distaste. Her instinct was to clutch the book protectively, but she opened her palms and let him take the thing in his hands. He thumbed to the table of contents. "You think this little book can bag you a husband?"

"Like a bird, you mean? I suspect the writer is not advising young women to aim firearms at prospective fiancés."

He laughed, and the sound of it, low, warm, and honest, seemed to vibrate in her, an effect that must be due to the close confines of the carriage.

"Nevertheless, Miss Fawkener, you must admit the writer's title suggests that women are in pursuit of a prize."

"An odd sort of prize, since it is the husband who will control his wife's fortune, her style of living, and her future." She had not thought of marrying in Halab, where fathers arranged such matters for their daughters. She wondered briefly if her father had thought of her marrying at all. They had laughed over the two offers he had received for her hand, and she had gone on with the routines of tending her father's house and aiding in his work. The husbands she had known in Halab were her adversaries in the souks, merchants who bargained hard, and men like Bilal, the camel trader, who always offered the weakest of his lot first, or Nisos, the Greek map dealer with the inflated prices. Dealing with them had sharpened her wits, but it had not inspired dreams of a husband.

"So, why do you wish to hunt a husband, Miss Fawkener?"

Too late Jane realized she'd revealed thoughts best concealed. She reached for the book. She wanted it back in her possession. "Do you dispute the writer's premise? Do you think that a woman in London has no need of a husband?" She might wish it were true, but she thought of her two hundred pounds. As long as she lived with her father, she'd had no need of money. Now that she was on her own, she had no source of it.

"I'll take the book, thank you." She put steel in her voice. She could not be sure that Hazelwood did not already suspect something about the book, and until she could examine the little volume thoroughly in the privacy of her own rooms, she must not let him get too close a look. She had no way of knowing in which part of the book her father might have concealed his true message to her.

She held her palm extended, waiting for Hazelwood to return her possession. There was no avoiding his gaze.

He watched her closely. "I suspect there would be fewer husband hunters if more women had bank balances in their favor." He placed the book in her hand. "Do you know what you're looking for in a husband, Miss Fawkener?"

She knew what she did not want—a man who would see through her and interfere with her plan to recover her father. She tried to think what Hazelwood expected an earnest husband hunter to say. "A man with connections, with a respectable name, and a decent income."

"That's setting the bar quite low. You don't require any distinction of person or character?"

"I suppose you think every maiden dreams of meeting a handsome prince."

He shook his head. "Not at all. In my experience princes are fat and dissolute with mistresses old enough to be your grandmother. But if you've so few requirements, we should be able to find you a husband in a fortnight. A ball here and there, an appearance or two in an opera box, maybe a few circuits of the park, and some fellow will fall to his knees in the accepted form and offer you his hand and a generous allowance."

That *we* bothered her. She might be seasick, or land-sick, or whatever it was that kept her feeling so unsettled, but she wasn't stupid, and she'd dealt with men trying to maneuver around her before. The Englishman was different in his tactics, but not his aim, after all. There was a word for his attitude. It was something her father would say. It would come to her in a moment.

Just as she became accustomed to the carriage with its ripple of movement over the cobbles like bumping over rapids in a mountain stream, it stopped.

Hazelwood's hand was on the door. "I'm sure when you open the book, you'll discover that the author recommends the services of a milliner and dressmaker before you level your weapon at a likely bird." He descended and held out his hand to her. "I'll collect you at ten tomorrow morning."

The word for his manner came to her then—*cheeky*. Her rescuer was a *cheeky* fellow, full of easy confidence that he could make things go his way.

"I think I'll read the book first."

*A brief word of caution is now in order. Upon arriving in London and beginning to go about in society, the Husband Hunter will observe many more gentlemen than she is used to seeing at home in her country town or village. Neither the village church nor the local assembly has likely ever drawn more than a few gentlemen into her orbit, while it is the nature of the great metropolis to draw men of all ranks and characters to mingle together seeking both prominence and pleasure as their individual characters direct them.*

*The Husband Hunter will not know at first glance which of these gentlemen has the respectable character she seeks. All may appear equally fashionable, equally polished in manner. Rather than descend into giddiness at the apparently limitless supply of gentlemen, she must develop the habit of listening carefully to a man's speech and discerning from it, his true character. Where there are any hints from his manner of speaking of that he may be at heart a scoundrel, she must take steps to find credible informants to further elucidate his character.*

—*The Husband Hunter's Guide to London*

# Chapter Four

When Hazelwood returned to the club, his fellow spies, Blackstone and Clare, stripped to their waists and wearing padded leather gloves, were sparring with words and fists at one end of the cavernous coffee room. Nate Wilde, the club's man of all work, was setting out a tray of sandwiches and liquid refreshments. Occasionally, Wilde offered a word of approval or advice to the pugilists.

Wilde, a youth in his early twenties, rescued from a life of crime nearly ten years earlier, had acquired the manners, accent, and above all, the wardrobe of a gentleman, though no fashionable gilding could hide the youth's rough compact build, his toothy grin, and pronounced ears. He made excellent coffee, knew London's streets intimately, and didn't hesitate to back up his gentlemen in a fight.

As sobriety was a club rule, the steaming punch Wilde set out would likely be made from tea, spices, and hot milk. Neither Hazelwood nor

Blackstone minded the ban on spirits, though Clare grumbled about it. The irony of Hazelwood's disguise in the past year had been that he'd been perfectly sober while wearing claret-stained cravats and waistcoats reeking of brandy. He liked being sober, liked a clear head and quick reflexes. He had willingly accepted the benefits of sobriety in spite of its less-visible disadvantages. Sustained sobriety was humbling. It tended to make a man acutely aware of past follies, misjudgments, and character failings.

His friends exchanged another flurry of blows before Blackstone got in a solid hit. Sweating and panting, the two opponents let Wilde remove their gloves and hand them towels.

Hazelwood helped himself to the punch while the other two toweled off. He was particularly fond of the club's coffee room with its high, curved ceiling, long comfortable sofas, and absence of feminine objects. He didn't have brothers, and his school friends had fallen away from him as his fortunes sank. In Blackstone and Clare he had new friends, men of keen intelligence and a proper appreciation of a good fight.

"Hazelwood, did you meet the girl?" Clare asked, picking up a mug of punch and wrinkling his nose over the steaming drink.

"What girl? A new case?" Blackstone toweled his head dry. "Has Goldsworthy removed you from night work?"

Hazelwood nodded. "The girl is the daughter of that agent that went missing."

"George Fawkener? Remind me where he disappeared." Blackstone tossed his towel aside and accepted a mug from the discreetly hovering Wilde.

"Somewhere between Kourdistan and Kabul."

"What happened to him?" Blackstone took his first taste of the drink.

Hazelwood lifted a brow. "You think Goldsworthy would tell? Fawkener was strangled, or beheaded, or tossed off a minaret in Bokhara. In any case, left for the birds and dogs."

"And the government has done what for the poor sod?" Clare asked.

The three friends looked at each other. They knew the answer to that one. Exactly nothing. The Foreign Office had a way of regarding lost agents as private travelers for whom no help or ransom could be offered. Two years earlier Blackstone had spent his personal fortune ransoming his half-brother and a dozen other captives from a Greek warlord.

Hazelwood felt a pang of sympathy for Jane Fawkener. Her father probably mattered to her. "The Foreign Office has arranged for his royal highness to bestow a posthumous knighthood on the dead hero."

Clare snorted and put down his drink in disgust. "Some consolation. A silver trinket in a velvet box."

Hazelwood stretched out on his favorite couch. "Ah no, my friend. There's to be a full investiture ceremony with bunting, a band, and royal personages. Fawkener's daughter is to receive the honor in her father's name. That's where I come in. I'm the protocol officer assigned to see the girl through the ceremony."

Clare saluted him. "Is she pretty?"

The question shouldn't throw him. It was the expected question after all. They had joked for a year about their mysterious benefactor and spymaster Goldsworthy having an ugly daughter tucked away somewhere that he planned to foist on one of them. But Hazelwood found he didn't quite know how to answer. Jane Fawkener wasn't pretty in the conventional sense, but he had wanted to wake her with a kiss, an odd impulse in a man of his experience.

Blackstone spoke up next. "More to the point, Hazelwood, why the government charade? Why does the Foreign Office want you to shadow the girl?"

Trust Blackstone to focus on the main point. Hazelwood took a pull on his mug of punch. "It's more a case of keeping British secrets from the enemy. Goldsworthy suspects they will try to get some papers off of her."

"No one entrusted dispatches to her, did they?" As a professional soldier, Clare hated it when the government used unreliable civilians for its business.

"Not at all, but the girl insists her father's alive, and she seems to know his route. In other words, she knows more than she should about the government's secrets."

They were silent a moment.

"So your real job is to keep her from falling into the enemy's hands." Blackstone was instantly grim. He knew from personal experience how dangerous England's enemies could be and how easily they could strike within London itself. "The Russians won't be kind."

*And we will be?* Hazelwood finished his punch. He meant to keep the girl from the Russians, but he doubted she'd appreciate his efforts. He couldn't be sure, but he suspected that he had pushed her into declaring her intention to become a husband hunter. After years of living abroad, she would have no idea what that meant.

Wilde picked up the mug Hazelwood had put aside, and Hazelwood had a thought. "Wilde, I could use your help with this one."

"My help, my lord?" The youth set down his tray.

"I'd like you to get a copy of this book for me tomorrow." Hazelwood found a pencil on the table and scrawled the title and publisher's name on

a two-day-old copy of the *Morning Chronicle*. "Go to as many booksellers
as you need to, but get it."

Wilde studied the scrap of paper, a dismayed expression on his face,
his ears reddening. "*The Husband Hunter's Guide to London*? But, Lord
Hazelwood, sir, you can't be serious. I can't ask for this book in…"

"Public? Afraid of a little humor at your expense, Wilde?"

"Sir, I'll be laughed out of every shop I enter."

"You could say it's for your sister."

"Don't 'ave a sister, my lord." Wilde's old accent slipped out
with his unease.

"I know what. Take Miranda with you. Tell her she'll be doing me a favor."

The youth's face changed instantly at the girl's name. Miranda Kirby
was the daughter of the club's in-house tailor. With her fiery hair, smooth
rosy cheeks, china-blue eyes, and lush figure, she possessed Wilde's heart.
Whether she would eventually return Wilde's admiration or not was the
subject of a wager between Hazelwood and Clare. Hazelwood was glad to
give the lad another opportunity to win the girl's affections.

"Yes, my lord. Tomorrow, my lord?"

"If you can manage it, Wilde."

As soon as the youth left the coffee room, Clare turned to Hazelwood.
"You'll set the whelp back," Clare grumbled. "He was making a good
recovery by staying away from Miranda for weeks."

Hazelwood shook his head. "He's not going to get over her, Clare, and
he needs all the help he can get."

"*The Husband Hunter's Guide to London*? Doesn't sound like your usual
reading, Hazelwood." Blackstone turned the discussion back to the case.

Hazelwood sat up and swung his feet to the floor. "Not in the least. But
tell me what you think. Fawkener used his bankers, the Hammersleys, to
deliver one thing to his daughter."

"This absurd book?" Clare asked.

"Exactly. And the girl holds on to the book as if it were the Holy Grail."

"So?" Blackstone raised a skeptical brow.

Hazelwood leaned forward. "I think that if her father wanted to get a
message to her without the idiots in the Foreign Office—"

"Or any spies—"

"—knowing what that message was, he'd send it through his bankers. We
all know the Hammersleys are skilled at codes and at getting information
across the continent."

Blackstone nodded. "And you're going after a second copy
of the book—why?"

"For comparison's sake. I want to know what's in it, so that when I get my hands on her copy, I can catch what's been added or altered."

"What do you think her father is trying to tell her?"

"That depends on how much she already knows." It would be Hazelwood's job to find out.

"Her father's probably trying to tell her to stay out of the spy business and get herself a husband as fast as she can," observed Clare, setting down his cup.

Hazelwood laughed. "Goldsworthy is working up a list of eligible young men."

"The girl's doomed then. Better all the matchmaking mamas of London than Goldsworthy. Does she have family? Does she have money?" Clare was on the girl's side for sure.

"Little money, I suspect." Hazelwood turned back to Blackstone. "Your banker wife will know."

"And Violet will never tell. But you think this Jane Fawkener knows that her father was a government agent and not merely a merchant?"

"No question about that, and she believes she can prove that he's alive. She seems to have information that differs from the government's account of things."

"Then what if someone else gets their hands on the book? The Russians will try."

"It will be time to break heads and throw bodies down stairwells. I expect you gentlemen are up for whatever it takes." Hazelwood grinned at his two friends. In the end, they'd be in it together.

\* \* \* \*

Nate Wilde passed through the bare garden in the back of the club and entered the rear of the tailor's shop. A long, narrow hallway led to the front of the shop, which faced a fashionable street and masqueraded as a chemist's establishment selling gentleman's toiletries—soaps and brushes, salves and pomades, toothpowders and scents. Though Kirby & Sons was the name on the door, there was no son, only a daughter—Miranda.

From the time he'd come to work at the club, Nate had been unable to resist the chemist's shop. One day he'd seized the biggest chance of his life to leave behind his childhood in a notorious London rookery, and the next he'd met Miranda Kirby, and discovered how powerful a hold the most insignificant things could have on a man's mind, things like chestnut curls against a white throat and the swell of a silk-covered bosom.

He closed the rear door behind him. Coming in the back way meant that no shop bell jingled, so Miranda had no warning of his approach. He liked to catch her at her work and tease her about it afterward. She waited on gentlemen who were in awe of her beauty, or she helped her father with the fitting and measuring of the spies for their disguises. Miranda regarded every gentleman who came through the door as a potential husband, a man who could make her a lady, not a shopgirl.

He paused on his side of the crimson velvet curtains that separated the hall from the shop to listen for the presence of a customer. Miranda had a story she liked to tell her gentlemen clients about her French mother as a child escaping from the Revolution in spite of the silver buckles on her shoes. She believed that her mother had named her Miranda like a duke's daughter in a play to remind her of her lofty origins. Nate was pretty sure that she'd had an Irish mother who'd come to London and got herself in trouble until old Mr. Kirby rescued her.

Still his Miranda was shrewd and alert, so she readily sorted out unlikely candidates for her plan of becoming Lady Somebody, but her shrewdness did not protect her from Hazelwood. The disgraced viscount with his easy charm and laughing eyes appeared to Miranda as hers to claim. To her way of thinking, no lady of his own class wanted him, so he was hers, like some rich cake sent back to the kitchen because the lofty guests had already had their fill.

Yesterday she had been thrilled to hear that Hazelwood's new assignment meant no more stained and stinking clothes. She had been beside her father as he fitted the viscount for his new clothes.

Nate heard no voices, so he pushed aside the curtain and entered the shop. Miranda looked up from her needlework, something fine and silken with small covered buttons, most likely a waistcoat for Hazelwood. She wore fingerless gloves with a blue woolen shawl draped over her shoulders.

"You could use a brazier of coal," he observed. He could see his breath in the shop.

"Did you bring one then?"

"Easily managed."

"No need. I'll close up soon for tea."

With a quick pump of his arms, he boosted himself up to sit on the broad marble-topped counter. He wanted to show her that he'd healed from the injury to his collarbone, and he liked to look down at her. She tilted her head when she worked. Her left ear peeked out from her burnished curls, and the slight rounded curve of her breast rose above her lace tucker. Today her skin was very white against the blue wool of the shawl. Usually, he could not detect her scent in the competing odors of the shop—the citrus, bergamot, and lavender of the soaps and pomades, the rosewater of various lotions, and the cloves and cinnamon of toothpowders, or the peppermint of lozenges. But today Miranda was the only warm thing in the shop, and she smelled like the almond milk lotion she used on her skin.

"Make yourself at home, then."

"I am home." In the spring, he'd been beaten and tossed for dead by a pair of hired fists in Wapping when he'd come too close to their lair on a case. Since then he'd spent some time away from the club with his grand friends in their fine London houses. The time away was supposed to cure him of his attachment to Miranda. "The shop is club premises, isn't it?"

"What makes you idle then? No one needs you on the other side?"

He shook his head. "I've been given a commission to get something relevant to the latest case." He liked using big words to describe the jobs they gave him.

She shot him a suspicious glance. "So you can get yourself knocked senseless again?"

He shook his head. "Not a chance with this assignment. You could go with me."

"Go with you? The places you go? Hah!"

"Not this time. You would have to dress as a lady, if you wanted to come."

"As if I don't always." She gave a haughty toss of her head that set the curls bouncing.

He concealed a grin at having riled her. With her eye for detail, she always dressed like the real ladies he knew—his friends' wives, Cleo Jones and Helen Jones, and the grandest lady of them all, the Marchioness of Daventry. Miranda just never talked the way those ladies did; no she sounded more like the women of Bread Street where he'd spent his early days.

"You think I want to be seen with you?" He noted that she hadn't turned him down yet.

"You might. I've been asked to go around to some booksellers."

"Booksellers?"

"For a book."

He could almost hear her calculating little brain spinning, like a turnspit dog racing to keep the roast from burning. She'd be thinking of the great bookshops—Hatchard's and Lackington's—and he'd take her to those places first, and hope that they wouldn't need to comb the rubbishy bins outside the used book dealers on Holywell Street. He didn't want to take her to his old haunts.

"What sort of book could possibly help solve a case?" His Miranda didn't lack for wits.

"You won't believe it." He pulled the newspaper with Lord Hazelwood's scrawl from inside his coat. He felt foolish even reading the title to her. He cleared his throat. *"The Husband Hunter's Guide to London."*

She shot him a skeptical glance. "You're bamming me. How is such a book to help one of our gentlemen catch a spy?"

He pushed off the counter. He admired her brains, but he didn't want her getting too smart on him. "They think the book contains a code, like that Spanish bank note I showed you last spring."

"They?" she asked. "Whose case is it?" She put aside her needlework and slid from her stool. "It's Lord Hazelwood's new case, isn't it?" Her eyes lit up.

He nodded, momentarily distracted by the effect of her quick movement on her bosom.

"Of course I'll go with you. When do we go?" She bounced a little on her toes, and a very distracting motion ensued. Nate's privy member, not his brain, took note.

"Tomorrow morning." He swallowed hard. He'd won and lost simultaneously. He'd have hours of time with her while she thought about her viscount. It was full dark and bitterly cold when he passed from the back of the shop to the club again.

* * * *

Clive Walhouse leaned against the gold-flocked wall of a discreet gaming establishment in Cleveland Row admiring Lady Pamela Ravenhurst as she placed her bets at the faro table. The eager gleam in Lady Pamela's violet eyes and the candlelight gilding the half moons of her breasts rising from the dark blue velvet of her gown stirred his cock to a pleasant state of anticipation. He had no trouble imagining how Pamela's capacity for losing herself in play would translate into wanton abandonment in bed, or even in the closed carriage, which would convey them from the club later in the evening.

She played recklessly, as she did when her marital frustrations were driving her. At nineteen she had married a man fifteen years her senior, whose interest in the minutiae of foreign policy was profound enough to close all of Argus's famed one hundred eyes. Clive had heard it said in the Foreign Office that Ravenhurst slept more often with his red dispatch box than with his wife. Nevertheless, in seven years of marriage Lady Pamela had produced three credible replicas of her husband and was now apparently free to pursue her own interests. Clive would be her first, her liberator from the toils of the marriage bed.

He raised a glass of the house's very tolerable claret in a silent toast. He owed it all to his father's dead cousin George Fawkener. *Rest in peace, cousin.*

A stir at the door of the card room drew his gaze from Pamela's charms. Clive's friends, Lutrell and Archer, had arrived with Count Malikov and the usual group of young blades that surrounded the Russian émigré. Lutrell and Archer headed straight for Clive while Malikov, ever attentive to the ladies, bowed over the hand of the club's hostess in her purple gown and turban.

"Walhouse, you sly dog," Archer began. "I thought you were out of the game, up to your frayed collars in debt."

Clive came away from the wall and shook his friends' hands. "Never count the Walhouses out, my friends. We always come about." He signaled a waiter to bring the drinks tray.

"Must have been a very rich cousin who popped off, Walhouse." Lutrell accepted a glass from the waiter. "I saw your esteemed pater in Tattersall's Thursday dropping his blunt on a pair of showy grays."

"A baron must be seen to live like a baron, my friends." Clive tipped his glass to theirs. It was his father's chief principle of money management. Theodore Walhouse, Baron Strayde—Teddy to his friends—had run through his own inheritance long before Clive was out of short coats, and had subsequently worked his way through his wife's fortune as well.

From across the room Pamela caught Clive's gaze and smiled an intimate smile at him. Their exchange of glances was not lost on his two friends. Gentlemen inclined to wager on such things as a married woman's first lover had put their money on his rivals. Clive enjoyed the satisfaction of knowing that tonight those bets were lost.

"Now that you've stolen the fair Pamela from under our noses, Walhouse, the least you could do is stake us to a *rouleau* for the EO table. Each," Archer suggested.

"Of course." Clive had no objections. With his father enjoying George Fawkener's vast fortune, Clive at last had an allowance that permitted him to live like a gentleman and not a mere clerk. He offered Archer a fat wad of notes, and when the two friends went in search of the EO table, Clive resumed his study of Lady Pamela's bosom.

Since his university years he had been *poor* Walhouse, the butt of jokes, the one fellow in his circle of friends with barely enough money to scrape by from one quarter to the next. Poverty had ultimately obliged him to take a job in the Foreign Office as an undersecretary to Lord Chartwell. It was the sort of position for which he had been told to feel grateful as the son of a titled but impoverished gentleman. Clive, however, had been unable to summon much gratitude for a position that required piles of tedious work and a degree of anonymity that grated on his sense of himself. He had ideas. He wished to be heard. But no one solicited his opinion or imagined that he had one.

He had chafed under the burden of mounting debts, which arose not from extravagance, but simply from the effort to live as a gentleman in London, and he resented the duns that gathered on the family doorstep. His father only gave a helpless shrug at the duns and pointed out that Clive had been provided with a fine education and could make his own way in the world. "And besides," his father had added, tossing a scrap of paper at him, "Fawkener may die, and with the entail I'll inherit his bloody fortune."

The words on that paper started Clive thinking how handy it would be if his father's cousin Fawkener, on assignment for the Foreign Office in some benighted place of sunbaked camel dung and feuding warlords, would die. From that moment Clive had taken an interest in George Fawkener's career. Clive supposed he would have gone on toiling for Chartwell and hoping for news of Fawkener's demise except for Lady Pamela. One night at an endless musicale while watching Lady Pamela slide her fan along the thigh of the scandalous Lord Blackstone, Clive had confessed his hopeless infatuation to Malikov. His career frustrations and his family's appalling dependence on an inheritance that might never come got mixed into his account of the folly of Lord Chartwell.

His Russian friend reminded him to be patient and offered the comfort of the old saying that—*Graveyards are full of indispensable men.* The sympathetic count further suggested a way that Clive could earn some money while he waited for George Fawkener's inevitable demise. If Clive were willing, he could help Malikov shape a more favorable political climate for himself back in Russia.

After that, Clive's job had become easy and profitable. It was nothing to slip a letter here, or a document there to a man Malikov knew in return for the allowance Clive's father could not provide. Almost at once he had been able to enter the competition for Lady Pamela's favors, and he had seen what even Malikov missed, a way to the lady's heart. And now with Fawkener's death, Clive had resigned his post under Chartwell. He could at last live as a gentleman with no need to work or to sell scraps of paper. And he had Pamela.

He smiled as Malikov at last headed his way. Though Clive no longer helped his friend directly, they remained on good terms. Really, it was impossible to be at odds with the affable Russian. Malikov moved in the first ranks of London society and knew nearly everyone connected with the Foreign Office. He had come to England at the end of the long war with Napoleon and found it convenient to remain. With his easy manners and tall, fair good looks he was invited everywhere. Tonight the count's apparent good humor left Clive unprepared for the sober face that looked into his when his friend approached.

"You've had bad news about the situation in St. Petersburg?" Clive asked, straightening from the wall.

"Not at all, my friend." Malikov glanced at Lady Pamela. "You've won the fair lady, I hear."

Clive permitted himself a grin.

Malikov gave him a congratulatory thump on the shoulder. "I knew you'd be the one, no matter the odds in the clubs. You'll make her happy."

The count studied him rather earnestly.

"But you didn't come to congratulate me, did you?"

Malikov looked down into his drink, giving the wine a swirl in the glass. He shook his head. "Ah, no. My news concerns you, my friend. Nothing, perhaps to be too alarmed about, but nevertheless, a prudent man…" The count glanced around the room as if they might be overheard, but there was no chance of that.

Clive saw that Pamela was absorbed in the game and that the pile of chits in front of her was still sufficient for her to continue playing. "Tell me."

"Your cousin's daughter has returned to England."

"Her return was to be expected, wasn't it?" He studied the count's face and found it surprisingly blank, devoid of its usual sympathetic warmth. "Jane Fawkener inherits next to nothing, a thousand pounds at most."

"It's not the immediate loss that should concern you."

"What then? She has no legal recourse, has she?"

"She's gone to the Foreign Office."

Clive swallowed a substantial mouthful of claret. Malikov was making him uneasy, and he suspected the man enjoyed it. "Well, then I think my family has nothing to fear. We all know the level of confusion and error that reigns in that department."

Malikov laughed, though Clive noted a distinct lack of warmth in the sound.

"Jane Fawkener claims to have proof that her father is alive."

"Alive?"

Malikov watched him carefully.

Clive felt his self-command was just equal to that scrutiny. "Unlikely, isn't it? And the Foreign Office will hardly act on some waif's hopes." He took another swallow of his wine.

Malikov's glance shifted to Pamela. "You're right, of course. I mention it only because apparently the Foreign Office tried to pass her off to your family, and your mother declined to take her in."

"You think we should?"

Malikov shrugged. "It is up to you to protect your own interests, of course, but in your shoes, I'd want the girl where I could keep a close watch on her."

Clive got the hint. Malikov was putting him on his guard, offering him a way of dealing with the situation. His parents were hopeless. They would go on spending, without heeding the threat the girl posed and without making any provision to hold on to what George Fawkener's death had won them all. His sisters and younger brother who had not yet felt the worst effects of the family's spending habits would now suffer. Clive was the one who would have to do something. He would have to seek out this Jane Fawkener, discover her secrets, and make sure her father stayed dead.

Pamela gave a laugh of delight and leaned forward to receive a pile of chips. Clive promised himself that he would not let anything or anyone keep him from enjoying what he had won.

*The Husband Hunter must be seen, and therefore, must take great care of her appearance. This attention to appearance is not vanity but an effort to present her best self wherever she goes. The first element of her appearance is color. The Husband Hunter needs to draw from a consistent color palette flattering to her complexion. The second element of her appearance is fashion. The Husband Hunter must take care neither to be in the vanguard of fashion, dressed in styles that will pass before the Season ends, nor in the arrears of fashion in clothes that suggest more her mother's youth than her own. To this end a reliable dressmaker and a friend with a discerning eye are invaluable aids.*

—*The Husband Hunter's Guide to London*

# Chapter Five

Jane stood at the hotel window, the little blue book in her hands, trying to compose a suitably shriveling curse for a government functionary with an irritating sense of command. The world outside the glass was an uninspiring gray from the leaden clouds above to the damp cobbles below. She did not wish Hazelwood ill health or a tragic fate, but she could not shake the niggling feeling, like a grain of sand in one's boot, that he was more than a protocol officer.

The point of a curse her father had taught her was to imagine vividly a host of indignities heaped upon one's foe. It was a technique to quell fear, to remind a woman that whatever her enemy's power over her, he was no grander or less mortal than she, and just as subject to misfortune and shifting circumstances. She and her father had vied to invent the perfect one.

Yesterday, Hazelwood had delivered her to the hotel and into the hands of two competent and helpful women—Mrs. Augusta Lowndes, Lady Violet's former governess, and a young maid named Nell. In short order Jane had enjoyed a long bath, eaten a leek soup and roast chicken, and had her few possessions arranged in her suite. Then she had been left in solitude in a magnificent canopied bed to recover from her journey. She had no quarrel with the arrangements except their cost. Every penny spent now was a penny she would not have to mount a search for her father. Even London-bred Nell had been shocked at Mivart's costs and had refused to give Jane's private garments to the hotel for laundering when she learned what they charged per item.

The window rattled with a sharp gust of wind. Jane wondered if she'd lost the capacity to devise a curse now that she was so far from her old home. The previous day's curse had had no effect on *The Husband Hunter's Guide*. She had spent half the night reading the little book. It had not crumbled to dust as her candle burned to a stub, nor had it yielded any obvious clues to her father's whereabouts. When she'd wakened from dozing over its pages, she felt no closer to him. The book was full of wry observations that made her smile, and advice she would never need. A book was not a father.

His annotations in the margins appeared throughout the book, more than a dozen pairs of letters on the left or right page of text. Her tired brain knew the letters were part of code, but she needed the other half of the code, which would be a map. But the only map in her book was of London, not of the East, where her father had likely disappeared along the branching lines of the old Silk Road. Besides her father's notes, there were some in a hand she did not recognize, and she could make no sense of those markings at all. It all meant that she was precisely nowhere in her search.

Over the years Jane had come to understand that her father was not really a merchant. Rather he was a sort of geographer, one who mapped not rivers and mountains, but rather friends. He knew the family histories of dozens of small rulers back to the Battle of Kerbela, the intermarriages, the slights, the losses both avenged and unavenged that would be remembered when the time came to choose sides. He could find an English-friendly caliph or Bedouin chief and know to an exact degree how each man's binding kinship connections and loyalties would tie him to England or send him over to the other side in a moment of crisis. And he believed that crisis was coming. Russian railways stretched farther and farther south to bring the Czar's troops and supplies.

Now when her father needed rescuing, when he had done his best for England, the government refused to help him, and his daughter had missed some important clue. The sting of the government's ingratitude, the lost weeks of her journey at sea made her feel desperate to begin, but desperation was pointless. Patience was needed and steady attention to detail. Somewhere there was a prison or a cave. There were guards and cooks, who had cousins and neighbors. There was a commander overseeing the prison. He, too, had a wife and servants and relations, and he reported to a ruler. In the ruler's palace there was perhaps a servant holding a basket of apricots and nuts, hearing the talk of the palace, a servant who would, for the right favor, reveal what he heard. That was the way of the East.

Behind the thick clouds the sun rose, brightening the landscape almost imperceptibly, though there were no blue domes to sparkle in its light. Her world had stopped rocking, and in her borrowed gown, she had the appearance of an English gentlewoman. With Nell's help she wore stays that did not cut off her breathing. There was no danger of fainting into a stranger's arms. She picked up her bag and tucked the little blue book inside. One notation she thought she understood was the phrase *Madame Celeste* next to a passage about the number and style of gowns a serious husband hunter should have. The dressmaker's shop would be the starting place of her search.

In the street below, an open black vehicle with a high-perched seat pulled up. A groom stepped forward to hold the horses' heads, and Hazelwood leaped down. The perfect curse came to her.

*May the cold wind toss your hat into the gutter. May your snowy cravat wilt like jasmine in the desert heat. May dirt find the folds of your silk waistcoat, and may the mud and muck of London streets mire your boots from tassel to toe.*

At a knock on the suite door, she turned, and Nell, her maid, hastened to open the door. Making a hasty dip of her knees, she admitted not Hazelwood, but two strangers.

They were golden-haired and blue-eyed with long faces and such a strong similarity of appearance that Jane immediately knew they were brother and sister. They were as bright and colorful as a spice seller's cart, the young woman in a fur-lined, rose silk bonnet, and the young man in a bottle-green coat over a bold green and gold striped waistcoat. Beside the lady's beribboned hat, Jane's bonnet sitting on the desk looked like an overdone loaf of brown bread.

"Cousin," the gentleman said with a bow. "We've come to welcome you back to England."

"Are we cousins?" Jane could not keep the note of disbelief from her voice.

The gentleman laughed. "Miss Fawkener, you must forgive our presumption. We certainly are related. Our fathers were cousins, and that makes us cousins, too." He bowed again. "Clive Walhouse. May I present my sister, Allegra."

Allegra's sharp, measuring gaze roamed the crowded sitting room taking in the desk at the window, the blue velvet sofa, and the rose-striped chairs by the white marble hearth. She glanced through Nell as if the girl did not exist.

Clive's smile never wavered from Jane's face. "We've come to offer you a tour of the amusements of London, cousin."

His sister added, "You must be dying for good company after living abroad so long."

"Thank you." Jane regarded the first family she'd seen in years. There were eight words in Arabic for *first cousin* and sixteen for *second cousin*, and none of them seemed to apply to these two. Jane had no idea what to do with them. In her father's house in Halab she would invite them to sit on low, cushioned divans and offer them coffee, bread, and tomatoes. They did not look prepared to sit on cushions and eat tomatoes, however.

"Well," said Allegra, "do you wish to join us? Clive has the barouche, so we'll be quite comfortable."

Jane looked from one to the other. Like Hazelwood, they wanted to take charge of her, and like him, they assumed she was helpless to do anything on her own. She supposed she would have to set them straight, and hoped she could do it without giving offense. Even if she could not hire a guide and a pair of donkeys, she was sure she could manage to get to a London dressmaker without special assistance.

Clive stepped forward. "Cousin, you look uncertain. I'm afraid we've surprised you, but Allegra and I want only to welcome you to the family and ease your way in London society." Clive glanced at his sister as if for confirmation, but Allegra was adjusting the fall of her bonnet ribbons over her cloak.

Jane smiled the diplomatic smile her father had taught her. A polite refusal seemed best. "Thank you, but I must decline the invitation. You've caught me unexpectedly. I have a prior engagement this morning."

Allegra expelled a huff of breath. "Where could you possibly be going? You haven't any acquaintance in town, have you?"

"Nevertheless, there are matters to which I must attend." Jane detected a momentary flicker of annoyance in Clive's eyes, but it passed.

"Don't let us detain you." Allegra's chin lifted to reveal the elaborate bow of her bonnet. "Come on, Clive."

Clive stayed Allegra with a hand on her elbow. "Forgive the unexpectedness of our call, cousin. We would in no way be remiss in duty to a family member."

"You can't go about London unaccompanied, you know," Allegra added.

"I won't."

"And you do know you must not stay in a hotel on your own." Allegra glanced disdainfully at Nell.

Clive shot his sister a sharp glance. "Jane, may I call you Jane, cousin?" He waited for an answering nod from her. "Please forgive my sister's frankness. She means well. Surely, you would be more comfortable with family than in a hotel."

Jane did not think she had heard the word *cousin* quite so many times in her life, but she was sure the connection did not entitle these strangers to take charge of her.

"Oh, you must not worry about my situation. Let me introduce you to my companion." Jane sent Nell to call Mrs. Lowndes, who stepped into the salon just as a jaunty staccato rap sounded on the suite door and snapped all their gazes around again.

\* \* \* \*

From the doorway, Hazelwood took in the scene. He found the room distinctly overcrowded for his purpose. In addition to Jane's formidable chaperone Mrs. Lowndes at her side, Clive Walhouse and his very pretty sister occupied a prime stretch of carpet facing Jane.

Mrs. Augusta Lowndes was a full-figured woman with waves of sandy hair under a lace cap. Her ample bosom and firm erectness of carriage reminded Hazelwood of a certain tall, upholstered armchair in his father's study from which Lord Vange had been fond of handing out blistering reproofs. He felt a brief spasm of sympathy for Walhouse. Augusta Lowndes's respectable figure in gray silk had a dampening effect on a man's designs.

He shifted his gaze to Jane's guarded face. She looked as if she found her cousins' company smothering. He didn't know whether she was the sort to be taken in by protestations of familial feeling, but his job was to keep her with him. His mission depended on it.

"Jane, I hope I've not kept you waiting. I know you want to make an early start on our errands." He crossed the room, taking care to pass between Jane and her relations, making the pair of them step back. He kept his gaze on Jane, showing her as he passed, a basket in which was nestled a flannel-clad bundle. She cast a puzzled glance at his bundle, until she caught its aroma. Her eyes widened appreciatively. He'd not been wrong in guessing that she had a morning coffee habit after her long years in the near East. He deposited the basket on the desk and stood beside her.

Only then did he turn to the others, assuming a rueful face, as if he'd just noticed them. "Beg your pardon. Morning, Walhouse, Miss Walhouse. Don't let me interrupt a family visit." He bowed slightly.

He met Walhouse's expressionless gaze and watched Allegra stiffen, her mouth a taut line of disdain as she turned on Jane. "*Hazelwood* is your prior engagement? You prefer *him* to family?"

Hazelwood pulled Jane's arm through his. She made no resistance. "Jane and I are old family friends." Saying her name was a deliberate provocation, and he waited to see how much of a problem Walhouse meant to be.

Walhouse's smile faded. "I didn't realize you had family friends, Hazelwood."

"Surprising perhaps, but as you see, I count Jane as one of them."

Allegra tugged her brother's sleeve, her outraged stare directed at Jane. "Don't let *us* keep you, Jane, when you have such friends."

Walhouse removed his sister's hand from his sleeve. She glared at him and spun on her heel for the door. He turned to Jane and smiled again, drawing an envelope from his coat. If Jane Fawkener was any good at reading smiles, she'd see that Walhouse's smile was as false as wooden teeth.

"Cousin, even if you are not prepared to accept our invitation today, I hope you will join us for a family musical evening my mother is hosting." The man leaned close enough to give Jane a whiff of the scented pomade keeping his golden curls in such artful disarray. "You are quite new to London, and I hope you will let your family guide you. We can steer you away from many difficulties."

"Thank you, cousin, for this morning's call." Jane took the envelope, disengaging her arm from Hazelwood's. "And please thank your mother for the invitation. It is my second *evening* invitation, and I shall value it accordingly."

Hazelwood admired how neatly the girl did it. She put Walhouse in his place, and he'd never even seen it coming.

The man had no choice but to bow and follow his sister out the door.

As the door closed, Jane turned to Hazelwood. "You lied to them."

"You're welcome." He withdrew the flannel bundle from the basket, and had the satisfaction of feeling her draw closer. No one made better coffee than Nate Wilde. Hazelwood had counted on that and on her long years of living in a world where next to a leather water bag, the coffeepot would be the most valued household item. He'd not been in the East himself, but he'd heard the stories often enough in the clubs.

"I wasn't thanking you," she said as she watched him unwrap the coffee flask.

"Oh, I think you were." He grinned at her. "But perhaps you'd feel more grateful if I'd taken stronger measures. I'd be happy to toss your cousin Clive down a stairwell if you like, or offer Allegra's bonnet to a starving goat."

She gave him an arrested look before she spoke. "Surely your role as protocol officer does not include dismissing my family."

"Oh, I think you dismissed them. Handily. I was just part of the rear guard, and Mrs. Lowndes, of course."

"Entirely unnecessary," she said, letting her gaze slide from his.

The alert Mrs. Lowndes set a tray of cups on the desk, and Hazelwood unstoppered the flask, releasing the coffee scent into the air. He began to pour. "What brought them to your door at such an early hour?"

"They invited me for a tour of the amusements of London." She watched him pour the coffee.

"You've met your first fellow husband hunter, you know, a rival."

"I see that my appointment with the dressmaker is urgent if I am to compete." Jane accepted the cup he offered and lifted it to her lips. She closed her eyes and inhaled deeply, the pale flowered cup pressed against the dusky pink of her lower lip. For a moment the coffee clearly transported her to some other time and place. He looked away, offering a cup to Mrs. Lowndes, who declined it, and pouring one for himself.

Jane's eyes opened again with just the slightest hint of surprise at her surroundings. "Where did you get this coffee?"

"My secret, but I'm prepared to provide it every morning."

Her dark eyes turned wary. "At what price?"

"All part the service. And I can provide a London tour."

"And why should I accept your invitation when I just refused my cousins'?"

"Because I will give you the husband hunter's tour."

She put down her coffee and reached for her bag, drawing out the little blue book. "The dressmaker first, I think." She flipped through the pages. "There's a recommendation here." She looked up. "Madame Celeste."

Hazelwood schooled his face to meet her gaze. He did not look at Mrs. Lowndes, who gave no sign that she recognized the dressmaker's name, though Hazelwood suspected that she did. Celeste's clients included the most fashionable women of the demi-monde, those whose protectors opened deep pockets to dress a mistress. Once, he'd been one of them.

"What?" Jane glanced from one face to the other. "You both frown as if I had mentioned the unmentionable."

"Not at all." Hazelwood turned to Mrs. Lowndes. "But let's send Mrs. Lowndes ahead with a list of your requirements, so that Celeste will be ready for you."

Mrs. Lowndes met his glance with a steady one of her own. They understood each other. "A good notion, my lord. I will let Madame know the sort of client Miss Fawkener is and what she will want in the way of day dresses and evening gowns. I assume the girl needs a court presentation dress?"

Hazelwood nodded, and Mrs. Lowndes excused herself to get her coat and hat.

When he turned back, he found Jane regarding him with an assessing glance.

"*My lord?* That's something you neglected to tell me yesterday when you introduced yourself as my protocol officer. Should I be calling you *Lord* Hazelwood?"

In spite of himself he looked away from that direct gaze. He returned his cup to the tray. "Don't be misled by the title. In my case the 'lord' is a mere formality. There's no ancestral pile surrounded by vast acres, and no ten thousand pounds *per annum*." He picked up her cloak from the back of a chair and held it out to her.

She regarded him coolly without moving. "It cannot be usual practice for the government to employ lords as protocol officers for mere misses."

"Nevertheless, as my family doesn't object, the government is quite free to make use of me in the service of the British nation. You may call me Hazelwood without fear of offending." He kept his voice flat and unrevealing. She had seen the Walhouses' reaction to his presence, and she would hear soon enough how polite society regarded him. "Now, shall you have that tour of London? What does your book advise you to see?"

She turned to accept the cloak he held. He draped the wool folds over her shoulders. It was a common gesture of gentlemanly etiquette taught to him at an early age. He had practiced on his mother from the time he'd passed her in height. Since then he'd held a lady's coat indifferently or impatiently hundreds of times, so he should not suddenly feel that he was offering protection rather than politeness, and it should not matter that his fingers brushed her shoulders or that her scent rose to dizzy him a bit.

She turned and tied the cloak strings with swift assurance. "Do gentlemen usually accompany ladies to their dressmakers?"

"Protocol officers always do."

She was halfway to the door. "And when did I become 'Jane' to you?"

"When we became such old family friends, remember?"

She stopped and looked back over her shoulder. "And if we are such old family friends, then surely I know what sort of 'lord,' you are."

"A viscount," he said through his teeth.

\* \* \* \*

Not twenty minutes after his fruitless interview with Jane Fawkener, Clive watched from his barouche as Hazelwood drove off with the girl, and without the chaperone.

Clive's plan to offer his orphaned cousin the shelter of their family's home and name had gone badly wrong. It had been a mistake to bring Allegra along, but it had been Hazelwood's unexpected arrival that caused the most trouble. How the devil had such a disgraced wastrel come into the girl's life? And what did the dragon of a chaperone mean to let Hazelwood drive off with her charge?

Clive tried to think of the last place he'd seen Hazelwood. Clive was sure that the man had neither been sober nor perfectly upright at their last encounter. His claim of a long-standing friendship with Jane was a problem. Their mother would not want to take in the girl if her ties to Hazelwood were generally known.

Hazelwood's carriage turned the corner. The barouche could not follow the lighter vehicle easily, but Clive noted a fellow in a slouch hat on a hired horse who took off in pursuit. The thought that Malikov arranged it crossed his mind. Malikov's information about Jane Fawkener had been incomplete at best, and now perhaps his Russian friend wanted to know more. The question was why.

Beside him Allegra twitched her cloak around her knees, and settled her muff in place. "Can we go now? I'm freezing, and Mama will not be pleased when I tell her what you got us into this morning."

"You won't tell her anything."

"Won't I? You take out the barouche and offer an invitation to my party to a plain girl with no fashion sense and very bad taste in friends."

"She's our cousin."

"Humpf! She's old. She should be wearing lace caps, and she's nothing like us. Did you see her bonnet? Really, my maid wouldn't wear such a thing. Worse still, she's a friend of Hazelwood's. Mama won't like it at all that you exposed me to his company."

Clive signaled the coachman to start his team and turned to his sister. "Jane Fawkener is family, and we're going to keep her close."

"Since when have you cared about family? You're always wishing you had any family but ours."

"You mistake me, Allegra. I want only the best for our family."

"Well, Mama will be vexed. You know Hazelwood's reputation better than I, I dare say, and I have to be so careful, you know. It's my Season."

Clive took Allegra by the shoulders and pressed her back against the carriage squabs. She had no idea in her pretty little head how much her season depended on George Fawkener's fortune remaining in their father's hands.

"Forget Hazelwood, Allegra. You may tell Mama that we invited our poor, orphaned cousin to a party, our cousin who desperately needs Mama's guidance as she has no idea how to get on in London."

Allegra tried to squirm out of his hold. "Clive, stop. You'll bruise my shoulders."

"Give me your word, Allegra, that you'll say nothing to Mama."

She nodded, glaring at him, and he let her go. In one way Allegra had helped him. He found his mind quite clear. He had to get Jane Fawkener out of Mivart's Hotel and into his mother's house.

*It is a rare woman who can rate her merits as others do.*
*She can consult her mirror or her fond friends in vain for a*
*true estimate of her personal recommendations, for both will*
*flatter her. She can note with what care persons unknown to*
*her scrutinize her visage in the crowded sphere of public life.*
*Again she is likely to miss the mark in estimating her worth on*
*the marriage mart. So how is a sensible woman to determine*
*whether her aspirations in regard to a certain gentleman are*
*reasonable, or likely to invite private disappointment of the sort*
*that may diminish her bloom and lessen her chances for real*
*happiness?*

*Is she a gentleman's daughter? Is he a gentleman? So far,*
*all is well. Or perhaps she is the daughter of one of the great*
*merchants of London, and he is the son of another. All is well.*
*It is not unreasonable to look for a rough equality in the station*
*of one's parents and the parents of a prospective husband as a*
*first indication of the appropriateness of a match. On the other*
*hand, it is dangerous to set one's sights on a gentleman whose*
*rank far exceeds the rank of even a lady's most distinguished*
*relations. In such cases all the initiative in the acquaintance*
*must come from the gentleman, and all caution, must be*
*exercised by the lady.*

—*The Husband Hunter's Guide to London*

# Chapter Six

*Viscount* Hazelwood was proving to be a bigger problem than Jane had at first anticipated. He had seen through her effort to escape her cousins, he'd made it impossible for her to escape his company, and he had separated her from her chaperone.

She concentrated on overcoming the sensation of being lifted into his carriage by a pair of strong hands at her waist. As the impression of those hands faded, other sensations intruded. Hazelwood's shoulder under the capes of his wool coat rubbed against hers with the movement of his hands on the reins. Their hips met on the narrow seat, and their bodies leaned in unison each time the carriage took a corner. With her face deep in the poke of her bonnet, Jane had to turn her head to see either her companion or the landscape, and it was much safer to look at the scenery. Hazelwood was too near.

At least at the moment he was attending to his driving and not looking at her. She'd already figured out that he was like Papa in the way he appeared to take no deliberate notice of others, while seeing a great deal, too much really. And then there was the problem of his voice, the pull of it, the warm gravelly undertow of it that came and went with his audience. It had been instructive to hear him speak to her cousins in a different voice, an icy drawl that disappeared as soon as they left.

His vehicle, drawn by a matched pair of coffee brown horses with black manes, rolled smoothly over the cobbles. She concentrated on the feeling, which was nothing like riding a swaying camel. The height gave her a view of velvet curtains framing elegant rooms in rows of houses pressed together like the spines of books on a crowded shelf. By the time the first street opened into a wide square where the cold wind hit them, she felt herself ready again to deal with her companion. They angled across the square's end, turning south a block until Hazelwood pulled up across from the columned portico of substantial church.

"St. George's, Hanover Square," he said, the distinct drawl back in his voice. "The husband hunter's ultimate destination."

Jane regarded the church's columned portico jutting into the street, and its heavy stone recesses overshadowing small windows. "It looks suitably solemn and dignified."

He laughed. "You mean it looks gray and dull, as institutional as a bank or a prison. A fitting place to begin a life sentence."

She refused to be drawn. "There are other churches, I'm sure, where one may marry." She wondered if he had ever considered marrying—an odd thought to have.

He looked back over his shoulder before pulling into the stream of traffic and spoke a word to his groom.

In a few quick turns and one dash across a wide thoroughfare, they reached another square, a long oval actually, with dozens of tall plane trees in the center park, bare now in winter. At the southeast corner of the square, Hazelwood drew up the carriage again, next to the iron railing around the square's center.

"What am I to see here?" she asked. The square was nearly empty in the cold with rain threatening.

He gestured with one leather-gloved hand at a shop on the corner. "Gunter's Tea Shop. You'll want to be seen here, and you'll order your wedding cake from Gunter, himself, that is, from his son."

She glanced at the shop. Her father had brought her here once in summer to eat a violet ice under the trees in the center. The square had been crowded with open vehicles. She remembered ladies with bonnets and parasols to shade them from London's heat, and laughter, lots of laughter. The waiters had dashed back and forth through the traffic of the square with orders and trays of confections.

Hazelwood glanced at the sky of sagging dark gray clouds. "I doubt it will rain before noon. Can you hang on for a few minutes?" He leaped down from the carriage before she answered.

"Where are you going?" He shrugged out of his greatcoat and tossed it across her knees.

"For warmth," he said. Then he reached into the carriage, and snatched up a large black umbrella that had been lying at their feet.

"Where are you going?" she repeated.

He glanced across the square. "There's a fellow in a slouch hat who takes too great an interest in our carriage."

"Is it a grave offense, then, in London, for one to stare overlong at another's vehicle?"

"Quite grave. You must never do it yourself." With a grin, he strolled off.

For a moment she sat stunned. What did he expect her to do in an open carriage without an umbrella?

They were parked at the lower end of the long oval square. Jane's bonnet obscured her vision except of what was directly in front of her. She tugged the strings loose, looking out slightly to her right over the horses' backs, where she could see a portion of the square and Hazelwood strolling along, the umbrella over his shoulder, as if he had not a care in the world.

He disappeared from her view about midway, entering the square on a path that must take him through the park to the other side of the square. In a minute she heard his voice call a cheerful greeting.

She pulled off her bonnet. A man in a slouch hat, standing beside a horse, started as Hazelwood approached him.

The next instant Hazelwood snapped the black umbrella open under the horse's nose. The beast snorted and shied, hooves flailing. Slouch Hat stumbled back, trying to keep his feet and losing the reins of his plunging horse. Hazelwood caught the horse's flapping reins and pulled the animal's head away from the umbrella. Slouch Hat grabbed the umbrella, and Hazelwood released it, letting the man stagger backward.

In the next instant Hazelwood flung himself up onto the horse's back and into the saddle, keeping the horse's head turned, and leaning back over the cantle to keep his seat. Slouch Hat scrambled to his feet and brandished the open umbrella overhead like an axe. Down it came. The pointed tip of an umbrella rib missed Hazelwood's face, but connected with the shoulder seam of his jacket and caught. Slouch Hat stumbled again, his weight pulling the umbrella down, ripping Hazelwood's sleeve free of the coat, and scraping his arm from shoulder to elbow.

Hazelwood leaned low over the horse's neck and urged the animal forward. In a minute they came trotting around the square. He slid from the horse, tied the animal to the back of their carriage, and vaulted up into place beside her, taking the reins. His groom climbed up behind the carriage, and they set off as Slouch Hat came huffing around the park toward them, waving the umbrella and yelling, "Stop. Thief."

Hazelwood glanced her way. She supposed she must be gaping a little, as one did when a sudden view appeared, when the mountain path opened on a sheer drop and the stones disturbed by the donkey's feet bounced and rattled down the steep walls of a canyon endlessly while one waited to breathe again. Now she understood what Hazelwood's close-fitting English clothes revealed—how muscle and bone and height and strength—might be employed.

He lifted a dark brow. "You'll want to put your bonnet on, Jane. It's going to rain."

The skies opened up as Jane tied the strings under her chin.

* * * *

Nate held the umbrella as Miranda left the carriage. The heavy rain forced her to take his arm and stay close as they entered Lackington's. They handed over the dripping umbrella to an attendant at the door and turned to admire the shop.

In spite of the rain, tall windows along the street let in long shafts of light, in which Miranda glowed. She looked particularly fine, and she knew it. They caught the eye of an alert clerk as soon as they entered, and the man hurried to greet them.

"How may I assist you?" The fellow might have addressed the question to them both, but his stare was fixed on Miranda alone.

She gave Nate's arm a subtle squeeze. She had learned to her dismay at Hatchard's that as soon as she spoke, her accent quite spoiled the impression she made with her beauty and taste. Now she wanted Nate to do the talking, so that she could preserve the illusion of being a lady a little longer.

Nate assumed his loftiest manner. "My *sister* and I are looking for a particular title, but first, she would like to find a novel of manners and morals, something by a gentlewoman, and I would prefer a history."

The clerk managed to draw his gaze briefly from Miranda's face. "Sir, you'll find the histories on the far left wall. If miss would care to follow me, we have all of Mrs. Ross's work, Miss Musgrave's latest novel, and more."

Miranda shot Nate a look that said she did not want him leaving her with the clerk. He grinned. At the moment she was not thinking about Hazelwood. In truth he could see that she was a little cowed by the grandeur of the shop and would need to recover some of her spirit. He could help with that.

He leaned toward her behind the clerk's back and whispered, "Just nod and smile, and try not to gape like a bumpkin. I'll find you in a few minutes."

She shot him a quick glare before she turned a bright smile to the clerk.

Lackington's was nothing like her father's dark and narrow premises. The huge shop held thousands of books in vast two-story blocks of shelves from floor to ceiling with more books stacked on the floor. Tall ladders attached to rails rolled along from one end of each long wall to the other. Clerks in tailcoats scampered up and down the ladders or assisted the ladies and gentlemen gathered around the large circular counter in the center of the store. Miranda, a shopkeeper's daughter, would know just how to calculate the value of so much merchandise.

Nate found the histories, and glanced at the prices, but kept an eye on Miranda, as the clerk pulled a volume from the wall to show her. On another day, Nate could spend hours and too much money in the shop, but today, he made his way back to the large circular counter. He could see that Lackington's kept only its first-rate, mint condition merchandise on the main floor. An inquiry of one of the clerks at the counter told him that if he and Miranda ascended the wide stairs to the lounging rooms, they would find the books cheaper, but, the clerk warned, in less good condition. The true bargains would be on the top floor.

As Nate approached them, he saw that Miranda's clerk had spread out on a table a number of volumes for her to consider. He laughed to himself at the title that drew her eye, *The Marchioness*.

"She'll have that one, I think," he said to the clerk, pointing to *The Spinster's Journal*.

The clerk frowned and looked at Miranda. "Miss?"

Nate could see that she was longing to break out with her usual abuse of him, but she mastered herself, and smiled, shook her head, and put her hand on the first book, a shy, feminine gesture that didn't fool Nate. He laughed and directed the clerk to hold it for them at the counter, explaining that they were going to look for bargains on the upper floors.

As soon as they passed out of earshot, Miranda jabbed him hard in the ribs. "Nate Wilde, you beastly wretch, you make me want to sink through the floor."

"I just don't want you forgetting who you are, *sister.*"

"Thank goodness I am not your *sister.* I didn't come from the Bread Street gutters."

"Just don't get your nose so high in the air that you trip."

She glared at him, but looked down and lifted her skirts to manage the stairs. "Where are we going?"

"To find Lord Hazelwood's book. It'll be on one of the upper floors."

In the end they found it on the third floor with a little help from a condescending clerk who had seemed to regard the book as a joke when Miranda asked for it. But he'd checked his catalogue and led them right to the little blue volume. A water stain marred the front cover, but the pages were intact and the book was complete.

"Is the *lady* in search of a husband?" he asked. Plainly, he'd noticed that Miranda's accent was at odds with her appearance.

The man was a stick figure in a coat. Nate had both the breadth of shoulder and reach of arm to level the fellow with one good left. He settled for a bit of condescension. "My poor orphaned sister misses a mother's guidance at this time of her life. It will be a comfort to her to consult a woman in such matters."

At the main counter, he paid for Lord Hazelwood's book and the novel Miranda coveted.

She looked surprised. He shrugged. "For your part in the assignment." He couldn't be more generous than that, and he had his reward. Her face lit up with its prettiest smile.

But back in the carriage, it was Hazelwood's little blue volume she held in her lap as she traced the title with her fingertips.

"Do you think Lord Hazelwood will let me read it?"

"No harm in asking. You might be able to help him with the case if you know the book's contents."

"Are you going to read it?"

"Me! I don't need a husband, do I?"

"But you'll need a wife someday. You could learn how to court one properly."

"A wife's for old fellows in flannel waistcoats. I have to make my mark in the world before I marry." He wasn't about to let her know that he'd already picked the wife for him.

"Hah! As if you could make a mark in the world."

"It's what men do, and London's the place to do it."

"What about women, then?"

"They marry." He tapped the little book in her lap with his forefinger. She gritted her teeth. "You just wait then. I'll wager you that I can do better by marrying than you'll ever do."

"Be careful, Miranda. I might just take you up on that wager."

\* \* \* \*

In the rain with the carriage moving, Jane could do little but hold on. They stopped once under an awning for Hazelwood's groom to dismount and take Slouch Hat's horse away. Hazelwood explained that the blameless animal would be returned to the livery stable from which it had come. A brief argument ensued about whether Hazelwood should put on his greatcoat again. Jane did not win.

Madame met them at the door of her establishment. While Jane looked around at the pale green damasked walls and delicate gilt chairs, one of Madame's assistants carried off her soaked cloak and bonnet, and Madame turned her attention to Hazelwood. In an instant Jane realized that they knew each other.

Hazelwood stood just inside the door, dripping wet from the top of his hatless head to the soles of his mud-splattered boots as Madame peeled off his ruined jacket, the torn sleeve first. He was muddied, bloodied, soaked to the skin, and perfectly happy to be so. Jane's curse had hit its mark, but it had hardly humbled her adversary.

While Madame's assistants scurried for towels and a bootjack, Hazelwood tugged at the ruined neckcloth, undoing its soggy folds and wadding the sopping thing into a ball in his hands. Dark curls appeared at the base of his throat. A shop assistant held out a bucket for the ruined neckcloth.

Translucent with water, the sleeves of his linen shirt stuck to his skin over the bulge of his shoulders and the curve of his arms. His right arm had a vivid pink gash from shoulder to elbow, staining the linen. The rain had darkened his hair to the color of ink. He toweled it, leaving it tangled carelessly about his face like the curling script of ancient scrolls. Jane swallowed. Her throat felt unreasonably dry, her body warm, in spite of the dampness of her own garments. She gathered her wits.

"I have met eastern rulers, both satraps and beys, with numerous protocol officers used to bending so low their backs are permanently curved like willows over a stream. I've never met a functionary with such a taste for direct action."

His face was solemn, except for the laughing green eyes. "I believe things are done differently in the East." He tossed a towel aside with a smile for the assistant helping him. "You're in London now." He turned to Madame Celeste. "Has Mrs. Lowndes explained our needs?"

"She has, my lord," Madame replied. "Come, Miss Fawkener, let us see to you."

Jane gave him one last look. His hands on the buttons of his waistcoat stilled briefly. "Go," he said. "I'll soon be warm and dry, and you'll be fashionable."

* * * *

With a little help from Madame's girls and a package delivered from the club, Hazelwood sat warm and dry on the shop floor in a pile of pillows, his bootless feet stretched out before him. He listened to the murmur of female voices behind the rose velvet curtains of Madame's fitting area. As an assignment, he thought his beat any that Blackstone or Clare had had. His groom had ascertained the livery from which Slouch Hat had come, and Hazelwood contemplated his next move in the game against Jane Fawkener's enemies. A squawk erupted from behind the velvet curtain, followed by a single vexed syllable delivered in an outraged tone and a long rapid flow of words in an unfamiliar tongue. He recognized the low voice as Jane's.

"Hazelwood," she called. "I'm coming out."

He came to his feet. "Are you decent?"

The velvet curtain stirred, and Jane Fawkener, her arms extended from her sides, slipped through.

He felt his face change and worked to keep from staring at the slim form in the filmy white gown. Curves and hollows and sweetly rounded arms appeared, unveiled by the simple gown. The warm scent of her reached him. He must have looked as stunned as he felt because she flapped her arms like wings. "Hello, Hazelwood, please tell me this is not a shroud, and I'm not dressed to be entombed."

*Dressed for bed more like.* "White is the required color for a lady's first meeting with the monarch."

She looked at him as if he'd taken leave of his senses.

"Did you tell Madame that you preferred not to meet his royal highness?"

"I did, but apparently, your orders trump my preferences."

"Ah," he said, "connected as I am with the government, I do have a certain sway in this matter."

"The dress has no color. I would prefer not to look as cheerless as bleached bones on the side of a desert track."

"Is that how you think you look?" He closed the gap between them. "Arms tired?"

She nodded. "I've been standing like a signpost at a crossroads for hours. And there are pins. Hundreds of pins. I could run a stall in the souk."

He reached up and offered his open palms for her to rest her arms. She shuddered at the skin-to-skin contact. He kept his hands steady in spite of the desire to slide them along the silky underside of those arms. "You're used to being invisible, aren't you?"

She shook her head to deny it.

"Unnoticed then. What did you wear outside your father's house? The veil?"

"A head covering always, the garment of a modest woman in the public places of Halab. And sometimes the *chadri*, my own personal blue tent with a mesh screen to peer through."

He could imagine her veiled, only the dark eyes visible through the dark mesh of the headpiece, like the gleam of moonlight caught in a well. "Worried about being seen, are you?" He quirked a brow at her.

She shrugged.

"I assure you that no man in London will think of bleached bones in the desert when he sees you in this dress," he said it solemnly as a kind of promise. Then to lighten the mood, he added, "You do know the gown is not finished."

"Not finished?"

"It requires panniers, I believe."

Madame stepped out from behind the curtain. "Panniers, certainly."

"You mean what a donkey wears?"

Hazelwood tried not to laugh at the suspicion in her eyes. Clearly she was thinking of the woven baskets merchants strapped on donkeys to carry their wares.

"And I believe that there's an overdress required as well with yards of ribbon." He took his palms away from her arms and stepped back. Then he had to reach for her again. With the tips of his fingers he lifted her chin. "Have a little faith in Madame's skill."

When he next saw her, the white underdress appeared only as a thin column from her breasts to her toes, surrounded by pale pink silk ornamented with ribbons and lace and stretched on either side to cover the required panniers. Though they weren't quite the same as the baskets donkeys wore, they did give a woman a wide profile. The curves and hollows he'd admired were lost in the overelaborate court gown.

"How am I to move dressed in this absurd way?" she asked.

"Carefully." He kept a grin under control. "You won't want to make any sudden turns. You'll knock the king's guard down like nine pins."

"I'll fall flat on my face."

"As your protocol officer, Jane, it's my duty to see that you don't. We'll have to practice. For hours."

She slanted him a glance. "You'd like that, wouldn't you? To spend hours ordering me about."

He stepped back, giving her a quick sweeping gaze. "It's my job, my duty for King and country. You'll have to curtsy, kneel, stand, whatever I say."

She shook her head. "I think I shall insist on something from you in return before I agree to be tutored by you." She made a quarter turn to the right and sidestepped through Madame's open curtain as if she'd been wearing court dress forever.

He swallowed. She did not understand how her words might be taken by a man like him, but he could think of a dozen somethings he might offer her in return for her agreement to do his bidding.

*Some readers of this little volume may take exception to the term "Husband Hunter," imagining that it suggests a degree of forwardness unbecoming in a young person entering society for the first time. While this guide does not recommend bold or presumptuous behavior, it does not condone coyness. Coyness is indeed a crime, as the poet would have it, in a world in which there must always be a surfeit of young ladies in relation to eligible partners. Therefore, I must insist on a young woman's becoming a Husband Hunter, for no woman wishes to be mere "goods on a shelf" but an active seeker of her own happiness and well-being. Above all, a woman wishes to be in charge of her fate.*

—The Husband Hunter's Guide to London

# Chapter Seven

Jane stared at the door of her hotel suite and willed it to open. It was near nine. Her arms hung at her sides as dead as wilted as palm fronds in winter. Her empty stomach protested the long afternoon, sustained only by macaroons. Her busy brain contemplated what concession she wanted to wrest from Hazelwood—a true explanation of the episode with Slouch Hat in the park, an admission of whatever thing in his past had made him so disliked by her cousins, or a confession of how he had come to know Madame Celeste. Jane had insisted that the court dress remain at Madame's until she needed it.

Behind her, Hazelwood and Mrs. Lowndes exchanged a few words, and behind them, she knew came three footmen bearing boxes of tissue-wrapped garments for her new wardrobe as a husband hunter. The resourceful Mrs. Lowndes had arranged for the milliner to send bonnets for Jane to try at her hotel room the following day.

Hazelwood reached around her for the door, which swung open on a distraught Nell, her hands clasped together against her breast. "Oh, Miss, I'm so sorry. Someone's come to the rooms while I went to supper."

A surge of quick alarm replaced Jane's weariness. She reached out to the girl. "You're unhurt, Nell?"

Nell nodded, and Jane went straight past her to the bedroom for her father's letters, hidden in a red, Morocco-bound book, cleverly fitted out with a concealed hinge in the binding. She expected it to be missing, but it lay in a jumble of books scattered on the floor by her bed. She sank to her knees and took it up in shaking hands and slid the lock under the edge of the cover. The little box opened. The letters were still there, the blue ribbon in which she'd tied them undisturbed. She snapped the box shut.

Clearly, someone who knew she was staying at Mivart's had passed that information along to an enemy, accidentally, or deliberately. Someone believed she possessed important information. Her heart pounded.

When she looked up, Hazelwood stood watching her from the doorway. "Nell has gone for refreshments. When you feel more the thing, you can identify what the thief or thieves might have taken."

Jane nodded, grateful for the dim light of the room. Hazelwood's words were neutral, but he was not a man to miss the details. She looked around as he lit additional candles. The drawers and doors of the walnut armoire hung open, its contents dumped on the floor. Shoes and chintz-covered pillows had been flung about violently. A shield-back chair lay overturned at the foot of the bed. A kid half-boot had apparently hit the drapery and dropped to the floor.

Hazelwood had said "thief," not "spy," but Jane knew that the intruder had not come to find hidden bank notes or jewelry. She wore a warm new cloak supplied by Madame Celeste, and yet she clenched her teeth to keep them from chattering. She knew with cold certainty what the search of her rooms meant, and it had been a search, not a robbery—an enemy of her father's was here in London. She wished she knew whether that enemy came from within the government or without it, and what he had expected to find.

The little book was safe in her bag, one more thing she had left of him. She shuddered at the thought that it might end up in a spy's hands.

Hazelwood crossed the room and offered his hand to pull her up from the floor. "The fire's lit in the sitting room, and the footmen have gone."

He had removed his gloves. Jane took his hand. He lifted her to her feet in a swift, dizzying pull. Lightheadedness warred briefly with the sensation of his warm palm against her skin, not rough, but distinctly male. He let go, and she clenched her fist against a humming of her nerves. He didn't move, but stood close to her, looking about the room. "Hasty, weren't they?" he observed.

It was her thought, too, or else the spy would have noticed that the book with the concealed letters had not behaved like the other books. It had not fallen open along the spine. Its pages had not fluttered. She found that she'd been holding her breath, and she let it go. It was likely then that the man who had entered her room was a hireling with no real knowledge of what he was supposed to find. Her mind started ticking off the possibilities.

Hazelwood stood looking at her as she clutched the little box to her chest. He had a knack for catching her in moments of weakness. "What's missing? The family diamonds?"

She shook her head and relaxed her hold on the box, as if it were a mere nothing. She offered him a blank look. "No diamonds. I suspect the thieves were after money."

He scanned the room again. "It's a bold thief that enters Mivart's." His watchful gaze came back to her.

She made herself put the book box lightly on the table by the bed, and reached down to gather the other fallen books. Hazelwood scooped up two of them, and she stacked them on the table. She did not think he had noticed the trick box, but she could not be sure.

"You said there's a fire?"

He nodded and gestured for her to lead the way back to the sitting room. She found Mrs. Lowndes arranging a plate of sandwiches and cups on a tea tray, and Nell standing by, looking anxious. Jane sent Nell to put the bedroom to rights and told the girl she might go to bed. Then she accepted Mrs. Lowndes's help with her cloak, and settled on a small sofa by the hearth with a cup of tea.

Hazelwood stood staring at the sitting room desk. It, too, had been searched, its drawers left open. Hazelwood's gaze settled on her cousins' invitation, leaning undisturbed against the lamp where Clive had put it. The thought crossed her mind that she was imagining government spies in Lord Chartwell's office. Perhaps her cousins had talked quite innocently about their visit to her at Mivart's, and some enemy of England had heard their talk. There were such, she knew.

A knock at the door called Hazelwood away briefly. When he returned he accepted a cup of tea and turned to Jane, a harsh cast to his usually laughing features. "I've arranged for a man to stay outside your door tonight, but we need to move you to a safe location."

Jane shook her head. Hazelwood took his duties as protocol officer quite seriously, but she had no intention of letting him or the government control her movements. "I'd rather not rely on the government overmuch, but on a more secure and committed protector."

He appeared to choke on a sip of tea, and then recovered.

Jane turned to her entirely unruffled companion. "Mrs. Lowndes, can you tell me what protocol I've offended now?"

"Not *protector*, my dear. The word implies that the gentleman in question has not offered marriage before accepting its full rights."

Jane put down her cup. "Hazelwood, how very challenging a job you have to keep me from social peril."

"Forgive me," he said in an unrepentant voice, "I was momentarily more concerned with the peril to your person."

Jane waited to reply until he lifted the teacup to his lips again. "Quite right. Especially after we were followed to the dressmaker's today."

Once again she made him start and gulp the hot liquid down. It had taken her awhile to work out what had provoked him to confront Slouch Hat. The encounter had not been over an imagined social offense.

Her gaze held his for a moment while Mrs. Lowndes did her best imitation of a stuffed armchair.

Hazelwood put his teacup on the mantel. "Do you have your book, Jane?"

"In my bag." She pointed.

He retrieved the little blue book. With a look, he made her shift her skirts to make room for him on the sofa. In his hands the book looked quite small and helpless.

She grabbed a sandwich from the tray. "Here, let me. I know where to begin. I read most of it last night."

"Eager for the hunt, are you?"

She ignored the sarcasm. Her job was to follow her father's guide wherever that led her. "We want to start with the chapter on a woman's first appearance in society." She found the page. "Here."

The fire popped and hissed and sent out welcome warmth. Every outing in London so far had chilled Jane to the bone. She handed Hazelwood a sandwich and slipped out of her shoes, folding her legs under her on the sofa. In Halab she would have left her shoes just inside the door. For a moment, as she thawed, she felt almost comfortable. While turning the pages of the little book kept Hazelwood occupied, she considered what to do about the spy or spies. There was no question that she must take action, but she was already learning that a woman in London had a different set of restrictions placed on her than a woman in Halab. New rules appeared as fast as she broke the old ones. The sooner she could figure out where her father's travels had taken him, the sooner she could act.

She nibbled a sandwich while he read. She missed the flat, warm bread of home with the raised brown bubbles like freckles that one wrapped around meat and vegetables, but she approved the yeasty sweetness of English bread. Mrs. Lowndes rose and excused herself. "I'll leave you two to make plans for tomorrow."

The atmosphere in the room changed. Jane felt it at once. Though neither had moved on the little sofa, the distance between them had shrunk and become charged. In his hands the book looked small and feminine. He turned past the chapter she pointed out, flipping through the book to a page where her father's annotations were plain in the margin, his thumb coming to rest next to her father's notes. She held her breath.

"Do you want to tell me what you're hiding in your bedroom?"

"No more than you wish to tell me who followed us today."

"Ah, we've reached another impasse."

She smiled cordially. "Except that we've agreed that I'm to continue my husband hunt."

The teasing look was back in his eyes. He was not a man to push foolishly against a locked door. "Not a moment to waste. A woman must seek marriage while she's young. Her great attraction, beauty, is entirely ephemeral."

She twisted on the sofa to face him. Teasing talk was a game to him. "You claim a man's attractions are more lasting than a woman's?"

"Obviously. A man may always marry unless he's poor. He may be a gout-ridden octogenarian, but if he has property, he'll find a willing lady. Indeed, he may find himself more sought after the shorter his apparent lease on life."

She pretended to consider it. "I had not thought of older gentlemen, but perhaps I should aim my efforts in that direction."

"And where will you find these potential suitors?"

There was a note in his voice that she was beginning to recognize. It irked him when she appeared to be in earnest about her husband hunt.

His voice was a dangerous reminder of the intimacies of the day. One could dash through the rain and emerge to shake a few drops from one's hair or coat, but she had stood in a downpour of Hazelwood. From their first meeting, their eyes and hands and voices had been free to meet in ways she had never imagined in Halab. She reminded herself that such touches and glances were commonplace to him. It occurred to her that he knew Madame Celeste because he had come to the shop before with a woman whose wardrobe he was buying not so that she could meet the monarch, but so that she could please Hazelwood.

Jane took the book in unsteady hands, and opened to a passage she remembered and read in an only slightly shaking voice. "The Husband Hunter prepares for her first appearance in society by calling upon those family members and acquaintances with the power to introduce her to willing partners in the ballroom."

He tapped the page with his finger. "I thought your Walhouse cousins put you off your London family."

"I don't know them. I suppose I must give them a try." As she said it, she recognized that the letters in the margin next to Hazelwood's thumb were likely initials. The *EF* could be her father's mother Lady Eliza Fawkener. *TD* could be her uncle, her mother's brother, Thaddeus Drummond. Most of her father's codes over the years had involved the names of his relations. She cast a glance at Hazelwood. He was chewing a bite of sandwich, giving no sign of having noticed her father's marginalia.

Her father had always described his extended family as the cast of a farce. He had stressed that it was only possible to endure their company by seeing one at a time, and that a visit to any of them was a major exercise in diplomacy. Now it occurred to her that he might have been using such a characterization of their family to signal information about the rulers he met in his journeys across the near East.

She sat up a little straighter at the thought, and Hazelwood turned to her with a penetrating look. It was time to send her protocol officer away. She reached for the sandwich tray. He took hold of her wrist, arresting her movement. "Jane, what are you thinking?"

She offered him her blandest smile. "You know, I'd like to visit my grandmother tomorrow."

"You felt such a warm, family-feeling from your cousins this morning that you wish to connect with the rest of your relations?"

"One must always seek family connections. My father's mother is an invalid, I believe. My mother's brother lives precariously by gaming, and my father has a pair of twin cousins who could not interrupt their schedule of social engagements to take me on. Are you shocked?"

"By a lack of family feeling among the aristocracy of Britain? Hardly. Only by your desire to visit your grandmother."

"She may know an octogenarian widower or two." She covered a yawn with one hand. Her relations might not have welcomed her to London, but they might be willing to help her find her father.

She looked up and found him watching her. "You must be tired, too, and eager for your bed." She saw his half smile and knew that she'd blundered conversationally again. "What?"

"I'll bid you goodnight then." He stood and offered a hand. She took it and let him lift her from the sofa, but the foot she had tucked under her caught in her skirts and she fell forward. Putting out a hand to stop her fall, her palm flattened against his midriff.

"Steady," he said. "Foot go to sleep?"

She nodded, looking at her hand pressed against the hard, flat surface of his middle, her senses trying to comprehend the unfamiliar message buzzing along her nerves from her fingertips to her toes.

He laughed. "No need to break my ribs. I'm going."

She dropped her hand and recovered her sense.

With a brief bow he was gone, and she was left wondering what she'd felt, as if she'd had a brief glimpse through a door left ajar of some unexpected view and now could not say what she'd seen.

*The Husband Hunter in London will soon observe that a
gentleman in town unlike a gentleman in the country has a rival
domestic arrangement to his home. By training, at school, in
the army, or aboard the glorious ships of his majesty's navy,
gentlemen learn to live in wholly male societies. In his club the
scale and color of the furnishings, the objects in view, the food
and drink served, the rhythms of the day, and the very paintings
on the walls are wholly male.*

*In general, the Husband Hunter should not be alarmed to
discover that a gentleman of interest to her has a capacity
for friendship with the members of his own sex. The Husband
Hunter herself must form dear and lasting friendships with
women.*

*Nevertheless, the serious Husband Hunter will want to
ascertain about a prospective spouse the level of his devotion to
his club, which is to say his tribe. By observing him closely and
listening to his talk, she will determine whether he is capable
of forming a serious attachment outside of his circle of male
friends. You do not want your home to be the island to which
he occasionally rows from the mainland where he finds all his
comforts, save one.*

—*The Husband Hunter's Guide to London*

# Chapter Eight

When Hazelwood returned to the club, a dozing Wilde staggered to his
feet from a couch in the coffee room. The youth to took Hazelwood's coat
and hat and offered him a second copy of the little blue book.

"Found it at Lackington's, sir." The youth yawned. "Goldsworthy's
in his office."

Wilde didn't say, nor did he have to that their leader expected Hazelwood's
report. Hazelwood clapped the youth on the shoulder. "Off to bed with you
now, Wilde. I've got another job for you in the morning."

The youth looked over his shoulder at him. "Sir, Miranda wants to read
the book, if it's no trouble."

"If it helps your cause, Wilde, I'll give her a crack at it."

Hazelwood made his way to the spymaster's office. In the whole time he'd lived at the club, scaffolding had hidden its façade along Albemarle Street. The interior rooms, except for the coffee room and the bedrooms, were draped in canvas. Passersby were meant to think the place empty and undergoing renovation, and not housing a nest of spies. During daylight hours, most of them passed through the back of the house and out through Kirby's chemist shop on Bond Street to disguise their comings and goings.

The under-renovation disguise was pronounced in Goldsworthy's office, which had the tented look of a military field headquarters. Hazelwood found two men in the office, Goldsworthy, behind his huge desk, and Captain Harry Clare, at ease in one of the club's green leather armchairs facing their leader. Seated, Samuel Goldsworthy was no less monumental than when he rose to his towering height. A dozen candles illuminated the desk and cast the big man's imposing shadow over the canvas-draped wall behind him.

Hazelwood took the leather chair next to Clare, opposite the big man. In his scarlet regimental jacket, Clare looked like a faded print of Wellington's annual Waterloo banquet.

"Hazelwood," Goldsworthy greeted him, "just the man I wanted to see. What's the report?"

"The enemy is after the girl. We were followed from Mivart's to the dressmaker's this morning, and around seven this evening, while her maid was at supper, the girl's rooms were searched."

Goldsworthy's shaggy russet brows lifted. "And? Any papers taken?"

"Not that the girl will admit to. She showed alarm over one Morocco-bound book. As soon as she found it, she had little further interest in the work of the thieves."

Clare sat up a little straighter in his chair. "Bold customers, I'd say to enter Mivart's. Looking for what?"

"That's the question I've been pondering." Hazelwood watched Goldsworthy, trying to read any tic or twitch in the bluff ruddy face. The big man's expression was as readable as lichen on a boulder. Goldsworthy was not one to give away government secrets. "What information would Fawkener give his daughter that the other side badly wants?"

Goldsworthy showed no sign of hearing him. "Has the girl made any further claim that her father is alive?"

"Not a word." Hazelwood held up the little book he'd received from Wilde. "She's got herself a copy of *The Husband Hunter's Guide to London,* and plans to give the Season a go. I've offered to help, of course." He held on to the information that the guide had been delivered to her from her father through his bankers not the government.

Goldsworthy nodded approval, while next to him Clare snorted.

Hazelwood turned to his friend. "You doubt my ability to be of service to a maiden navigating the perilous seas of her first London Season?"

Clare assumed an innocent expression. "I'm sure that if she's looking for a reliable shot, or a man who can break heads, you're her man. Is that her object?"

Hazelwood shook his head. "I think she rather expects to find a fellow of dull and respectable domesticity plus a tidy income."

"You're safe then," Clare quipped.

Goldsworthy cleared his throat with a rumble that could be mistaken for a coal cart passing. "Gentlemen, may I remind you that the girl in question likely has information vital to His Majesty's government and that we must have that information."

Goldsworthy's tone reminded Hazelwood of certain unpleasant interviews he'd had in his youth with the Headmaster of his school. Goldsworthy had a sense of humor, but he also had a presence that squashed rebellion. Now he fixed Hazelwood with a grim stare.

"The government expects you to do what you do, Hazelwood. Persuade Jane Fawkener to tell you what she knows."

"Do what I do?" He kept his tone neutral in spite of a sudden distaste at his employer's suggestion.

Goldsworthy offered a dismissive wave of one of his melon-sized hands.

Clare interpreted. "He means, Hazelwood, that you are to use that polished address for which you are so well known to get the girl eating out of your hand."

Hazelwood had not misunderstood. Goldsworthy wanted him to be his old self, the man he was before he'd been recruited as a spy. He had been only too willing to respond to female interest from the first blushing housemaid who'd giggled at him to the highflyers who'd offered their services at the going rate. He let Goldsworthy wait.

If he could figure out what information the government wanted, maybe he could avoid being a complete villain in the girl's life.

"My guess is that whether Jane Fawkener realizes it or not, her father has left her in possession of the names of his friends in the Middle East, and that every one of those friends would be in grave danger if that information fell into Russian hands."

Goldsworthy assumed a sudden deafness while he rustled through a pile of loose documents on the vast desk. Hazelwood and Clare exchanged a glance. The big man's feigned disinterest was as good a sign as any that Hazelwood had hit it right.

A moment later, the papers shuffled to his apparent satisfaction, Goldsworthy pulled an envelope from the pile and lifted his head. He fixed Hazelwood with another fierce stare. "Can you do it?"

"You mean can I captivate the girl? Make her smile at me, look my way when I enter a crowded room, ignore all other partners, and offer me her confidences? Of course."

"Good. Do you know who followed you today?"

"A hired spy, a local, and not a serious tough. He scared off easily. Tomorrow, I'll send Wilde around to the livery stable where the fellow came from to see who sent him. Anything more, sir?"

"You've secured the information tonight?"

Once again Goldsworthy's attitude left him with a vague distaste for the assignment. "Protected the girl, you mean? I left a guard outside her door."

Goldsworthy nodded his approval. "Here's an invitation to a dinner party next week. Take the girl. See what you can learn." He tossed an envelope across the desk, and with a wave of his hand, he dismissed them both. "Goodnight, gentlemen."

Hazelwood and Clare rose. They passed through the darkened coffee room without speaking until they reached the foot of the stairs, where they stopped to pick up candles, and Clare spoke again. "Do you think Malikov's behind these attacks on your girl?"

Hazelwood took up his candle. He needed to get his head straight. He had been thinking of Jane Fawkener as his, which was a sure way to make mistakes and muff his assignment. "If Malikov is involved, then someone inside the Foreign Office is sharing information about the girl a little too freely. Her Walhouse cousins were at her door at an uncivil hour this morning."

"Chartwell could have told the family that she'd returned," Clare suggested.

"True, but I don't like it that we're lying to the girl at every turn."

Clare laughed. "It's your last case, and you're complaining because you've been ordered to make love to a pretty girl. Just do it, and be thankful you're not facing a Spanish fort with French guns trained on you."

"Clare, is that envy speaking? Remind me sometime to ask you about your faults, if you have any. Has Goldsworthy saddled you with something particularly disagreeable or dangerous?"

"Worse than that. Dull. I'm looking for a blind man, who may be mad."

"Ah." Hazelwood understood. Clare liked to lead charges in battle, sword drawn, facing the enemy head on. He had no stomach for lurking in dark places listening to random talk, seeking crumbs of information.

"So far my blind man hasn't turned up in any of the usual places, nor is he known in the almshouses. Usually, a blind man has his territory, and the neighborhood folks look out for him or know how to avoid him. I don't think this fellow is doing any begging."

"Then someone is sheltering him. Why does Goldsworthy want him?"

"He may be the only witness to a murder."

"A blind witness?"

Clare shrugged. "That's Goldsworthy for you. Our inscrutable leader won't share what he knows until you're up to your neck in assassins."

At the top of the stairs, as they prepared to go their separate ways, Clare had a last question. "Have you made plans for leaving the redemption club?"

"'Redemption club?' Is that what you're calling it? No plans. You?"

"None." Clare grinned at him and they parted.

Hazelwood sought his own rooms. Though he could joke with Clare, Hazelwood didn't like the part he'd been assigned to play in Jane Fawkener's life. He had thrown himself into youthful love affairs, but he had never deliberately deceived a woman for gain.

He entered his room, set down his candle, and began to undress. Goldsworthy's club was not the Albany, but the original owner of the club had designed spacious rooms for lordly tenants. Hazelwood liked his single and quite comfortable bed with its fresh herb-scented linens. The handsome dark furniture and the Turkey rugs suited him. There was a good hearth, a leather chair, and a desk and bookshelves. He realized he had come to think of them as his, too, though, nothing in the club belonged to him. And he would have nothing of his own in the world until he finished his service and his debts were paid.

And he liked his work steering young men away from Malikov, which had been his job for nearly a year with occasional episodes of facing foreign assassins with Blackstone and Clare.

He shouldn't let lying to Jane Fawkener trouble him. He knew what Clare would say. There were Englishmen in dangerous spots on the other side of the world who depended on them for good information about the enemy and on English secrets being kept. Why should it matter to him, if, years from now, Jane Fawkener, Lady Somebody-or-Other, came across a fan or a ribbon or a glove that stirred an errant memory of the time in her life when a man named Hazelwood played the villain? She'd be the wiser for any deception practiced on her. Besides, Jane Fawkener was smart. The chances were that she would see through him.

To get access to her book, he was supposed to seduce her into trusting him. He'd given Goldsworthy his assurance that he could do it, but as he thought of Jane, he realized she was unlike his former flirts. She had surprised him that first day by refusing the honor offered her father and claiming that she would turn husband hunter. Seeing her in contrast to her cousin Allegra confirmed his impression that Jane had a cautious, skeptical turn of mind, and an eye for anything that rendered a person ridiculous. He suspected that she'd take exception to some of the *Husband Hunter's* advice, and yet she seemed determined to follow the guide step-by-step. At least by reading it, he could anticipate her actions, like her desire to visit her grandmother.

Only when he had settled himself in bed with a brace of candles and his copy of *The Husband Hunter's Guide to London* did he remember a thing that had bothered him about the ransacked hotel room. The thief had left Clive Walhouse's card of invitation untouched on the desk.

\* \* \* \*

Clive tried to give the appearance of indifference as he passed Lady Pamela in the crowded salon of a prominent Member of Parliament's house. Just when Clive was growing accustomed to a daily dip into the pleasures of her lush body, she was required by a visit from her in-laws to be rather more circumspect than usual. There would be no late-night meeting between them tonight.

He accepted a fourth glass of wine from a passing footman and steeled himself for his friends' conversation about sport. Talk about guns and horses and numbers of birds bagged in the fall was inevitable. He'd never been particularly keen on any of it. Perhaps because his father's chief road to ruin had been overspending on dogs and horses.

He fixed a properly affable smile on his lips, positioned himself to watch Lady Pamela from across the room, and allowed himself to recall a recent interlude between them in the little house he had taken in St. John's Wood.

Malikov's voice in his ear startled him sufficiently that his arm jerked and a few drops of claret caught the lace of his cuff.

"I take it you were unable to persuade your cousin Jane to remove to your home?"

Clive switched his glass to his other hand and shook the claret from his fingertips. "Good evening, Count."

"You look out of sorts, tonight, Walhouse. Are you and the fair Pamela already on the outs?"

"Not at all." Clive recognized the attempt to needle him. Malikov was up to something. "Her mama-in-law is in the house. Discretion required, you know."

"I see your sister is having quite the triumphant night."

"Is she?" Clive frowned. He had probably erred there, ignoring Allegra's movements. He wondered whether the Count had sought her out and coaxed the story of their morning visit out of her. It would be easy enough for a man of his address to get Allegra babbling about her grievances. Clive found himself a little irked with his friend.

He didn't really want the count sniffing around Allegra. The man was acceptable company but hardly a match for his sister.

Malikov lifted his glass in a toast. "To a splendid match for your sister and a final defeat of the duns at your door."

Clive swallowed the angry retort that bubbled up inside him. He now regretted his unguarded sharing of his monetary woes with the Russian. "Thank you. You can be sure that our family will look out for Jane Fawkener."

Malikov clapped him on the back. "Just the thing. Keep her in the family fold, where she can't hurt your fortune."

*The role of family in the Husband Hunter's quest is first and foremost to provide those connections through which helpful invitations and introductions may be obtained. No family tie, however slight can be ignored, especially where considerations of rank may weigh. One's second cousin, once-removed, the Dowager Duchess of Grandpark, is as worthy of a visit as the dearest godmother of your heart.*

*—The Husband Hunter's Guide to London*

# Chapter Nine

By nine Hazelwood stood before the tall mahogany-framed glass in the back room of Kirby & Sons chemist's shop while Kirby examined the fit of a new blue coat that was to replace the one ruined by Slouch Hat the day before. Kirby's fitting room was as plain as Madame Celeste's establishment was ornate. Yellow painted walls, heavy solid tables and chairs, a Kilim-rug padded bench, and open shelves of fabric and tools gave the room its comfortable masculine air. Only Miranda hunched in the corner over *The Husband Hunter's Guide to London* added a feminine touch. This morning her father had to speak sharply to her when he required his chalk or tape.

Hazelwood smiled at Miranda's absorption. He had found a night of reading the book quite enlightening. Had he read the thing a decade earlier, he would have known how to signal his unavailability to the hopeful mothers and daughters of three seasons who had wrongly imagined he wanted to be caught. Had Isabella Walhouse, Teddy's youngest sister, read the thing, she would not have sent him a letter of distress over her impending marriage to Stafford begging him to rescue her. The first of many scandals would have been avoided. In the end his father's action against him had reduced him to a permanent state of ineligibility as a husband. Now he could read the guide with disinterested amusement.

In the few minutes he'd had to study Jane's copy, he'd noted on page twenty-six the letters *EF, HC,* and *TD.* Last night he'd penciled that brief marginalia into his own copy. It was a start. Each time he got hold of her copy, he'd collect another piece of its notes, but that was hardly fast enough to suit Goldsworthy. The enemy, it appeared, was working just as fast to steal the information away. The one advantage their side had was that the enemy did not know about the book Jane had received from her father. Hazelwood very much wanted time to examine her copy thoroughly.

Kirby smoothed the new jacket across his shoulders and nodded his approval of the fit. "I've put some give in the shoulders, should yer lordship 'ave to take a swing at another bully boy."

Hazelwood thanked him and turned to Miranda just as Wilde entered the room, dressed for the task of tracking down Slouch Hat.

"Sir, your rig's ready and the coffee flask you wanted."

"Thanks, Wilde. Let me take you as far as the hotel. I'll let you know the target as we go."

Miranda still did not look up. She was hunched over the book, her shining chestnut curls falling forward across her creamy cheeks. Hazelwood reached down and put a hand over the pages.

"Oh, do you want it back, my lord?" She was plainly reluctant to part with her treasure.

"Tonight, Miranda."

"Don't encourage 'er, yer lordship. She's got 'er work to do," Kirby said sternly.

Hazelwood looked into a pair of sweetly imploring eyes and shook his head. "Miranda, pay close attention to the parts that will teach you to steer clear of charming rogues with bad intentions and not a groat to their names."

"Don't worry, about me, Lord Hazelwood. I'm not a flat."

"See that you don't turn into one when some silver-tongued idiot starts an ode to your eyes."

"As if I would fall for poetical nonsense."

"Good girl. And don't forget the book is for a case."

\* \* \* \*

After coffee and a brief debate about which should be the first of their errands, Hazelwood agreed to take Jane on a late-morning trip to the bank. There, in a private meeting with Violet, Jane turned over her father's letters for safekeeping and arranged to send letters of her own through the bank. When she and Violet ended their conference, Violet reported that her grace, Lady Penelope Frayne, had invited them to a select dinner party.

Hazelwood once again drove the curricle. He claimed she had no need of her chaperone to visit her grandmother. He drove with careless confidence, never flinching as approaching drivers rushed into the shifting openings in the throng. A pewter sky pressed down on the chimney pots and slates, but no rain threatened. Instead, London had turned beastly cold with patches of slick black ice on the streets and people slipping as they passed, some wearing no more for warmth than hats and long wool scarves wrapped around their throats.

Jane had not remembered how many horses there were in London. Even English persons of low condition appeared to think nothing of hopping onto a horse's back or whipping an animal drawing a laden cart. In the desert cities where her father traveled, it was a high crime, punishable by death, for an infidel to ride a horse, and though he disguised himself as a believer, her father never rode a horse in the East.

She clutched the edge of the high seat, and thought about the likelihood that they would be followed again after the invasion of her room the night before. She still wore the borrowed bonnet that impaired her vision. They passed close enough to persons on the flagstones for her to touch the rabbits dangling from a stick across a hawker's shoulder or to snatch a ginger cake from the head-top tray of a man selling them. None of the passersby appeared to note or follow them.

She had lain awake thinking about the intruder and what he had wanted, and she'd concluded that he must want the names of her father's hosts as he traveled on his secret journeys across Asia. If she possessed that information, it must be in code either in his letters or in the book he had given her through his bankers. His letters were now safe in Hammersley's Bank, and she would guard the little book with her life.

The government believed her father's last journey had taken him east from Halab and south along the River Oxus to his inevitable death in some hostile caliphate on the road to Afghanistan. But Jane believed he had traveled north to Tabriz and Baku and made his way across the great sea to the steppes and the road to Askabad in search of the Russian engineers laying plans for a railroad that would take them deep into the belly of Asia and allow them to take Merv. She pictured him along his route, stopping for the night with other travelers, sitting around a fire, drinking black tea with the old men, a lump of sugar between his teeth to sweeten the bitterness.

She felt that telling Lord Chartwell she believed her father was alive had been a mistake. Now an enemy wanted to know what Jane knew, and that meant whoever betrayed him still had access to Foreign Office information.

"Do you think anyone follows us today?" she asked Hazelwood as they passed through a narrow gate, leaving the Strand behind.

"If we've acquired a watcher, we probably won't spot him until we reach your grandmother's neighborhood, where he won't have the crowds for cover. By the way, what is your grandmother's ailment?"

"I don't know, and you're changing the subject."

"She's chosen her address well for a lady in ill health. Her neighbors on Conduit Street are London's most fashionable doctors."

"*Fashionable* doctors? Wouldn't a genuinely ill person seek an effective doctor?"

"Not in London." He turned another corner. "We'll make only a brief call."

"Are you opposed to maintaining close family relations?" she asked as they crossed a wide, open square in which every sort of vehicle and several flocks of animals mingled like the churning waters under a dam. The height of their vehicle made them visible above the crowd. She almost missed his answer as she turned to scan the sea of bobbing headgear around them.

"Not at all. I'm sure there are families in England in which warm and genuine affection prevails. I'm opposed to leaving horses standing long in cold weather."

She studied his profile and noted the tightness of his jaw. "What did happen between you and your family? You might as well tell me. Someone will."

"Let them," he said. "Nothing's more boring than a man sharing his grievances."

She looked at him again. For a minute their eyes met, his that rare green like cool, shadowed grass. "I should think you'd like a chance to dwell on your faults." It was almost the first thing she'd noticed about him, his capacity for self-mockery. She'd not met a man like that before.

He laughed. "A true leveler. You're dangerous, Jane. You see right through me."

They passed uphill to the north leaving the square for a narrower street. She turned back again, obliged by her bonnet to twist in the seat. "And, do you think, we might now be able to tell whether we're being followed?"

"More likely we'll catch a common pickpocket. The girls are notorious." He gave his full attention to the traffic.

"Girl pickpockets?" Jane had seen girls with the thinnest of shawls around their narrow shoulders.

"Are you shocked?"

"I'm impressed. You must know that girls in Halab have no such avenue of self-reliance."

He'd laughed again. "An admirer of female enterprise, are you?"

"I am. A woman can always do what necessity requires, you know." She twisted to look around, but no seemed to note their passing.

"I have been followed before. I wouldn't let it cause you any alarm."

"And what have *you* done to invite a dogged pursuit through the streets of London?"

He gave a slight jerk to the horses' mouths at her tone. "It's what I've *not* done. You'd think any self-respecting tradesman would be good for thirty-four pounds, six and eleven, but Poole and Davies hound a man as if he'd borrowed the whole of the royal treasury."

He meant it as a joke, she knew, though he might have creditors, and creditors in England might be a ruthless lot. But it was an evasion as well to pretend that he was the one being followed. His hotel room had not been ransacked. He was unwilling to acknowledge that he was something other than a protocol officer. She would do well to remember that he was the government's man and as interested in her father's information as the enemy was.

At the house on Conduit Street, habit stopped her from entering. There was one door only, through which both men and women passed.

He read her hesitation as something else. "Are you sure you want to do this?" he asked. "Tell me. What do you remember of your grandmother?"

"Almost nothing."

"And what do you want from her?" The warm rumble of his voice was almost gentle. A sudden ache rose in her throat.

She closed her eyes. What she wanted was in the word *grandmother* itself. She had heard the term for grandmother often enough in the souks of Halab—*teta. Teta*, the word conjured warnings about the evil eye and offers of sweet treats and always fierce pride in a child. So what did she want from her English grandmother? *Kindness. A warm welcome. A chance to talk about my father. Support for the search.* She opened her eyes again. It was probably foolish to want those things and definitely foolish to admit that she did.

"My book says that one's relations are the best source of introductions to potential husbands. Perhaps my grandmother knows a rich widower."

He only raised a brow at her and reached for the door knocker.

A solemn butler of advanced years and stooped aspect greeted Hazelwood's knock and ushered them into a black and white tiled hall with no place to shed their shoes. Jane looked. A footman took their outerwear, and the butler led them up to a blue-walled sitting room crowded with dainty furnishings and warmed to roasting by a crackling fire in a white marble hearth.

"Remember," Hazelwood advised on the threshold, "a short visit."

The butler announced their presence sonorously to the room's two occupants. Jane's grandmother, Lady Eliza Fawkener, daughter of an earl and widow of a wealthy gentleman, was a diminutive woman with a shock of white hair under a lace cap. Her pale, blue-lined flesh was pared down to the thinnest covering over her bones. She sat in a red and gold tapestried armchair, swathed in a silver silk wrapper, her slippered feet resting on a low red velvet ottoman. A collection of jars and vials vied for space on a silver tray at her right hand. The other woman, Margaret Leach, who looked perhaps forty, with soft rosy features, chocolate brown curls under her lace cap, and round wire spectacles on her nose, stood at Lady Eliza's elbow, offering her a drink from one of the vials on the tray. Margaret offered Jane's grandmother each of the vials in turn in a ritual of medicine-taking.

After a final sip of water from a glass, Lady Eliza spoke. "Margaret, don't hover." Margaret retreated to a chair on the opposite side of the fire, taking up a closed book and holding it in her lap. Lady Eliza curled a pale, fine-boned hand to urge Jane closer. "Let me see you, girl."

Jane stepped forward, conscious of a small pang of disappointment. She could see nothing in Lady Eliza's appearance or manner to remind her of her father. She guessed that her grandmother meant to frighten her by the frankness of her scrutiny, but Jane felt her courage rise under the icy blue stare. Hazelwood had temporarily deserted her to stand at the window looking down into the street.

"I suppose my wayward son sends you as a peace offering for getting himself killed. You know that you must marry now," Lady Eliza began, her strong voice at odds with her frail appearance.

"So I've been told, ma'am."

"You're twenty-three, if you're a day."

"It's true."

"You're on the shelf. What was your father thinking to stay away so long?"

Jane had no answer for the obvious, and Papa would advise her not to bait an angry person.

"And what am I to do with you? You've none of your mother's beauty, have you? Oh, you're tall enough, that's something. Nothing to be done about your nose and chin, but with the hair there's some possibility of improvement. Do you own a curling iron?" Lady Eliza twirled a boney finger vaguely in Jane's direction.

"I doubt any man will notice her nose." Hazelwood spoke from the window, his back to them, his voice a low rumble, lazy and distinctly masculine in the frilly room.

"How right you are, Lord Hazelwood. Gentlemen don't fall in love with noses, do they?" added Margaret from her chair.

"Don't spout twaddle, Margaret," scoffed Lady Eliza. "Margaret reads romances, you know. What gentlemen will fall in love with the girl at all? She has no fortune. I don't suppose you have any of the usual accomplishments, do you girl? Languages? Drawing? The pianoforte?"

"I speak Arabic and Greek and read Latin." Jane did not mention certain other skills her father had taught her, like detecting when one was being followed and relying on tact when under verbal assault.

"Humph. You might as well be mute as let a man know you've outdone him in the schoolroom."

Hazelwood laughed and turned from the window. "She does that every time she opens her mouth."

Lady Eliza made a most unladylike snort in reply. Jane shot Hazelwood a glance to say that he wasn't helping. In reply he crossed to her side with his lazy stride.

Lady Eliza fixed her sharp gaze on Hazelwood. "The girl's too solemn, too colorless, too old. Men like flutter and vivacity." She paused to pick up the water glass at her side. "And what is my granddaughter doing in your scandalous company, young man, if she hopes to enter London society?"

"You must blame the government, ma'am. I am Miss Fawkener's protocol officer."

"Impudent jackanapes, you and protocol have never been remotely acquainted."

A racking cough seized Lady Eliza. Jane reached out to steady the glass of water wobbling in her grandmother's hand. Competing scents from the silver tray assaulted her nose, a strong vinegary smell from a pierced silver box, something salty like the sea from an open jar, saffron and cloves, and sweet wine and boiled meat. In the warm room the combination was quite overpowering. Her father would never approve of her grandmother dosing herself with half a dozen questionable remedies that must be at odds with one another in her slender frame.

When Lady Eliza had recovered from the coughing fit, she stared at the fire, her thin hands fretting the folds of her wrapper. "I suppose you expect me to launch you in society."

Jane shook her head, but her grandmother appeared not to see the gesture.

"At my age, I can't do a thing."

"I thought, Grandmother, that you might have some of my father's things, his books or his boyhood treasures."

"Why would I keep maps and heathen gewgaws? Your father should have made arrangements for you before he went off on some fool trek in the desert." Lady Eliza stared into the fire with unseeing eyes for a long moment before she turned back to Jane. "I suppose I could present you as a novelty. You probably ate lamb brains and wore next to nothing."

"Not at all, ma'am, I assure you. A modest woman in Halab must be covered from head to toe at all times in public places. I wore the veil." Jane was being provocative, but she couldn't help it. Her grandmother's ignorance of Papa's world was appalling.

Lady Eliza shuddered, and the coverlet over her shoulders slipped. Margaret rose and crossed the room to right the fallen cover.

"You could take her to services on Sunday, ma'am," Margaret suggested.

Lady Eliza sagged against the chair back. "Go to services in my condition? I've not been in months."

"Not been to services, Grandmother?" Jane asked. Somewhere inside the cross and hurting woman in front of her was a *teta*, and Jane wanted to find her. "An outing will do you good, I'm sure, and I'd be happy to accompany you."

"Hah! If you think you'll meet some eligible beau on the back bench of Grosvenor Chapel, you're as romantic as Margaret. What's that group of yours called, Margaret?"

"We're the Back Bench Lending Library. We have the last pew, you see, and we do have three single gentlemen members of our group."

"Foolishness," commented Lady Eliza. "What was Fawkener thinking to die in some heathen country and leave a perfectly good fortune to those wretched Walhouses? In two years' time, Teddy Walhouse will burn through what has taken generations to build."

"Ma'am, if I may be so bold," Hazelwood interrupted.

"You've always been a bold one, boy."

"The king himself has taken an interest in your granddaughter. He intends to bestow the Order of St. Michael and St. George on your late son. Miss Fawkener will receive the honor in her father's name."

"The king favors her, does he?"

Jane stiffened at the sly gleam that came into her grandmother's eye. Her chin came up. "I do not plan to attend any investiture ceremony."

"Not attend when the king is honoring your father? You will if you want me to have anything to do with you."

"Of course she will, ma'am," said Hazelwood, turning to Lady Eliza. "She has a gown for the investiture ceremony. You will receive an invitation, and Miss Fawkener will be glad to accompany you for Sunday services."

Her grandmother looked from one to the other of them. "Well, you'd better bring her round, boy. Be off with you now. I'm tired."

\* \* \* \*

On her grandmother's doorstep, Jane's breath frosted instantly, and Hazelwood caught her arm as her foot slipped on an icy step. By turning her head, she could look down Conduit Street. Neat townhouses lined the flagstones on either side. No twists or turns offered hiding places for lurking villains. A few doors down, at number thirty-seven, a group of ladies and their attendants waited for admittance where a sign on the building indicated a doctor had his practice. Turning in the other direction, Jane saw only a gentleman's carriage moving at a brisk pace.

At her side, Hazelwood signaled his groom to bring the horses forward. "I rest my case about families," he said.

"At least my grandmother was frank about my prospects as a husband hunter."

"Prospects, which you did nothing to improve by deliberately setting her back up." He grinned at her.

"I had some excuse. She's woefully ignorant of the East, and she thinks London is the center of the universe."

"A bear with a toothache is equally ignorant, but one doesn't poke him with a stick."

"You didn't help the situation any."

"Didn't I? Haven't you heard of drawing the enemy's fire? And didn't she agree to go to services with you?"

"I hope she does. It cannot be good for her to spend all day in such heated rooms abusing that sweet woman and mixing draughts of who knows what." Somewhere behind her grandmother's peevish voice and medicinal odor was a *teta*. An outing to church would help Jane find her.

"Dr. Sydenham's formula, I expect."

"What?"

"A potent brew of opium, saffron, cloves, and canary wine. It does wonders for a cough apparently."

"Oh dear."

"Feeling unlucky in relatives?"

"Not at all. My grandmother just needs to get out in the world." He was too perceptive. She did feel an unexpected disappointment. No matter what she'd been told about her family, she had expected to feel a more instant connection with her grandmother, but she would not give up yet on Lady Eliza.

He cast her a doubting glance as his groom brought the carriage to her grandmother's door. Hazelwood helped her up to the high seat, vaulted up after her, arranged a rug over their knees, and set his horses in motion. She tucked her bag between them on the seat. It made a slight barrier between his hip and hers. She stared straight ahead.

Hazelwood was right about Lady Eliza being cross as a bear. Jane might deplore her grandmother's attitude, but she could not help but notice that it was resentment that drove Lady Eliza. Her son had deserted her for places whose mysterious attractions she could not imagine, and then he'd been so foolish as to die and leave her with no one on whom to vent her displeasure. Jane wasn't willing to be that person, but she could see that she had to push her grandmother to empty some of those vials and leave her drawing room.

"Taking my grandmother to services will be good for her, but don't think to use my grandmother to get me to that investiture ceremony."

Hazelwood cocked one dark brow at her. "Perhaps over a luncheon, we can consult your book again, lest we forget that your aim is to find a husband not to soothe angry bears."

He turned the carriage into a main thoroughfare, and they found themselves abruptly trapped. A wide cart had lost a rear wheel and spilled its cargo across the road. Heavy bags of grain had split open, spilling fragrant malted barley onto the cobbles. The driver of the cart appeared to consider the situation hopeless, for he had taken a seat on the curb opposite to fortify himself with swigs from a jug. A gentleman in a stalled carriage ahead of theirs stood berating the luckless driver for bringing his cargo up a hill in icy conditions.

As carriages pulled up behind theirs and drivers shouted to clear the road, an elderly crossing sweeper threw down the tools of his trade, and with his hat began scooping up the spilled grain. His action drew the notice of several other passing persons who began using whatever they had handy to collect the grain. At that the driver roused himself, waving his arms and shouting to stop the wholesale plunder of his cargo. He set down his jug and seized a skinny boy who was shoveling barley into a large round wicker basket almost half his size. He tossed the boy aside, and another scavenger swung at him.

For a moment the scramble reminded Jane of Halab, of the jumble and confusion one day in the main souk, when a donkey got stuck between the narrow walls, and a crowd of boys had emptied its baskets of pomegranates.

"I don't like it." Hazelwood turned to his groom, who came forward to take the horses' heads. "We're getting out of here," he told Jane.

As he turned to leap down from the carriage, Jane felt a violent tug on her left arm, jerking her sideways, dragging her up over the edge of the seat. A startled cry escaped her. She twisted, clutching her bag, trying to see her assailant.

Hazelwood caught her about her knees and held on. Her assailant dropped his hold, and her shoulder slammed against the sharp upper rim of the wheel. She couldn't see beyond the brim of her bonnet. Hands clawed at her cloak. Hazelwood shouted for his groom. The man yelled at her attacker. The horses sidled uneasily, jerking her out of her assailant's reach, and Hazelwood pulled her back up onto the seat.

For a moment he held her in a tight embrace. Her heart raced madly, and her breathing came in gasps. Black dots danced before her eyes as she stared out from the depths of her bonnet. She gave vent to her feelings in the only words that came to her in the moment, pouring out a satisfying curse in the general direction of Hazelwood's shoulder, heaping indignities on assailants and spies.

After a long moment Hazelwood relaxed his hold. She took a deep breath and straightened, facing forward. A dozen or more persons old and young now swarmed around the spilled grain while a pair of laborers under the direction of the first angry gentleman helped the carter shift his load so that his horses might drag the ruined wagon to the curb.

"Do you have your bag?" Hazelwood asked. She showed him. "Good. Don't move. I'm going to get us out of this crush."

She nodded. The carriage tilted as he climbed down and disappeared into the crowd beyond the brim of her bonnet. Her heart had stopped racing. Her vision had cleared, and her breathing slowly steadied. Her left arm and shoulder ached. The cold made her breath a cloud, and the energy of the fight drained from her limbs, so that they trembled. Papa would say it was time to take stock of what she'd learned from the encounter.

By the time she heard Hazelwood's voice giving orders and felt him settle beside her again, she had reviewed the events of the past few minutes right up to Hazelwood's embrace.

He was angry. She sensed that anger in the deliberate care with which he adjusted the carriage rug over their knees. "Jane, I can't see you."

At a gentle tug on the brim of her bonnet she turned to meet his fierce green gaze.

"What hurts?" he asked.

"My arm. I suspect it's bruised. But nothing's broken," she assured him. "May we return to the hotel now?"

He didn't move. She regarded his gloved hands. Carefully, he secured the reins and turned to her. The soft leather tips of his fingers under her chin warmed her to her toes.

"You need a new a new bonnet, you know. If you're going to be attacked, I want you to see your assailants coming." He tilted her chin up and began undoing her bonnet strings, his fingers quick and clever against her throat.

She swallowed. "Wouldn't a big stick be handier than a new bonnet?"

"Handier, perhaps, but less fashionable. Perhaps your attacker simply took offense at this disastrous bonnet. It certainly offends me." He lifted her bonnet from her head and frowned at the thing, which now had a fist-sized dent in the crown.

She looked away, an unaccustomed warmth burning in her cheeks. She had not batted his hands aside, as a respectable woman of Halab would have done had a man outside of her family presumed to touch her in a public place. She knew that no one regarded them in the tangle of horses and vehicles, but she felt exposed with her head bare, her hair uncovered, her thoughts unruly.

Next to her Hazelwood turned the bonnet around in his hands, studying it as if it were a puzzle to be solved. "Of course, it might be *my* hat, to which our assailant objected. There are legions of men in London who object to a high-crowned beaver worn at a jaunty angle. Our assailant might have been trying to get to me through you."

*Our assailant.* He made of the attack a shared adventure, willingly taking on her enemies as his. She considered telling him what she really believed about the attacks.

She stole a glance at his profile. In spite of his customary joking tone, his mouth had settled into a taut, implacable line. Without the deep-poked bonnet her glance could range as freely as his over their surroundings. He'd anticipated danger from the moment he'd seen the broken cart. Yesterday, he had made a game of danger and acted with a cheerful lack of hesitation in the face of it. He'd returned to the dress shop, his fashionable clothes soaked and torn, his face and arm scraped, indifferent to the damage. He had saved his most severe frown, his brow contracted in displeasure, for her poor bonnet.

What she'd been thinking, before he'd touched her and stalled her brain, was that the ferocity of the attack confirmed the value of the information her father had gathered. Her father knew something truly vital to this game between England and Russia. His enemies believed he had passed the information to her, and now they were here in London. In protecting her, Hazelwood protected her information. He was, after all, the government's man, not hers.

She had, somewhere on her or with her, information for which her father had risked, and perhaps given his life. She could not give that information away until she knew for certain who had betrayed her father.

"Husband hunting in London is more dangerous than I supposed. I did not imagine it would lead to being tugged violently by opposing forces and dropped like a sack of lentils."

He looked up from her damaged bonnet with an unreadable gaze. "Ah, sadly, husband hunting is not for the faint of heart. You're not afraid to carry on, are you?"

She understood him. His answer told her it was a game they were playing, different from the one England and Russia played, and she did not yet know the moves. "Apparently, my situation raises doubts in some quarters about my sincerity as a husband hunter."

"Then we must do our best to let it be widely known that the objective of your London visit is to bring a man to his knees in the most honorable way possible. An advertisement in the papers might do. Newly arrived from abroad, Miss Jane Fawkener seeks an eligible gentleman with whom to contract that lifelong partnership sanctioned by the church—the holy bond of matrimony. Only men of means need apply."

"You are absurd. Are you never serious?"

His expression changed again, startled recognition sharpened his gaze, which caught and held hers. "No matter how many despicable cowards object to your bonnets, Jane, as your protocol officer I will defend you."

She turned away. He spoke nonsense, but she thought that her hair might escape its pins and tumble down her shoulders from the look he gave her. With a self-mocking laugh, he sent the bonnet, its black strings fluttering, sailing out over the crowd of scavengers, and took up the reins.

*The female visitor to London is right to regard the bonnet as an indispensable item of fashion. She notes with astonishment, and perhaps envy, confections of silk and ribbon adorning the heads of ladies of every station and condition. Her first impulse is to seek a known milliner with a reputation for elegance, and to purchase, at great cost, a bit of headwear that will secure her reputation as a woman of taste, forgetting the very reason for which bonnets were devised.*

*While she accepts the compliments of her friends, the sun beats down, mists rise off the Thames, winds howl, and rains descend. While she, with smug complacency, repeats the name of her clever hatmaker, a half a million chimneys spew into the air the smoke of sea coal, which settles as a fine soot on every street and dwelling and blackens the whitest stone. The Husband Hunter who would preserve her fair beauty wears a bonnet not to advertise her taste or fortune, but to protect her hair and face from the elements.*

—The Husband Hunter's Guide to London

# Chapter Ten

Hazelwood put down the book and looked up. He had not touched the girl since they'd returned to the hotel. While they were calling on her grandmother, three bonnets had arrived for her. He'd taken a seat as far from Jane Fawkener as the hotel sitting room permitted and occupied himself with reading aloud to her while she tried on the bonnets. The plan was to distract her, to keep her focused on husband hunting, not on England's enemies or her agents. Instead he was the distracted one, worried that England's enemies could get to her all too easily. The boldness of the attack bothered him.

She was neither a green girl nor the waif Goldsworthy described. She'd stood up to her grandmother and an assailant without flinching. If Hazelwood let her think, her busy brain would figure out more than he wanted her to understand about the attack and his response to it. He had gone far beyond the brief of any protocol officer.

Now he ventured a look at her. "Sensible advice. I'm inclined to revise my estimate of the usefulness of your little guide."

She glanced at him from under a fetching blue velvet cap. "I'm sure the author would be gratified."

"She should be. Perhaps I could provide a commendation to appear in the front matter of any further editions." He put the book on the table beside him. Later he would add to his copy more of the notations her father had penned in the margin of certain pages. If George Fawkener were using the book to pass along information, it was in code, and the letters in the margins of the page needed examining.

Her father's notes were a further reminder of the mission. Hazelwood had had an unfortunate moment earlier in the public street when his anger at her attacker had opened the way for other feelings. Looking up from the ugly bonnet in his hands, he'd seen the beauty of the ordinary, the round cheek, the clear, frank gaze, and the resolute chin. He'd felt as if he'd let his guard down and taken a direct hit from some fourteen-stone bruiser wearing weighted gloves.

It did not help his frame of mind that the milliner from whom the bonnets had arrived had been one Mrs. Paxton, proprietress of an establishment with which he was quite familiar. The last woman for whom he'd purchased Mrs. Paxton's bonnets had been a high flyer of a sportive temperament who had been as familiar as he was with *Aretino's Postures* and whose reputation had helped to prompt his father's legal action against him. Jane Fawkener might be a woman of spirit, but she had no experience of desire or its consequences.

She was studying her reflection in a glass and trying to tie the bow under her chin. The close-fitting cap of cerulean blue velvet framed her face perfectly and gave her skin a pale gleam like pearls.

He took up the book again. "What makes you trust a woman writer, likely a spinster, to be your guide?" he asked.

"Who better?" She was holding her head perfectly straight.

He leaned back on the sofa. "Why a man, of course, the object of the hunt. Wouldn't a woman like to hear directly from a man how he may be ensnared?"

"I doubt any man would reveal such a thing." She let go of the black ribbons under her chin to begin again. "Besides, a husband may be the object of the hunt, but as a treasure rather than a trophy to mount on the wall."

"You make husband hunting sound quite mercenary."

"You are being deliberately provoking." She looked away from the mirror and had more success tying the bow. Of course, she tied it primly, with perfect symmetry, directly beneath her chin.

"Am I?" His fingers itched to adjust that bow.

"Of course. The guide is for a woman of sense who looks upon marriage as…as a partnership." She frowned at herself in the glass. "In the East the poets write that marriage is *the free will of the two partners based on love*."

"I'm not sure a man sees marriage in those terms." He put the book aside and crossed the room, threading his way through the furniture. He had to fix that bow.

"In what terms then, does a man see marriage?" She appeared surprised to see him so near.

"As a catastrophe to be avoided until the last possible moment." He took her by the shoulders, turned her to face him, and once more tilted her chin up.

She gave him a wary glance. "And how did you escape the catastrophe?"

He tugged the ends of the hat ribbons undoing her insipid bow. "In my youth—"

"And you are now in your dotage?"

"Flannel waistcoats are next." He pulled the ribbons to one side and began to tie a bow in the hollow between her right ear and the edge of her jaw. "In my youth I resisted the prescribed path laid out for my father's heir. I courted women of the demi-monde. I speculated in trade. I refused to marry a lady of birth and rank to whom my father had betrothed me. It was a great scandal. For my sins, my father cut off my allowance, and when that measure did not seem to arrest my downward slide, he went to parliament to cut me off from him in a more permanent way."

"He ruined you."

He smiled at her plain speaking. "I ruined myself. My father merely contained the damage to a single generation."

"And your lack of fortune makes you ineligible?"

"In the eyes of husband hunters, like yourself." He gave a shrug. "Nevertheless, my friends tell me to beware the woman with maternal ambitions who will take me in order to become the mother of the next Earl of Vange."

"Such a hopeful outlook on conjugal bliss. No wonder you doubt my guide's wisdom."

He turned her to face the glass again. "Always tie your bow on one side or the other, Jane, or you'll look a complete dowd."

Hazelwood thought for a moment that he'd succeeded in turning her mind from the conversation they'd been having. She looked pretty, her eyes bright with the argument. He rang the bell for Nell to bring his greatcoat, hat, and gloves.

Jane twisted away from the mirror. "How does your mother feel about your father's casting you off?"

Nell entered with his things, and he thanked her and shrugged into his coat, letting the question of his mother's feelings go unanswered. When Nell left, he started a different conversation.

"We need to practice the investiture ceremony, and I know a place that might give us room and privacy."

"Privacy?"

"To spare you any embarrassment." He picked up his hat and gloves and moved toward the door. "You may find it quite difficult to manage the kneeling and bowing."

Her expression shifted rapidly from exasperation to shrewdness. "I'll manage. You didn't answer my question."

"Didn't I?"

"About your mother?"

He shrugged. "She has washed her hands of such a son as I am. You know—hang, beg, starve, die in the streets."

She watched his face closely. She doubted he understood how his mother felt about him at all. "It is a good thing, then, that you are reading my guidebook. Likely, it will help you as much as it helps me."

"Help me?"

"Oh yes, because marrying well will be your best revenge on those who underestimate you." She turned her head slowly from side to side. "I like this blue hat best. It lets me see the most."

\* \* \* \*

Hazelwood walked back to the club from the hotel. Ordinarily, he would find a walk in the night air a good head-clearing exercise, but London was turning arctic and he hastened his steps. He went straight to Goldsworthy's office, but found no sign of the big man. In the coffee room minutes later, Hazelwood shed his greatcoat and shouted for Wilde.

"Here, sir," the youth called. He jumped up, looking abashed, from one of the sofas, leaving Miranda Kirby sitting next to the spot he'd left. "We've been reading your book, sir."

Hazelwood halted, stripping off his great coat and handing it to the youth. He looked at the two faces turned his way and read the signs of a quarrel in progress. "Find the book helpful?" he asked.

"We're in some disagreement about that, sir," Wilde said grimly. "Coffee, sir?"

Hazelwood nodded. "I'll hear your report in a minute."

"Sir." Wilde strode off.

Hazelwood turned to Miranda. The girl was striking, and he could see why Wilde was smitten. He wondered what made him immune. *Age,* he thought, *or a distaste for petulant beauties like Miranda, with her pretty mouth drawn up in a pout.* "Are you to hunt a husband, too, Miranda?"

"Doesn't the book say I must?" Miranda stood and offered him the book with a brief curtsy and an irritated swish of kerseymere skirts.

"But you'll have your father's shop some day." Hazelwood took the book to a reading table and opened it to one of the pages he remembered as marked.

Miranda followed him. "A shop's no substitute for a husband, Lord Hazelwood."

"Ah, so you want a man to be something more than a reliable source of revenue."

"How you men talk as if marriage were a business. You sound as cold as Nate Wilde."

"Then you must not take me seriously." He found a pencil, and concentrated on filling in from memory the notations he'd seen on several pages of Jane's book earlier. One thing was clear from the day's events—Jane's enemies rather desperately wanted the information she possessed. As Hazelwood saw it, that information was contained in the book her father had sent her through the most secure means at his disposal, his ever-so-discreet London bankers. Piece by piece he would extract her father's notes from her copy of the book, but he also had to decode them, and he suspected that only Jane Fawkener herself possessed the key to understanding her father's marginalia.

The enemy seemed to be ahead of them on that point. Their attention to the girl's movements and the attempt to snatch her from his carriage made it clear they believed she knew something.

Wilde put a cup of steaming coffee at his elbow. Hazelwood took a swallow and let the rich liquid warm him. He finished inscribing the notes he remembered then turned to Wilde for his report.

"The stable sacked the fellow who followed you yesterday, sir, but I found the man in the Dog's Head, drinking and complaining about horse thieves and bad luck. According to his story, a toff hired him to spy on you for a wager."

"Did our luckless fellow remember anything else?"

"He said the toff told him there was a bet in his club on where you'd go first with your new…mistress, and he wanted to beat the other fellows out."

Hazelwood nodded. It had been a clever ruse, and it explained why Slouch Hat had not taken great pains to conceal himself. "Did he remember what the man who hired him looked like?"

Wilde shook his head. "I pressed him, sir, but he just kept saying the fellow was a toff like every other toff. Said the fellow had a fine hat. Sorry, sir."

"You did well, Wilde. We were attacked today, and I did no better at getting a look at the attacker."

"Attacked?" Miranda asked.

"Someone staged an accident in the street, trapping us in the confusion, and sent a hired fist to pull Miss Fawkener from the carriage."

Wilde gave a low whistle. "You think that changes things, sir?"

"I do." He was looking at the notes he'd collected so far. A pair of letters appeared on the left or right page under the number. Was there a sequence? Was there a relationship between the page number and the letters? Did the left or right position mean anything?

The thought that had occurred to him while he held the girl's trembling body against his was that book did not merely contain information about the friends of England in the East, but that it might also contain information about Russian plans for the region. The repeated and escalating attacks might mean that the Russians feared that information about their plans might fall into English hands.

He opened the fold out map of London. It charted a journey from the east end to the west end of the city in six vertical columns. As he pondered the map, he became aware of an argument growing louder behind him.

"It's no place to take a lady," Wilde said.

"It's the most fashionable park in London. *The Husband Hunter's Guide* recommends that a young lady be seen there."

"Not at a fool stunt for a wager. No one will be looking at you, Miranda."

"You're the one who said a man must make his mark in London."

"Not by driving four blood horses and a blacking van over pond ice that could open under him and every other nodcock that's skating about to watch his foolishness."

"Hah! You don't want to take me because you don't know how to skate, and you don't know how to drive."

"I know better than to do something idiotic." Wilde's usual toothy grin had vanished.

Hazelwood felt the moment had come to interrupt. "Children, I have not the pleasure of understanding this dispute."

Wilde seized the opening to make his case. "Sir, everyone's saying that the Serpentine's going to freeze over, and Orator Hunt's son has wagered a hundred guineas that he can drive his father's blacking van across the lake and back over the ice. Madness."

"Ah, and when is he to test this claim?" It sounded like the sort of thing Hazelwood would have done in his youth.

"Saturday next at two."

Hazelwood turned to Miranda. "You'd like to witness the event?"

"I would, my lord, and Nate Wilde should not have told me about it, if he didn't want me to go."

"If you go, you may witness a scene of injury and death to horses and men."

Miranda brought her hands to rest on her hips in the universal gesture of female frustration with men. "You men, you chase after danger and adventure and insist that women sew and sit and pour tea, as if we hadn't any courage or spirit. You were attacked yesterday, Lord Hazelwood. And Nate Wilde has just mended from his injuries last spring."

"You are not advocating that women get their heads broken regularly, are you?"

Miranda exhaled a breath of frustration and raised blue eyes full of appeal. "I'd be perfectly safe in a carriage with *you*, Lord Hazelwood."

Hazelwood sobered instantly. He didn't want Wilde cut out.

Miranda went on pleading, indifferent to the bleak expression on the youth's face. "It will be exciting. All London will be talking about it. I want to be there."

Hazelwood stood. Maybe he'd been wrong to encourage the youth's passion for a very young and slightly selfish beauty.

"Sorry, Miranda, I'm in the middle of a case."

Miranda's ripe lower lip quivered ever so slightly. Her eyes filled with the bright glitter of tears. "I know, Lord Hazelwood, I just thought to leave the shop one afternoon for a lark." Hazelwood knew he was being played, but the girl did it very prettily.

"If we go," he said, "we will naturally take Wilde, as he's a good man to have on hand should any danger arise to threaten you. We will refrain from going out on the ice. And you must have your father's permission in any case."

The beauty's tears vanished. She flashed a triumphant look at her adversary. "I'll ask my father," she said. "But I know he'll say yes." She was gone in a rustle of skirts.

In the coffee room Hazelwood turned to Wilde. "I'm sure there's a lesson in this for both of us. You told her about Hunt's wager?"

"I did, sir." His shoulders slumped. "She sees the idiot as some kind of hero. She needs a steadier hand than someone who'd do such a mad thing."

"And you tried to explain that?"

"I did." Wilde's voice was a mumble.

"I'm not sure she's worthy of you, but I'm on your side, Wilde."

"I know, sir."

"Let's hope for a thaw. Now, I want your opinion on this code."

*If the Husband Hunter is to judge rightly the degree to which a gentleman's attentions please her, there is a sense she must cultivate above the other, common senses. This new sense has, at present, no name in our language, yet it is as valuable to the Husband Hunter as the eye to the marksman, the ear to the musician, or the nose to the cook. It is a sense that begins to operate as soon as a gentleman enters her presence. It is chiefly through the skin and the movement of the blood through the body that the Husband Hunter observes this sense acting to inform her of her pleasure or disgust in the nearness of a particular gentleman. Much unhappiness in life may be averted by careful attention to the difference between a shiver and a shudder of awareness at a particular gentleman's nearness. Perhaps in this modern age that looks forward to so many advances in knowledge, there will come a scientist whose study of the nature of love between women and men will lead her to name this sense for us.*

—*The Husband Hunter's Guide to London*

# Chapter Eleven

"You want me to do what?" A bead of sweat trickled down Jane's back in short, ragged runs beneath the layers of her English clothes. It was not so much what he'd said, as the way he'd said it. The distinct note of satisfaction in his voice made her rebel.

And then abruptly he seemed to forget his own command, as if he were one of Tamerlane's great astronomers seized by some sudden realization, the solution to a deep cosmic mystery. She waited for him to return to his peremptory self.

Most of the day he'd been angry, well not angry perhaps, but underneath all that charming civility, he'd been at least miffed. He didn't like it that in the morning she'd accepted her cousins' invitation to the musicale, and he'd taken it out on her in hours of ordering her about in the name of protocol as if he'd bought her in the slave market in Khiva, instead of being assigned by the government to help her through a hollow ceremony that would not bring her father back.

He thought to wear down her resistance by numbing her mind and making her limbs tremble with fatigue. He could order her about all he liked. She would not change her mind about her cousins' party.

They had left the cold behind for an oasis of tropical warmth in the central courtyard of Hammersley House. He had let Mrs. Lowndes off to visit with her former charge, Lady Blackstone, and brought Jane here, where the servants were invisible. They could not be more alone if he had strapped her on a donkey and taken her to his desert tent. Tall, potted palms arched overhead. From somewhere came the splash of water in a fountain as if a spring gurgled up from underground. The black and white tiled floor underfoot was warm from some hidden heating source, and a glass ceiling far above them admitted wan winter light. Round, white-painted iron tables, each with a cluster of chairs, stood under the palms at the edge of the room, leaving the open center, where she and Hazelwood practiced for the investiture ceremony.

Jane felt flushed and heated. She breathed the fragrant air of the place and let her tired limbs rest a minute. Though she had heard her father's stories of meeting lofty personages in distant palaces, she had not imagined how hard it was to move in such a controlled fashion, to bend her knees just so, while dipping her head, and holding her skirts in a way that was both courteous and prudent. Only once had she made it through the entire sequence of moves without stepping on the sheet tied about her waist. Now he wanted her to kneel again. Even if her spirit had been willing, which it wasn't, her knees refused.

"Remind me how practicing for the investiture ceremony helps me to a husband."

Hazelwood stepped forward to adjust the pillows and the Holland cloth he had tied about her waist to approximate the panniers she was to wear. "To be the daughter of *Sir* George Fawkener gives you a distinction you would otherwise lack."

"People in London take such minor distinctions into account?"

"They do, and so much more. That's why you need a protocol officer."

It was easy for him to say. He was not the one sweating. He had removed his jacket, but he had not exerted himself more than to raise his voice or position her limbs. She should be used, by now, to his close-fitting English clothes, and to his habit of touching her, but she wasn't. They were alone in their tropical garden, which had not seemed to matter while he instructed her to come forward, curtsy, take the handrail, kneel, wait, rise, wait, bow, and back away, always managing her skirts, until the separate steps of the process had begun to blur together in her mind.

Now that they'd stopped for a moment, her concentration shifted from her own limbs and movements to his. His least motion drew her eye to his person. Her fingers remembered being pressed to his flat middle.

He turned away and crossed to one of the tables where a footman had left a silver tray of tea and sandwiches. "Besides, you might need to know what to say to a fellow who leads you from a crowded ballroom to a conservatory, or a balcony, or a garden."

"As you have done?"

"Just so," he said without looking at her.

Jane studied his back as he poured the tea. There was nothing remarkable about his appearance. He had the same number of limbs in the same arrangement as any other man. He was person-shaped. His hair could perhaps be called interesting, dark as the darkest black coffee beans roasted in the Halab way, but not striking, nothing like the golden hue of her cousin Clive's curls. Though she stood perfectly straight, she could feel her whole inner being incline his way, like some leaning, earthquake-damaged tower.

Her inner leaning made no sense. She ought to thank him for his instruction and dismiss him. He might even be a social liability with his past scandals clinging to him. She could deal with her difficult, "un"familial relations and follow her guide to a husband without an interfering protocol officer.

He turned back to her, offering a cup of tea, and she had to admit that his eyes were not ordinary at all. The changeable green of them was sometimes like the first green of spring in the hills near the coast and sometimes like the dappled green under the leaves of a mulberry tree at noon in her father's courtyard. At the moment she read in them some alteration in the nature of his attention.

"You were, what, fifteen when you left England?" he asked.

She nodded.

"And you had not yet started thinking about young men? I thought most husband hunters began early."

She shrugged. "I had my father and my lessons. He had so much to teach me. I suppose I had his undivided attention for those lessons, and I could please him by doing well. How was a young man to compare?"

"Was there not some manly figure in fiction that stole your heart?"

She looked up from the tea. "You mean like Achilles or Odysseus? There was Hector. I suppose I did love him. Paris and Telemachus were simply annoying."

He laughed. "My schoolmates found all of them tedious and annoying. I meant was there not a Henry or an Edmund perhaps?"

"From a novel you mean? I didn't read novels."

"A flaw in your education, I think. What do you know of your feelings? How will you recognize an inclination for one of your dance partners?"

"I think I will know whether I like someone or not."

"Will you?" His voice dropped into its lowest register. "You'll be warm from the crowd or the dancing, and your companion will offer you refreshment, and the night air will be so pleasant, and the dark such a relief from the over brightness of the rooms."

"And?"

"In such a moment, some fellows are apt to lose their heads." He busied himself with a second cup of tea.

"Perhaps I should make it a rule never to leave a ballroom with a gentleman."

He nodded. "A wise precaution. But will you remain wise when you have dozens of suitors?"

"Dozens? No one imagines that I will have dozens of suitors."

"They underestimate you, I think." He put his tea down on a nearby table.

The distance between them had shrunk without her notice. He was standing within arm's reach, and she had the oddest feeling that he might seize her by the waist and whirl her around the open courtyard, pillows and all. Moments earlier he had just been a voice explaining the turn of the left wrist required to manage her skirts, while with her right hand she took hold of the rail of the kneeler and descended in a smooth move neither lowering nor raising her chin, but keeping her eyes respectfully downcast in the king's august presence. He had warned her that it might be difficult, that anyone, seeing the king in all his corpulent majesty for the first time, was apt stare.

He swallowed. "You see the challenge, I think, and we need a better practice space, one where you need not labor so hard to imagine the palace. This room doesn't do it justice."

She regarded him a taut moment longer. "Are we done then?"

"For today. Do you wish to sit?"

"If I may." She set her tea aside and reached for the ties around her waist, and he reached to help her. Their hands met. His fingers, warm and relaxed, tangled with hers, stiff, and unfamiliar with the knots. The moment caught and held them arrested, standing close in the dim light and fragrant air. His words of a minute before came back to her, but he was not a man to lose his head over some awkward girl standing with a pair of pillows strapped to her waist.

"Let me," he said. She held her arms away from her sides while he untied the ribbon holding the pillows and sheet in place. He tossed the pillows on a chair and concentrated on rolling the loose sheet into a ball. She sat in one of the chairs, taking up her tea and looking into the cup. A moment later he cleared his throat and asked, "Have I been too harsh an instructor today?"

"Were your own instructors so harsh?"

"Worse, for they were free to beat me or any boys in their charge for dullness or error."

"Did they? Beat you?" she wanted to know. Of course that was just the sort of question he would not answer.

"Come, let's return to the hotel. You will need to look your best for the duchess's party tonight. I'll drive you past St. James's Palace on the way, and you can contemplate the honor soon to be bestowed on your father."

* * * *

The inescapable topic of conversation at the Duchess of Huntingdon's supper party was London—its unusual icy weather, its superior shops, and its latest scandals. Jane listened and looked on, at a little remove from her fellow guests. In her white gown she looked like the other young women around her, but she could not quite catch their knowing way of speaking about London. Their conversation followed a pattern of allusions and jokes that, as an outsider, she could only guess at.

The duchess had stepped in more than once to remove Jane from the edge of one circle of friends and introduce her to another. From time to time she caught the duchess watching and smiling encouragement.

As the supper hour approached, she stood between one of the massive gold candle stands that lit the long gallery, and a tall, thin-shouldered young man with curly brown hair, whose attention had focused on Jane after the duchess's introduction. He extolled the antiquities of the Egyptian Hall in Piccadilly. "You'll not have more fun for a shilling anywhere else in town."

Jane liked him, but she knew in some perplexing way that she had no interest in him as a husband. It was strange to have such certainty in the matter on her first night of husband hunting. She kept her smile in place and told herself that her lack of interest must be because she was not truly hunting a husband, but searching for a father.

"Do you have a supper partner, Miss Fawkener?" her companion asked.

"I thought I did." She looked for Hazelwood among the shifting groups of guests in the vast hall. She had come to expect him to be at her side, and now he'd simply vanished.

"Lost him in the crowd?" her companion asked.

She ventured another glance down the room. "It's just that..." Her voice trailed off as a tall, stately white-haired gentleman in black approached the duchess.

"My dear, how is your party going?" He bowed over the duchess's hand. She smiled up at him. "It's a success as you see."

The gentleman gave no answering smile. A single round glass dangled from a pale blue ribbon around his neck. He lifted it to his eye and scanned the room. He turned back to the duchess with a little crease between his brows. "I understand Hazelwood is here."

The voice was mild, but there was no mistaking the rebuke. The duchess smile died. "He is."

"Ah, is that wise? You do not want to squander your influence on such a man, I think."

The duchess's fan fluttered. "You don't think anyone regards such old scandals, do they?"

The tall gentleman appeared to consider the idea, looking at the glass in his hand. "Ah but they do, my dear. Several of his mother's friends are here."

The duchess cheeks reddened, and she gave a quick look around. Her eyes failed to meet Jane's. She bowed her head.

"I'll have a word with him, shall I? We can't be seen to take in every stray, after all." The tall man patted the duchess's arm and turned toward the crowd.

"Who is that gentleman?" Jane asked her companion.

"His Grace, the Duke of Huntingdon."

Jane understood at once. Hazelwood was about to be humiliated in the most polite but devastating way. It would be public, too, unless there was another way out of the vast gallery.

She turned to her companion. "You've been here before?" she asked.

"Yes, of course, my sister and the duchess—"

"Where would one go to hide?"

"Hide?" He looked utterly perplexed.

"Be...private?" She had to find Hazelwood before the duke did.

His eyes widened.

"I need a moment to myself," she told him, glancing after the unhurried figure of the tall duke.

"Follow me, then." Her companion caught her sense of urgency, and taking Jane's arm, he led her across the gallery, around a pair of velvet settees, and through an arch wide and tall enough for a Roman emperor's chariot to pass. He pointed to a door just beyond the arch. Jane thanked him, and passed through the door into a cool, dark dimly lit space that smelled of damp and earth. Its inner wall stretched the length of the gallery. Its outer glass wall was frosted over. She looked to her left at a series of alcoves furnished with benches and lit by candles in glass lanterns.

"Found a husband already?" Hazelwood's voice came from the shadows. She moved toward its low rumble. "You knew you would be shunned tonight."

He came to his feet in the darkness. She could see the white linen at his throat and the faint gleam of his eyes. "The potted palms made no objection to my presence."

She assumed they were alone in the long room, but she moved close enough to speak softly. "How long have you been here?" It was cold enough that the flesh on her arms puckered.

"Long enough. Did you find a suitable octogenarian?"

"No. I did find a promising young baron." She stepped closer to him.

"Much better. Is he coming to meet you here?"

She took hold of his coat and tugged. "Of course not. You warned me against such a rendezvous."

"So I did. Yet, here you are, alone in the dark with…me, tugging at my coat. A man might misunderstand."

"Well don't. I'm here on a mission."

"I know. To get a husband." He leaned forward, his forehead touching hers. She stilled at the contact. Their frosty breath mingled. She shivered. "At the moment I have a more immediate goal—to keep my protocol officer from being ejected from a select party by his host."

He straightened away from her. "Ah, the duke is here."

"He is, and he strongly objects to your presence, which has been noted by friends of your mother's apparently."

"It's the way of things in London. I assure you I deserve their censure for my youthful indiscretions."

"So you say. Nevertheless, I don't wish to see my protocol officer publicly ejected from a party. Do you know another way out?"

He reached up and took her hands from his coat. "That's one thing we pariahs always know. Come on."

*The danger of fairy tales we are told is that they mislead
girls into dreams of marrying Prince Charming. We are to
believe that unless we snatch from our girls' hands the stories
of Cinderella, Snow White, and Beauty, and insist on the
reading of Fordyce's Sermons, they will marry badly. And yet
the heroines of these tales are as humble, cheerful, competent,
and caring in the domestic sphere in which each lives, whether
castle or cottage, that each must be considered a model of
female virtue. If there is a danger in these familiar tales, it is
surely that the tales ignore Prince Charming's life. There is no
requirement that the heroine understand him, know his past,
know the work that he is called to do in the world. She is left to
imagine that the story is entirely about her rescue, not his.*

—*The Husband Hunter's Guide to London*

# Chapter Twelve

Jane did not want the service to end. For an hour she had felt English,
at home in her surroundings. The worn red psalter in her hands, the sober
cadence of the worship of the season, the light slanting down into the chaste
white interior of the chapel from its upper windows had transported her
back to that long ago time when she and her father had come to services
on Sundays to pray for Mama.

Until she'd entered the chapel with her Grandmother, she had remembered
little of her London childhood. As she crossed from the dark porch into
the church proper, memories rushed back in with the smell of candles
and the stirring notes of the organ prelude. She heard Hazelwood whisper
in her ear, "Any single man under forty in this lot is probably yours for
the taking." Then he vanished, after dogging her footsteps for days. She
did not yet understand the pattern of his disappearances and wondered
what on earth so alarmed him about a Sunday church service that he'd
fled her company.

She and her grandmother parted with Margaret at the rear of the church.
Margaret slipped into a pew in the very back on the right, squeezing in
with three ladies and two gentlemen, who nodded to her as she entered.

A trim white-haired gentleman noted her grandmother's arrival and
came to offer his arm to assist her. As they passed up the aisle, Jane heard

whispers in their wake. At the front of the church where Jane and her grandmother sat, the dark, straight-backed pews with their blue velvet cushions felt instantly familiar as if nine years had not intervened since Jane's last Sunday service but only the usual interval of a week. The service passed in a measured succession of creeds and collects and prayers for the king, clergy, and people. Only her questions over Hazelwood's abrupt departure interrupted her thoughts. Hazelwood had a way of doing that, occupying her mind when she meant not to think about him.

Now the worshippers in their pew stirred, taking hymnbooks into gloved hands. They were to stand for a benediction and the recessional hymn. Around her the onion-thin pages of the hymnbooks rustled and people cleared their throats. She helped her grandmother to stand. The unseen organist struck the opening chord of a hymn of praise. Just then a broad-shouldered gentleman in a blue coat jostled his way into the pew, forcing everyone to shift to the left. The congregation began to sing, and Jane found her voice. It was a stirring tune to rouse a martial spirit.

As the organ notes died away, a procession of elegant people filled the main aisle, those from the first pews leading the way. The business of helping her grandmother stand and step into the aisle occupied her attention for several minutes as the crowd passed. When at last they began to move, Jane's attention was caught by an elegant woman in dove-gray silk, her chestnut hair streaked with white at the temples. The woman's fellow churchgoers bowed and greeted her with apparently little expectation of a return greeting.

"The Countess of Vange," her grandmother whispered in her ear. "She's a great patron of this chapel and a regular at Sunday services. Your scapegrace friend, Hazelwood, is her son."

As soon as her grandmother spoke, Jane saw the resemblance. What little Hazelwood had admitted about his family came back to her. And something else. Hazelwood was wrong if he thought his mother felt about him as his father did. The countess's drawn face and her brittle hauteur were signs of a woman suffering from a great loss.

"Come, Margaret will be waiting of us with her Last Bench Lending Library group. We'd best get it over with."

Margaret made the introductions. The others smiled and nodded at Jane and looked awed by her grandmother. Hazelwood's words about husbands echoed in her head when Margaret introduced Captain Simon Mudge, a retired naval officer with a limp and brown military whiskers that curved from his ears along his fine square jaw, and Thomas Bickford, a tall, lean man of extraordinary pallor, a widowed barrister of the rank of King's Counselor. The surprise was that her father's indistinguishable twin sisters, Cassandra and Cordelia, in matching fox fur-trimmed pelisses and bonnets were part of the group, indeed its most elegant members. The final member was Lucy Holbrook, a young woman in a plain dark blue wool coat that could not limit her striking fair prettiness. Each of them clasped a book in hand.

"We are not Mudd's Circulating Library, but we do keep books moving," Cordelia confided, holding out her book for Jane's inspection. "Have you read Mrs. Raby's latest medieval romance?"

Jane shook her head.

"Hair raising stuff. I'll lend you Volume One when Cassandra's done with it. She's the slowest reader of the bunch."

"Yes, but, unlike Cordelia, I never forget what I've read. She's the one who slows the group down by re-reading a book she read a month earlier."

The group of friends moved toward the entrance. Margaret took over with Lady Eliza. Jane was looking for Hazelwood when the broad-shouldered gentleman who had entered late came up to her. "Jane Fawkener, is it? They told me you'd be here. Let me look at you." His hearty voice echoed through the emptying church. "It's your Uncle Thaddeus, niece."

Jane looked up at a rosy-cheeked gentleman with smiling blue eyes. Now that she could observe him closely, she saw the threadbare condition of his coat. "Uncle Thaddeus, hello."

"Doing my duty, don't you know." He looked around. "Used to come here after your mother passed. Put in a word or two, you know"—he glanced upward—"on her behalf. Not that she needed anything from the likes of a plain naval man like me. She always was a good sort of girl, even when she was mad for your father." He cleared his throat. "Now, he, mind you, he probably needs all the words you've got to say, eh?"

"He needs more than words, Uncle. He needs our help. I'm sure he's very much alive and probably in trouble." Jane spoke quietly but clearly, sure that no one else could hear her in the general murmur of leave taking.

Her uncle's brows shot up, and he glanced around. "Do you know what you're saying, niece?"

She nodded.

His brows contracted in a heavy frown, and he offered his arm to her.

Again, Jane felt that moment of hesitation, caught between the ways of Halab and the ways of London. She took his arm, and he turned them toward the church door.

The crowd was thinning, but her uncle looked about before he spoke again. "Did your father leave you a map? Always giving maps to people, as if we were all about to go haring off on an adventure."

"Did he give you one, Uncle?"

"No, but I have one, one he gave to your mother long ago. Don't know where the thing has got to, but if you've got one, best to keep it to yourself. Don't let anyone see it." He looked around again although the vestibule was now nearly empty.

She nodded. She had believed the map in *The Husband Hunter's Guide* to be significant from the moment she'd seen it. Now curiosity consumed her about her uncle's map. She glanced around. No one seemed to note their conversation. The Last Bench Lending Library friends stood at the foot of the chapel steps, exchanging talk and laughs.

Her uncle looked chagrinned. "Well, I'd best be on my way, niece. You've got other fish to fry, eh? Your grandmamma tells me you're on the lookout for a husband. Don't want to hurt your chances by talking to an oldster like me."

"I hope I may talk to family, Uncle Thaddeus, and still expect to attract a husband." Jane smiled at him. She didn't want to ask him outright for his map from her father, but she did want to see it. "May I call on you, Uncle? Is it done?"

His face brightened. "Of course, my girl. You've got some kind of companion, haven't you?"

"I do."

"Well, I've only my bachelor's digs in Hampstead, but my man can make a decent cup of tea. You'll come have a dish of tea, eh? This afternoon?"

Jane nodded. Her uncle had a map of her father's. She would get Hazelwood to take her. "Thank you, Uncle Thaddeus."

She joined the Last Bench Lending Library members as churchgoers waited for carriages to arrive. Margaret smiled at her. Her grandmother's companion looked different after her talk with her friends, livelier, brighter, almost cheerful. Jane would have to get her grandmother out more often. "Now that you know how we operate, Miss Fawkener, you must bring a book next time."

"I shall." Jane smiled back.

Across the narrow street Hazelwood emerged from behind his carriage, and she wondered whether he had seen his mother leave the church.

\* \* \* \*

In the end Jane could get him to say nothing about his family other than to admit that he had an older, married sister. When the conversation shifted back to the investiture ceremony, she was able to persuade him to take her to Hampstead by refusing to practice another minute and by agreeing that she would return from her cousins' musicale that evening in his carriage. Uncle Thaddeus's white cottage was tucked away among other houses on a hillside sloping toward the heath. A narrow lane passed by the high-walled garden, and the interior was fitted up like the inside of the ship that had brought Jane back to London with wood paneled walls, upon which hung the brass tools of the sailor's trade—clocks, barometers, and sextants.

Uncle Thaddeus settled them in the small dark parlor in heavy chairs with worn leather seats. His man brought the tea tray and set it on a battered old sea chest that filled the center of the room. The tea was weak, the old-fashioned dishes worn and chipped, and the plate of biscuits quite sparse. A meager fire burned in the grate. Her uncle was either very frugal or very short of cash. For a few moments they talked about the house and how her uncle's prize money had allowed him to settle there when he left the navy. A large square of blank paneling above the hearth drew Hazelwood's attention.

"Are you missing a work of art, Captain Drummond?"

Uncle Thaddeus put down his dish of tea and patted his whiskers with a napkin. "That I am, Hazelwood. Hoping to ask my niece Jane for some help in the matter, but first things first. Promised to show her one of her father's maps."

Thaddeus rose from his chair and signaled them both to stand, beckoning them across the room to a large desk under a round window like a ship's porthole. He lit a lamp.

"Didn't think I'd know where this was, but I found it right off." He unrolled a sheet of heavy yellowing paper and spread it on his desk anchoring the ends with a compass and some bits of sea-weathered wood and loops of iron that Jane did not recognize.

She bit back her disappointment when she leaned over to look and found that it was a map of the city of Oxford, the locations of the ancient colleges marked by shields of their coats of arms.

"I suspect that it's one of the early maps he sent your mother before they married," said her uncle. "Perhaps even the first one."

"And he sent her other maps?" Hazelwood asked. With one finger he traced down the center of the map from the Banbury Road along St. Giles street through the town to where the River Cherwell met the Thames in the south.

"It was their way," her uncle replied. "Do you see these notes?" He pointed to a pair of initials inked onto the map, like those Jane had found in her book. "EF, JL?"

"Yes, I see them. What's the significance?" Hazelwood asked.

"All family members' initials, you see."

"Oh?"

"EF, why that's your grandmamma, Jane, Lady Eliza Fawkener. And JL, that's your mother's mother, Julia Leigh."

Jane nodded. She did see. The inked pairs of initials dotted the map the way the pairs of initials dotted the pages of her *Husband Hunter's Guide*.

"George and Julia would have a good laugh about those initials, I guess. The families, you see, didn't want them to marry. Neither the Fawkeners nor the Drummonds. Julia was supposed to marry some fellow our parents picked out, so Fawkener and Julia invented a secret way of communicating."

"Communicating what?" Hazelwood asked.

"When they were apart, and he was up at Oxford, he would write to her that he planned to visit some family member. It was his way of telling her where he'd be and when. He had initials for special places in London where they could meet when he was in town."

"So," said Hazelwood, "she had the map, and when she received a letter, she would go to the map and know where to meet him?"

"Just so. He'd write something like—will visit Uncle Matthew for tea. Then she would know to go to St. Martin's or some such place. Or he'd write that he was coming to visit Henry, and she'd know that he meant for her to meet him in Old St. George's burial ground where Henry is buried." Thaddeus grinned at them, pleased to be able to explain. "This Oxford map was just the first. He gave her one when he went abroad, too, just after they married on his first mission." Uncle Thaddeus cleared his throat. "That is, adventure, wanted her to be sure she knew how to follow his journey. Damned uncertain times to be on the continent."

Jane studied the map. She recognized the same sets of initials she had detected in her book. "Uncle Thaddeus, do you know who all these people are? RD and HD?"

Thaddeus's brow wrinkled. "It's been a long time since I thought much about 'em, but those are my dead brothers—Richard and Henry." He tapped the map where JW appeared. "That's your Great Uncle John Walhouse, I think. And," he tapped another set of initials, "that's Frederick Walhouse that died young. Your grandmamma will have all these people noted either in her peerage or her Bible."

Jane kept her gaze on the map. She had not been wrong. Her little book was full of clues to her father's route, and now she understood her father's two-part system. To trace a journey of his, you needed the marked map, and the letters with their deceptive air of chatty news about the family. It helped to know the family tree, in which he had trained her well.

She looked up and found Hazelwood watching her, reminding her of one more thing she had—a protocol officer, who was the government's man and who now possessed the key to her father's secret methods of communication.

"You're welcome to take the map, niece. It was your mother's after all." Uncle Thaddeus gave her an awkward pat on the shoulder and began rolling up the map.

"Thank you, Uncle. I'd like that. I have little that belonged to her."

Thaddeus cleared his throat. "Niece, would you mind doing your uncle a bit of a favor?"

"If I can, I will, uncle."

Uncle Thaddeus tied a black ribbon around the rolled map and pointed with it to the bare wood above his mantel. "There's a picture of mine that your papa was keeping for me. Now your cousins have it, and I'd like it back."

"Picture, uncle?"

"It's called *Nelson Turning a Blind Eye.* Clever as can be. There he is the great man himself, in the thick of the battle, putting his blind eye to the telescope, so that he can disregard orders and win the day. Painted by one of those big-canvas, history painters, you know."

"How did it end up with the cousins?" Hazelwood asked.

Thaddeus shook his head. "When they took over Fawkener house, they claimed the furnishings, too. I was supposed to be there for the reading of your father's will, niece. Damned quick it was. Somebody from the Foreign Office must have told them your papa was gone, because they were reading the will before any news of him reached the papers. I was lucky to catch wind of it from talk at the Admiralty, but I was too late to get the picture with Lady Phoebe already in possession."

"Uncle, is it the large painting above the staircase?"

"That's the one. Quite on the grand scale, must be five feet across and nearly seven feet high, I think. Thing is, I can't see Phoebe caring about a picture like that. Not her style at all."

Jane nodded. She remembered that painting, more for what was behind it than what it looked like from the stairs. She would not be leaving the house tonight with her uncle's picture tucked under her cloak.

In the carriage, Hazelwood turned to her. "You do realize that your dear Uncle Thaddeus appears to be low on funds at the moment."

"I noticed."

"No doubt he intends to sell that painting. So are we stealing it tonight?" Jane turned to him. "On my second night as a husband hunter?"

"In a hurry to get a husband, are you?"

"How many gentlemen should I consider, do you think, before I make my choice? Five or six or a score?"

"You sound as if you're hiring for the position."

"Could I? Would an ad in the papers be a more direct method of finding just the man I want?"

Jane smiled to herself as he turned the carriage at the end of the narrow lane. At least for the moment she'd made him forget about paintings and maps.

* * * *

It was dark by the time Hazelwood returned to the club and growing colder by the hour. He had sent Wilde off on an assignment earlier, and Miranda had taken over the youth's duties temporarily, setting out a tray of sandwiches and coffee. He asked her to bring him what he called the club copy of *The Husband Hunter's Guide to London*.

Drawing a chair close to the fire, he settled down to review the pages of the little book, thinking about what he'd learned from Jane's uncle and what he still needed to know.

He had read dozens of George Fawkener's letters, which had been copied by a man in the Foreign Office, but Hazelwood had read them, as a man indifferent to family connections, skipping over the chatty news of tea with aunts, walks with uncles, and visits to cousins. He had been searching for anything that might reveal the state of England's friends in the East. He'd been wrong. He should, apparently, have been paying attention to the very thing he'd ignored, Fawkener's accounts of visiting his relatives. That was the code.

He stretched his feet out and propped his boots on the brass fender. The question was—how well acquainted was Jane with her father's code? This afternoon she'd given nothing away, neither in her face nor manner. Yet presumably, she knew her father's code, and with the book, she had a sequence of points on a map. He wondered, whether she had the corresponding map in her possession, as well. Had the code and the map given her the certainty that her father was alive?

He flipped through the little book again. The coded pairs of letters appeared on the left or right pages, in the upper or lower corner to convey some element of Fawkener's journey as yet undetermined. As he puzzled over the possibilities, a passage caught his eye, and he read:

*The Husband Hunter's first evening in society will be a success, if but one gentleman in the crowd takes note of her. However limited her beauty and accomplishments, the element of novelty in her appearance among the familiar faces of several seasons will assist her in drawing notice. Her youth and her eagerness to please and to be pleased in company will encourage gentlemen to stay by her side long enough to discover her charms of character as well as appearance. Young men will vie for her attention, and a prudent woman will not deny any an opportunity to make her better acquaintance until she discovers an irredeemable character flaw that requires her to dismiss a gentleman from her suitors.*

—*The Husband Hunter's Guide to London*

Tonight Jane would be that fresh girl at the party, a girl Allegra could never be. Few men might notice, but if even one man saw Jane the way she was, the game would change. Hazelwood didn't like it. He had all the advantage of private time with her, of a hundred opportunities to meet and hold her gaze, to make a joke, to touch in all the ways that he knew could awaken her sleeping sensuality. But he had none of the rights of a suitor. He could do nothing honest.

What he had was a job to do. He closed the little book and stood and stretched and turned from the fire. He needed to get his hands on Jane's copy of the book, the one she carried with her at all times. He must charm and mislead and deceive until he had possession of the book. And then he had to find the corresponding map.

If Jane Fawkener learned to flirt and dance and accept the attentions of dozens of men of fashion, it should not matter to him in the least.

\* \* \* \*

At Clive's request and over Hazelwood's objections, Jane arrived ahead of the other guests to meet her family. She was shown up to her cousin Phoebe's dressing room, where a pair of lady's maids were engaged in finishing Phoebe and Allegra's hair for the evening.

Phoebe gave Jane's appearance a thorough scrutiny. "I can't fault you, Jane, except perhaps to recommend the regular application of Gowland's Lotion for the freckles. We'll send a jar of lotion home with you tonight, and your maid can apply it at bedtime."

Her cousin turned back to look critically at her own appearance and direct her maid in adjustments to her coiffure, and Jane saw a chance to slip out of the room. Her uncle's painting beckoned.

Jane paused in the hall as the sounds of servants preparing for the party drifted up the grand staircase from below. On either side of her were concealed jib doors, made to look like the wall itself, one door led to the servants' stair and the other to a closet above the grand staircase behind her uncle's painting. A flash of memory of her younger self in the closet sent her hand reaching under the molding to push the concealed latch. The door opened, and she stepped into the dark.

She took a deep breath, inhaling musty smells of forgotten things. The scratchy folds of a wool coat and the slippery perfumed silk of some old evening cape enclosed her as if she were wearing the *chadri* again, that tent-like covering of a modest woman in the public places of the East. Behind the mesh face piece and under the blue concealing folds of her *chadri* she had watched her father's guests and hosts over the years. Silent and unobserved, she might as well have been in a closet.

When she was ten, her father had shown her the spy hole concealed in her uncle's grand painting. A panel in the wall slid to one side, exposing the back of the painting. Her father had given her the job of watching a group of men arriving for a meeting and telling him, if she could, which of them were on his side and which were against him. If only it were as easy now.

She found the latch and slid the panel aside. A beam of light shot through the hole. The trick was not to touch the canvas itself. Behind her the concealed door opened. She lifted her hand to cover the spy hole.

*It is necessary to cultivate the art of conversation. You must speak while dancing all but the most vigorous country dances and waltzes. But how is the Husband Hunter to learn the art of conversation? Practice, of course.*

*There is in every society a subject into which complete strangers enter readily and by which they signal their interest in continuing a conversation. In London that subject is the weather. Once you have established your partner's willingness to converse, you may learn much through the weather. In talking about the incessant rain, or a severe frost, or the dry weather for harvest, the Husband Hunter may judge of the affability, the wit, and the balance of concern for others and self-concern her conversational partner possesses.*

*Inevitably, the topic of weather will exhaust itself, as surely as rain clouds move off. That is the moment in which the Husband Hunter must keep her wits about her. There are a number of topics on which she must never speak. Do not speak of anyone's personal appearance, neither your rival's, nor your own, nor that of the oddest looking person in the room. Furthermore, avoid speaking of yourself, your accomplishments, or your family. You may, on the other hand, always speak of principles and art and the beauties of the setting in which you find yourself.*

*Are there subjects that arise about which you have very little knowledge, but which are of great interest to your partner? So much the better. His knowledge of cricket or the arrangements for the officers' living aboard his majesty's ships or the intricate points of tithing is an opportunity for you to exercise your curiosity. In encouraging him to speak, you are not so much learning a new subject, as observing the workings of his mind and determining his character.*

*—The Husband Hunter's Guide to London*

# Chapter Thirteen

"Jane, I know you're in here. Are you hiding?" The door closed, and Jane's youngest cousin Annabel pushed her way in among the cloaks and coats.

Jane released the breath she'd been holding. Her thirteen-year-old cousin was no threat. "I am scouting the terrain."

"Mama won't like it if you ruin your hair and dress."

"Promise you won't tell."

Annabel offered her solemn promise. "What are you scouting in the dark?"

"There's a spy hole over the grand staircase." *And perhaps a concealed map that will help me find my father.*

"Really? A spy hole? Not mice and spiders? Where are you?"

Jane reached out and found Annabel's arm. "Come stand on this box, but don't touch the...wall." She lifted her hand from the spy hole, admitting a ray of light that illuminated Annabel's face.

Annabel stepped up on the box and pressed her eye to the tiny opening. "Oh, you can see the whole entrance stair with everybody coming up. How cunning! But won't people see us?"

"They won't if we are careful not to touch the canvas." Her uncle's painting concealed the tiny hole in the end of Nelson's famous telescope from the Battle of Copenhagen. From below guests would see only the glint at the end of the telescope. Her father loved the joke.

Annabel moved back from the peephole. "I see what you're about Jane. You want to see the eligible gentlemen. I think it's a good plan."

"Do you see anyone eligible?" Jane wanted to laugh at her thirteen-year-old cousin. Obviously, husband hunting started early in London.

"You mean anyone young?" Annabel returned to her position looking down on the arriving guests. "I only see old married men and ladies so far, but don't worry. Mama's parties are famous, and young men always come late. How did you find this spy hole? I never knew it was here."

"My father showed it to me." Her father believed in watching the way people arranged their faces as they arrived at a meeting or a party. There were a dozen small gestures through which one could read honesty or falseness.

"Finally." Annabel sighed and stepped back from the peephole, and Jane leaned forward to take a look.

She saw a fashionable young man in black evening wear with cropped ginger hair, ruddy fair looks, and an utterly guileless manner. "Is he an eligible?"

"Oh, yes!" Annabel sighed again. "That's Cecil Eversley. He has dogs. Allegra won't talk to him because his fortune's too small for her. If it were my season, I would talk to him, but it won't be my season for three years, seven months, and three days."

"An eternity."

Annabel sighed again, and Jane watched a pair of girls in white gowns make their curtsies to cousin Phoebe and nods to Allegra.

"What do you see now?" Annabel tugged at Jane's sleeve.

"Allegra's rivals, I think. They look very English in their white gowns."

"Let me see." Annabel took Jane's place. "Oh, Lady Rivers's daughters. Their mother thinks they are great beauties, but you needn't worry. You look very English tonight, too."

"Do I?" She did not feel English. She should, she supposed, feel excited and on edge with anticipation about her second venture into London society. She felt instead as if she were going to a play, as if everything that would happen would happen to other people, and that she would sit in the darkness observing, moved briefly, perhaps by the players' distress or joy, but still on the outside. And later she would tell Hazelwood about it.

At the peephole Annabel gave a giggle. She stepped away and spun in a quick whirl, setting the coats in motion and stirring the musty air.

"What is it?"

"Just what Mama's party needs." Annabel pushed Jane back into place behind the painting.

A crowd of late arrivals, all young men, jostled their way up the stairs, talking and laughing, and tossing coats and hats at the butler, Bolton, and his footmen. Among them Jane spotted Hazelwood, bold as brass, flinging a cloak on the pile in a footman's arms. Hazelwood looked directly at the painting. From below, it seemed impossible to steal without ladders and accomplices, but if Jane told him about the panel in the closet, Hazelwood would steal it. The feeling of being at a play vanished. Instead she felt as if one of the actors had called her up from the audience to join him on stage.

Behind her, Annabel sneezed. "Jane, you should go down, unless you want Allegra to have all the gentlemen to herself."

Jane slid the panel back into place, secured the latch, and reminded Annabel to tell no one.

\* \* \* \*

Once past the beleaguered butler, Hazelwood took care to draw no attention to himself. He avoided any encounter with his hostess and her family, kept mainly to the window embrasures, and let his gaze slide away from anyone who gave him a puzzled glance of partial recognition.

An hour passed in which he listened to a florid Italian soprano, studied the pattern of Lady Strayde's carpet, and looked for Jane in the crowd. He wasted no thought on the painting. He had seen from the stairs that they would not have an opportunity to steal it at present. He might make Uncle Thaddeus a loan.

Waiters ignored him, and over-warm guests passed rather closer to one another than all but the most licentious waltz permitted. Every ingénue looked the same. In his outcast state, he had forgotten the tyranny of fashion, which dictated a uniformity of dress for respectable young women that made them nearly indistinguishable. A Broadwind pianoforte, as yet untouched, told him the evening was far from over.

He spotted Jane at last in the interval after the soprano's performance. She and Allegra shared opposite ends of a striped green and gold silk sofa. Allegra managed no fewer than four admirers from her end of the sofa with the cool command of a colonel of the line. Young men brought her refreshments, or held her fan, or gestured extravagantly to capture her flickering attention. At the opposite end of the sofa Jane talked quietly with a ginger-haired fellow, Cecil Eversley, who had her unwavering attention, and who, in Hazelwood's opinion, would never do as a husband for Jane.

Hazelwood had not taken her husband hunting seriously, or he had not believed that she took it seriously. But now that she was out in the world where other men were free to admire her, to discover that gleam in her eye when she was about to say something sharp, he feared a husband might find her. Her thick hair was up, her slender neck and the hollows at the base of her throat, exposed. The customary white dress looked as substantial as a cloud.

He wanted to tell Allegra's admirers that they had the wrong end of the sofa, but he realized that young men inevitably chose the wrong end of the sofa, as he had done years earlier.

* * * *

Jane had no idea where Hazelwood had gone. Once again he had entered a party, this time in violation of the agreement they'd made, where his hosts were likely to toss him out rather than offer him a seat of honor.

The rooms were crowded with guests, most of them in motion in the interval after the soprano. From her position at the end of Allegra's sofa Jane could see little beyond the skirts and waistcoats of passing guests. The young man Annabel admired, Cecil Eversley, had looked so downcast at Allegra's coldness that Jane had spoken to him.

"You like dogs, I hear," she had said.

He had brightened at once, and they had been talking ever since. To be honest, he had done most of the talking, but that had left her brain free to worry about what Hazelwood might be up to. He was not supposed to enter the house. He was to collect Jane at the end of the evening. That was the plan. He had spoken in jest about stealing the painting, and she hoped he would not attempt the impossible. But he had already gone beyond what they'd agreed to by entering the party.

She widened her smile and gave Eversley a reply to help his story of one of his dogs giving birth to a large litter of puppies. Poor man. He had all the qualities her guide admired, yet he'd never be a favored suitor as long as Allegra was doing the choosing. She wondered whether he would wait to choose a wife until Annabel's three years, seven months, and three days expired, and she tried to remember what the *Husband Hunter's Guide* said about persistence.

It occurred to her that if she were truly hunting a husband, she would choose very differently from the man in front of her. She would choose a man who was competent and fearless, indifferent to opinion, and inclined to confront authority rather than bow to it.

In the next moment Lady Strayde called on Allegra to display her musical accomplishments. Allegra stood. Eversley stopped speaking. His gaze swung from Jane to Allegra. She smiled at her other admirers and turned to Eversley. His face colored, a stunned look of pleasure came into his eyes, and he stuck out both his elbows, like a bird preparing for flight. With a toss of her head and a swift punishing glance at Jane, Allegra seized Eversley's arm and hauled him toward the pianoforte. Her followers hurried after her, and a general rearrangement of guests and chairs left Jane alone. She supposed she should be downcast, but she felt relieved to be alone.

She was thinking about that look in Eversley's eyes when a tug on her right wrist made her turn and glance over her shoulder. Hazelwood had her by the arm and pulled her between the heavy velvet curtains at the edge of a deep window embrasure. "Figured out yet how to get your uncle's painting back?"

"As a matter of fact, I have." She turned resolutely toward Allegra as the girl began to play. The guests now occupied irregular rows of little gilt chairs facing the pianoforte.

"You're not going to tell me?"

She disengaged her hand. "I'm not, because you should not be here, and my cousins must not see you."

"Thanks to the wonders of English architecture, I've been invisible these past two hours."

"We agreed that you were to collect me later." They had agreed that it was unlikely that an assailant would strike at her while Allegra Walhouse played the pianoforte. She wondered what had prompted him to change his plan. Now he took her by the shoulders and shifted her position. "If you stand here, just so, no one will see me."

"If you had an ounce of common sense, you would—"

"Stick to the plan? How dull! You don't like dull men."

"Don't I? I quite enjoyed talking with Cecil Eversley just now."

"Did you? Should I tell you how that exchange looked to me?"

She shook her head. He was far too perceptive.

"I think I must in the interest of your husband hunting plans. There was Eversley, prosing on, probably about his dogs. He's famous for talking about them. There you were, with polite and perhaps even kindly indulgence, letting him tell you about some mastiff's pedigree and the animal's astonishing cleverness, with your hands folded in your lap and your lips fixed in a bland smile just short of rigor mortis."

She laughed and drew a sharp reproving glance from a turbaned matron, even as she felt Hazelwood tug the blue ribbons dangling from her high waist and pull her farther back into the deep window embrasure. Jane had a feeling she was violating all the rules her guide recommended.

"You are so wrong. Is there no guide for young men? Eversley apparently has no idea about how to…"

"Talk with a woman? Flirt a little?"

"None. I like him the better for it."

"It won't win him Allegra's heart, that is, if she has a heart to be won." Hazelwood spoke directly in her ear, so that his breath disturbed a loose strand of her hair. She could not help a slight shiver at the sensation.

"He's already won a heart I think." She was thinking of poor besotted Annabel.

Her words were almost lost in the applause for Allegra's first piece, but Hazelwood gave a start as if he'd seen some danger. Jane glanced around but could see no threat as Allegra immediately moved to her next selection.

"Shouldn't you slip out while Allegra is playing?"

"Are you so eager to return to Eversley?"

"Merely hinting that great stealth is the proper protocol for an uninvited guest's leave-taking."

"Don't worry. I'll manage."

"It—"

"Jane!" At the sound of her name, she turned and saw Clive.

"What are you doing so far in the shadows? Didn't mother have a seat for you in the front?" As he caught sight of Hazelwood, his smile vanished. "How in the deuce did you get in here, sir? My mother will have an apoplexy if she sees you."

Hazelwood stepped from behind Jane. "Lady Strayde's house, is it? I must have mistaken the place for a more entertaining establishment. I'll take my leave."

"Just a minute." Clive's face flushed an angry red. "I don't know what permits you to claim an acquaintance with my cousin, but you can't go pulling her into corners in this shabby way."

"Worried that my presence will cost your mother an invitation to the famous Vange ball?"

Clive caught the eye of a footman and gave the man a curt order.

Hazelwood bowed to Jane, his eyes alight with unholy satisfaction, and turned toward the salon doors, his movement unhurried.

Clive pulled Jane's arm through his and patted her hand. "That fellow has no sense of how unwelcome he is here and elsewhere. He takes advantage of your ignorance."

"My ignorance?" Jane could not help asking. She made a note that if she were ever to write a guide to husband hunting if would include a list of those condescending gestures gentlemen made that really should disqualify them as potential husbands. Hand patting would be on her list.

"He's debauched, hopelessly in debt, and utterly cast off by his family. You don't know the story, of course, but his outrageous behavior nearly ruined my mother's sister."

"Can you tell me?"

Clive momentarily checked his tongue, his gaze on Bolton approaching with two footmen. He nodded to the butler and cocked his head toward Hazelwood's back. "Perhaps you should know." Clive hesitated. "Hazelwood interrupted my youngest aunt's wedding, stormed in really, sword drawn, and hauled her out. He claimed that they had an understanding and that she was being forced to marry Stafford. Of course, nothing could have been farther from the truth."

"When was that?" Jane asked. Across the room she could see Bolton and two footmen move purposely around the seated guests, who turned to stare after them, in spite of Allegra's cascading notes.

"Years ago. I was just a boy, younger than Percy. It must have been ought five or six." Clive, too, watched Bolton rather than his sister.

*When Hazelwood was twenty.* "And your aunt, did she ever marry?"

"Oh yes, Stafford, of course. She's quite the happy matron."

"I'm glad to hear it. It would be sad if one day's folly by an ill-judging young man had cast a shadow over a woman's whole life."

Clive laughed. "You're a sly one, Jane, getting me to admit that my aunt recovered."

Once, Jane and her father had broken a journey in the month of Moharren, to attend a mystery play that lasted ten days in which the slaughter of Imam Hoossein at the battle of Karbala was reenacted. Apart from her father among the women, Jane had been surprised when the audience reacted with a grief as keen and unrestrained as if the death had happened only that week and not centuries earlier. When she had asked her father about it, he told her that families were great keepers of grievances. Trust me, he'd said, families have libraries and chests full of them. She remembered the incident because her father had been uncharacteristically serious. No laugh or playful wink had accompanied the words. They had been spoken instead as a solemn truth.

Hazelwood had reached the salon doors when he simply stopped to look at her uncle's painting. Jane tensed, willing him to keep moving as Bolton advanced.

Allegra moved into the final flourishes of her performance, the audience stirred, and another footman, looking at his tray of glasses, oblivious of the phalanx bearing down on Hazelwood, stepped directly into the path of the oncoming men. At the collision his tray went askew, and glasses flew upward. Guests jumped aside as champagne rained down, and when Jane glanced back, Hazelwood was gone.

Jane was left staring at the painting. She joined in the polite applause, turning to watch Allegra take her bows, sure that Hazelwood had come to the same conclusion she had. The painting concealed the map.

*Contrary to what the Husband Hunter might expect this guide to suggest, she must not fall in love. It is no more advantageous to "fall" in love, than to fall from a horse or a bridge or down a flight of steps. The uncontrolled path of a falling object and the inevitable end of a fall in a broken head or broken limbs is no apt metaphor for the onset of deep and lasting affection. Love does not happen to us as a result of chance or a misstep. It is not induced by Cupid's arrows, nor by the juices of rare flowers applied to one's eyelids. We may discover that love has begun, or that we are in the midst of love with another person, but not because we have fallen but because, in a fertile garden carefully planted and tended, love has bloomed in its season and place when perhaps we were not looking.*

*—The Husband Hunter's Guide to London*

# Chapter Fourteen

Hazelwood handed Jane into the carriage and climbed in after her without speaking. He settled a rug over their legs and feet. The carriage lamps cast a faint light into the cold interior.

"Are you sure you want to leave? We could make a push to get your uncle's painting. Cut it out of the frame, roll it up."

"You already created a sufficient stir this evening, you know."

"Did I?" He knocked against the forward panel for the coachman to start the horses and leaned back against the leather upholstery. The dim light revealed his profile, the straight line of his brow above the deep-set eyes, the plain thrust of his nose, and the faint pull of a smile on his lips. In profile he looked almost ordinary, almost like the sort of man her guide would recommend, a sensible man of good character and respectable reputation. She reminded herself that he was no such thing.

"The clumsy footman, I take it, is an associate of yours?" She hardly needed to ask.

"Did Clive give you trouble on my account?"

"Clive forgave my ignorance in connecting myself with you."

"Generous of him."

"He explained how you offended his family at his aunt's wedding. Do you want to tell me your version of the story?" She could imagine how offhandedly he would tell the story, making light of his feelings for the bride. She guessed he might have been very much in love, at twenty.

"I'm sure Clive's version sheds a sufficiently glaring light on my faults."

"Must you play the hero all on your own?"

"The situation called for action. That's what I do. I act. Are you going to tell me what you discovered about the painting?" There was a touch of irritation in his tone.

"After you have confessed to a habit of independent action more likely to harm you than anyone else?"

"Clive's story is an old one. No damage done. You can see for yourself." He took her gloved hand in his, slipped it inside his greatcoat, and pressed it against his chest, his warm, hard chest. Through soft wool and silk and linen she could feel the strong beat of his heart. The sudden intimacy altered the smooth rhythm of her pulse.

The carriage rattled along over the stones, and under the rug her knee bumped against his thigh. Hazelwood's other hand slid around the back of her neck and pulled her closer. The wool scarf over her head slipped back.

"We didn't finish our conversation about how to behave alone with a gentleman in the dark."

She swallowed. "I decided never to be alone with a gentleman in the dark."

"Yet here you are." His low voice had that break in it that turned her insides to jelly and made the inches apart seem like too much. His mouth was near but not near enough. It was like the end of a desert journey, when the donkeys stumbled on their feet, and it was dangerous to even think of water.

He took her other hand in his and lifted it to his face. "Eversley's not the man for you, you know."

"He is exactly the sort of man my guide recommends."

He shook his head. "Let me show you why your guide is wrong."

"You mean tell me."

"Eversley's touch doesn't move you, and what's more, you know it."

She could not deny the truth of it. Though she had no experience by which to judge, some instinct of which she had been previously unaware told her as much. She had barely tolerated Clive's patting her hand, yet Hazelwood's tying her bonnet or tugging at her ribbons drew her whole person to him, like a wave sucked back to the sea.

She should lean away from him, but her body refused to move. "You know, I have had suitors before." She was not as green as he supposed.

"Have you?" He pulled the wool garment from around her throat.

"Once, the woodcutter's son asked my father what price he would accept for me. And another time the neighborhood widower who raised pigeons on his roof told my father that the sight of me in our courtyard had inspired him to think of marriage again."

"How is a fellow to impress a woman of such vast experience, I wonder?" She could hear the laughter in his voice. And felt the change in him when the laughter died.

He lowered his head and leaned forward across the narrow space where their breath already mingled in the frigid air. Then he kissed her.

At first it was a lazy, teasing kiss, lips meeting in a touch as light and airy as words and wit. It coaxed her along, floating lightly on the tide of their wordless exchange, until she was far out from shore, not anchored any more to the bench of a rocking carriage rolling through London. A deeper current of feeling welled up and knocked her off-balance. She clung to him more. He was solid and real.

His mouth took firm and unyielding possession of hers. The kiss became a question about who she truly was, the husband hunter she claimed to be, or a daring woman who would put her trust in a stranger who was still a mystery to her yet who seemed to understand her as no one ever had. The dark, rocking coach seemed made for their encounter. He slid so that his body angled down and made a hard slope against which she lay, held in place by his arm around the small of her back and his mouth on hers.

As long as she kept the little book secure, and as long as no one else discovered the map, her actions would not endanger her father. As soon as the thought occurred, she broke away, her breath warm and ragged, her body vibrating with sensation. "Thank you for the lesson. It was most instructive. I will know how to avoid being alone with any government protocol officer trying to persuade me to steal a painting from one of his majesty's subjects."

Their carriage halted. They had reached the hotel. She scrambled back on to the seat, rearranging her disordered skirts. It was time to break free of the hold he had on her, to remember that she had only one purpose in London, and it was not to find a husband but a father.

\* \* \* \*

An hour after the last guests had left, Clive found his mother at her dressing table as her maid undid her coiffure. At forty-six, Phoebe Walhouse had no reliance on dyes. What silver had invaded her gold curls was disguised in the intricate arrangements her expert dresser created.

Clive seated himself and waited for a flushed Allegra to finish recounting the attentions she had received from eligible admirers. As impatient as he was to keep his evening appointment with Pamela, he felt the fresh recital of Allegra's triumphs would dispose his mother to favor his request.

When Phoebe dismissed her maid and Allegra yawned, he brought the matter up. "Mother, don't you think we should invite Jane Fawkener to make her home with us this Season?"

"Her home?" Allegra squeaked. "Mother, you wouldn't. It's my season."

Clive countered, "So it is, dear sister, but you wouldn't want anything said against you when your cousin is received elsewhere and people wonder why we haven't taken her in."

Allegra opened her mouth, but Phoebe silenced her with a look. "Really, Clive, Jane Fawkener is no concern of yours. If your father is not troubled about the girl, you need not be either."

"Mother, what could be the harm in having Jane with us for a few weeks? The Season proper hasn't even begun yet, and there's no danger of Jane poaching any of Allegra's beaux."

"She kept Eversley to herself all night," Allegra protested.

Clive shrugged. "You don't want Eversley."

"That's not the point. He's my beau not hers."

"Children, this squabble is absurd." Phoebe waved her maid away. "The girl is plain enough. She makes a good foil for Allegra's brilliance. I distrust her eyes though. I think she has an unbecoming habit of judging for herself."

Clive thought about it. "She's merely ignorant and cautious."

Phoebe took a jar of cream in her hands and removed the lid. "Perhaps. I'm sure her father never taught her anything useful. And he certainly never taught her to regard family as she ought. You can't expect the Walhouses to do a great deal for her, Clive. After all, it is Allegra's season to shine."

"We could put her up in the spare room next to Annabel's for the Season? She'd be in nobody's way there. Her father did ask."

"You saw that letter, did you? I'm sure Fawkener never expected us to take her in. He never did the least thing for your father when he had difficulties."

"I thought they went to Eton together."

Phoebe gave him a condescending look. "Really, that old school ties thing is passé."

A rustling from under the bed made Allegra jump. Clive turned to see the bed skirts sticking out.

Allegra held her wrapper tight about her. "Mother, what is it?"

"It's me." Annabel wriggled out from under the bed in her night rail with a blue counterpane wrapped around her shoulders. "Couldn't we have Jane? I like her."

"Annabel," their mother said. "How long have you been under that bed?" Annabel stuck out her chin. "I wanted to hear about Allegra's party."

"You were spying," Allegra said.

"Just listening, not spying. Spying is when—"

"Annabel." Their mother frowned. "Hiding is a very bad habit. I must never hear of you hiding again."

Annabel hung her head. "Yes, Mama."

"To bed with you." Phoebe pointed toward the door, and Annabel trudged toward it, dragging the blue counterpane.

When the door closed, Phoebe turned back to her two eldest children. "Allegra, don't be a goose about Jane Fawkener. Clive, take the girls shopping tomorrow. Make sure Jane Fawkener won't embarrass the family. Goodnight." Phoebe's expression ended the interview. She dipped two fingers into her cosmetic pot and drew forth a dollop of aromatic cream.

Clive bowed. He'd won enough of a victory to enjoy Pamela's company.

*In the course of a long Season, the Husband Hunter will
inevitably hear remarks from married ladies about the nature
of conjugal intimacy. On hearing such remarks, she may doubt
that she can judge a man's character from his public manner
at a ball or in the park. Her natural curiosity about the more
private side of a man's nature may tempt her into situations of
the utmost peril to her honor and her reputation. Every man
in London knows his way to a balcony, an obscure anteroom,
or a palm-secluded corner of a conservatory in which he may
offer to satisfy the Husband Hunter's curiosity in these matters.
The Husband Hunter will do well to avoid such locales and
to remember that, until she is betrothed, the two intimacies by
which she may signal her favor are the pressure of her hand
and the warmth of her gaze.*

—*The Husband Hunter's Guide to London*

# Chapter Fifteen

A message brought Clive and Allegra to Jane's door early. Allegra
proposed a shopping expedition starting with Botibol's, the *plumassier* on
Oxford Street, where a lady could purchase ostrich plumes and flowers to
adorn her hat. Jane readily agreed. It was just the escape from Hazelwood
that she needed. The cold, clear light of day forced her to admit to herself
that she had been too much affected by his kiss.

From the moment she entered her cousins' carriage, Jane understood
that her unspoken rivalry with Allegra had heated up in spite of the bitter
weather. Jane offered no competition in the most visible hat category, for
Jane's close-fitting blue velvet cap came in a distant runner up to Allegra's
fur-lined rose silk bonnet with striking green ribbons. Nor could she
challenge Allegra's personal attractions. Allegra's golden hair gleamed
in large curls, and her blue eyes stood out vividly above her rosy cheeks.

Clive attended the ladies as far as a shop on Old Bond Street, where,
Allegra said, they would find "indispensable" ribbons. At the prospect of
ribbon shopping, Clive bowed and took his leave. A footman was engaged to
carry their purchases, and Clive promised to meet them with the barouche
at the foot of the street.

In his absence, Allegra linked arms with Jane. It felt awkward but daring to walk abreast in the street without her veils. At least Allegra's hat drew most of the stares from passersby.

"We are your family and must take an interest in you," Allegra said. "Clive wants you to come live with us, you know."

"Does he?" Jane concealed a smile at Allegra's way of making family into a millstone.

Allegra nodded. "So after last night, I feel I must advise you how to get on in London society."

"And what do you advise?" She wondered if her cousin had read the Husband Hunter's guide.

Allegra gave a great sigh. "First, you must take great care not to engage the attention of a man who is already the property of another woman."

"You mean a betrothed man, of course."

"Never!" Allegra nodded emphatically, her plumes bobbing. "But really the rule goes further. You must not admit attentions from any man with even a slight inclination in another lady's favor until *she* dismisses him. It's not done."

"Thank you for putting me on my guard."

"It's no trouble. As a cousin, I feel I must help you understand London ways. Your position in society is so precarious."

"Precarious?"

"In your situation," Allegra looked very grave, "you must forget you had a father. Oh, I know that sounds heartless, but what did he ever do for you but leave you penniless and wholly dependent on us?" Allegra gave Jane's arm a slight squeeze.

Jane could neither nod nor speak. Her certainty of her father's being alive somewhere was momentarily rocked by Allegra's blithe acceptance of his death. She concentrated on not betraying her feelings. Allegra intended no cruelty.

"I'm glad we understand each other. Now let me tell you about this part of London."

Allegra explained how most of the Old Bond Street shops catered strictly to gentlemen. When Jane asked why they looked at shops they would not enter, Allegra assured her that it was perfectly respectable to walk the street in the *morning* as long as they did not return the glances of impertinent gentlemen. Jane smiled to herself at the Allegra logic of inviting glances one did not mean to return, but she enjoyed the freedom of sending her own glance everywhere.

She looked into the stream of people coming their way, all strangers, and tried to determine the quirks that made them English. Allegra seemed to know instinctively which side of the pavement belonged to them and which they must yield to persons coming their way. Just when Jane thought she had it figured out, a man came toward them slipping swiftly through the languid strolling crowd.

His broad shoulders and massive head of shaggy russet hair rose above the crowd so that Jane could see his face clearly. It was a face she recognized instantly, and it stopped her in the middle of the pavement. She did not know the man's name, but she remembered clearly the parting handshake he had given her father on a street near the docks of Koron. The next day her father had left for his last journey.

The big man bounded up the steps of a small shop with two tall bow windows and passed inside before Jane could blink.

"Jane, what is it?" Allegra tugged on her arm. "You're standing like a gawk."

"I'd like to visit that shop." She read the sign, "Kirby & Sons."

Allegra gave the shop a doubtful glance. "It's a chemist's shop. For *gentlemen*. I've never heard of it. What could you possibly want there?"

"Soap." It was the first thing that came into her head. "I'll not be two minutes. Wait for me." She disengaged her arm from Allegra's, hurried up the steps, and opened the door. A bell jingled and a remarkably pretty girl in blue looked up from behind the counter. The door closed on Allegra's protest that she would not be left on the street and she would not wait.

Inside the little shop there was no sign of the big man and nowhere he could be concealed unless he lay on the floor at the girl's feet. It was as if he had vanished. Jane had assumed that he entered the shop to make a purchase.

"May I help you, Miss?" the girl asked. Her manner was frosty, but her voice was young and common. She gave no sign of having seen a large man enter her premises. Then Jane saw the red velvet curtains behind the counter sway as if disturbed by someone's passing.

"Soap," Jane said. She weighed the wisdom of dashing past the girl through the curtains.

"For a gentleman?" the girl asked.

"For a lady. Do you have any?"

"We do." The girl put aside her stitching and came from behind the counter.

Jane looked around as if the shop itself could explain the mystery. It was quite ordinary and not so packed with items for sale as the stalls of the soap dealers in the *souk*. Neat rows of bottles and jars lined dark wood shelves, arranged by use. Jane could see men's tooth powders and boar's bristle brushes, like the ones her father had given up years ago for fear of giving himself away as an infidel in the East.

The girl turned a key and pulled open a drawer under a counter that ran along one side of the shop. Jane glanced briefly at the curtain and tried to contain her impatience. Nothing would be gained by rushing into the situation without knowing more. She fixed her mind on the key point—a man present on her father's last day in Koron was here in London a year later, a man who might know something about her father's plans, a man who might be a friend or a foe. Until she determined which, she should proceed with caution.

She hardly saw the rows of round soaps wrapped in pale tinted papers that filled the open drawer. The girl placed a pink-wrapped soap in Jane's palm. "Smell. This one is rose-scented. Triple-milled, French."

Jane inhaled the delicate flowery aroma, like perfume.

"We have soaps in almond, lavender, and verbena as well," the girl said.

"Do you have an olive oil soap?" Jane asked.

"Olive oil?" The girl shook her head, took the soap from Jane's hand, and replaced it with another. "Try this one."

Jane obliged her. The lemony smell was lovely, but it was not the soap of home, not the brown-rimmed bars with the deep green centers of the richest soaps, aged the longest, for which the merchants charged the most. The soap in her palm was pale green like a three-month soap, the kind a woman of Halab would use only for washing her hands. Still Jane would buy it. Allegra must not suspect her of any other reason for entering the shop.

"Thank you," she told the girl. "I'll take this one." The shop name and number on the paper would help her find the place again.

"That will be twelve and six." The girl took the bar from Jane and stepped back behind her counter.

Jane faced the curtain. Was the big man Kirby, the proprietor of the shop? It made no sense that a London shopkeeper would travel to Koron to meet with her father. She was turning questions over in her mind as she reached for her bag when footsteps from the other side of the curtain made the girl turn eagerly. Jane held her breath and tried to calm herself. The big man would not recognize her. He had never seen her out of her veils. When he spoke with the shopgirl, Jane might learn his identity.

But the big man did not appear. Instead Hazelwood stepped through the curtain in white shirtsleeves and gray trousers, with a dark blue silk waistcoat in his hand. "Miranda," he said, "a button's come loose. Could you—"

He broke off as his gaze collided with Jane's. "You."

Jane nodded. Her throat had gone very dry. "Hazelwood."

"What are you doing *here*?" he asked.

Jane could feel Miranda's curious, alert scrutiny directed her way. It was not friendly.

"Buying soap." She had never seen Hazelwood at a loss.

He shifted his position to block Jane's view of the curtains, and she felt herself stiffen. She did not ask him what he was doing there. His obvious familiarity with the place and the girl spoke for themselves.

Hazelwood turned to the girl. "Miss Kirby, forgive me. I didn't realize you had a customer."

"It's no trouble, Lord Hazelwood. Leave the waistcoat with me. You'll have it as soon as I attend to the lady."

Jane gritted her teeth. She did not miss Miranda Kirby's signal. The girl was letting Jane know that Hazelwood belonged to her. It occurred to Jane that he might live there, above the shop, or in some apartment in the rear of the building. He might live where the big man from Koron had disappeared. He must know the man in any case. It could not be otherwise. Her mind shut down as a howling darkness descended like a sudden sandstorm.

She fumbled the unfamiliar English coins out of her bag. They spilled onto the counter, and Miranda picked out those she wanted, giving Jane a pitying look. Hazelwood did not move from his stand in front of the curtains. Their gazes met again. He had command of himself now. His eyes revealed nothing. He put the blue waistcoat on the counter.

Jane's face felt flushed. He had toyed with her in the coach the night before, rendered her witless with a kiss that meant nothing. She had to press her lips closed to keep from speaking. *You kissed me.*

"You were to remain in the hotel this morning." Just like that he assumed command of her.

"My cousins called for me."

He glanced from her to the watching girl. "Miss Fawkener, Miss Kirby," he said. "Miss Kirby's father is an excellent tailor, perhaps not as well-known as Poole or Weston but certainly as good. He has his fitting room here in the back of the shop. Miranda helps him with some of the fine work."

Jane absorbed the lies. She had seen her father lie smoothly and convincingly to bandits and greedy officials of every sort. The trick was to start with a grain of truth. So there was some truth in Hazelwood's words, the kind of truth that concealed the bigger lies, including the lies of omission. He was not telling her about the big man.

"Do you have a maid or footman with you?" he asked, as if he'd forgotten she was with her cousins.

"We do. We're meeting Clive at the foot of the street."

"Let's get you back to the hotel then."

She wanted to protest that she was free to go where she pleased, but her throat was tight and words did not come. She nodded.

"Your soap, Miss," Miranda said.

Jane did not know how she got out of the shop. Allegra and her footman were not waiting for her, so she stood on the steps looking blindly down the street for the barouche. Then she saw it coming her way with her cousins, apparently engaged in heated discussion.

She stepped forward, and the shop door opened behind her. Before she could turn, someone grabbed her by the shoulders, spinning her around. She looked up into Hazelwood's face, close to hers at it had been the night before when she'd trusted him and thought him open and kind and funny and a bit in love as she had been.

He had thrown on a greatcoat over his shirtsleeves, and the shoulder capes fell over her arms, enveloping her in the heavy garment. She tried to pull back from his hold when a blur of movement caught her eye and something struck one of the panes in the bow window beside them with a heavy thunk. Hazelwood pressed her face against his chest as the window exploded in shards of splintering glass.

For a moment with her ear pressed against his chest, she could hear only his heart pounding.

She lifted her head. Glass bits glittered against the fawn-colored wool of his coat. He turned her toward the street again, and gripping her arm, led her down the stairs. Her cousins' barouche pulled up. She caught the frown on Clive's brow and the pout on Allegra's lips. The footman scrambled to open the door and let down the steps.

Hazelwood jerked Jane forward. There was no time to speak, either to thank him or berate him. "See Miss Fawkener safely back to her hotel."

Clive gave a curt command to his servants, and the carriage drove off.

*Before the Husband Hunter orders wedding cakes from Gunter's, she would be wise to check her runaway imagination. An unchecked imagination is as dangerous to the Husband Hunter's happiness as an unbridled and spirited horse is to her limbs. Imagination, which so inspires poets and writers, may be a false friend, indeed, to the Husband Hunter. She, who is learning to read human nature deeply, and perhaps for the first time, may be led by a quick imagination to suppose that a gentleman thinks more highly or feels more deeply than, in fact, he does. When the Husband Hunter allows her too-rapid imagination to assume the conquest of a manly breast that seems hers for the taking like an undefended town, only one result is inevitable—mortification. Furthermore, the degree to which she has let her preference and her expectations be known within her circle of friends and even beyond, the greater the humiliation she must suffer.*

*—The Husband Hunter's Guide to London*

# Chapter Sixteen

Hazelwood closed the shop door behind him. Miranda stood with a broom and dustpan ready to sweep up the broken glass. He reached down and picked up a chunk of paving stone the size of a man's fist. It had been aimed at Jane's head.

He was angry. At Jane Fawkener for setting out to avoid him this morning and exposing herself to danger. At whatever form of hired lowlife would chuck a stone at a woman's head on a busy street. At himself, most of all at himself, for kissing her and for stepping through those curtains with Miranda Kirby's name on his lips. With one careless blunder he had undone all the trust he'd built up between them.

Stealing her book had been the only way to recover from his mistake.

Goldsworthy pushed aside the velvet curtain and stuck his large head into the shop. "Did you get it then?" he asked Hazelwood.

"I did." Hazelwood held up the little blue book he'd lifted from Jane's bag.

Miranda dipped a curtsy in the big man's direction.

"Nicely done, Miss Kirby. Very cool under fire." Goldsworthy offered the girl one of his rare smiles. His glance took in the broken window and the stone in Hazelwood's hand. "Close call, was it?"

"Did Miss Fawkener see you, sir?" Hazelwood asked. "I'm trying to puzzle out why she chose to enter this shop of all the shops on Old Bond?"

The big man turned to Miranda. "When did she come in, Miss Kirby?"

"Right on your heels, sir. Just as you went through the curtain."

Goldsworthy frowned, but he shook his great head. "A near miss then. No reason for her to recognize me. I met the father in Koron, but not the daughter. Concentrate on the book, lad. Crack that code and report to me. Only days until the investiture ceremony." With that he dropped the curtain. His heavy footsteps faded down the hall.

Miranda began to sweep the shop floor. "I'll get Papa to board up that window."

Hazelwood cleared his throat. "Miranda, I owe you an apology. I'm afraid I allowed Miss Fawkener to make an assumption about our connection that does neither of us any credit."

Miranda did not look up from her sweeping. "I'm sure you did it for the case, my lord."

"That doesn't quite excuse me. I'll set the record straight the next time I see Miss Fawkener."

"There's no need on my account, my lord." The girl colored prettily.

"There's every need, Miranda. I won't have *you* pay for *my* faults."

He went out through the back of the shop and across the frozen patch of garden. In the club he hesitated once at the foot of the stairs. He could settle down to figure out George Fawkener's code, or he could get back to Jane Fawkener's side. He hefted the piece of paving stone in his hand and took the stairs two at a time. In his room, he tossed the little book on the bed. He would tackle the code later, once he knew that Fawkener's enemies couldn't get at his daughter.

* * * *

Jane stood in the marble-tiled entry of her grandmother's townhouse. She had refused to return to the hotel where Hazelwood could find her, and she'd convinced Clive and Allegra to leave her here in spite of their reproaches for her behavior in entering the chemist's shop. She did not know whether the window breaking or Hazelwood's embrace shocked them more. She suspected the latter.

As she lifted her bag to find the soap she'd purchased, she realized the bag was open. She reached in and found the soap and her few coins, but not her book. She looked at once at the floor and at the footman holding her coat and gloves, but there was no book in her grandmother's foyer. Her mind made a quick scramble back through the carriage ride to the moment she'd last opened the bag to pay for her purchase when she'd fumbled with the coins. She was sure she had not dropped the book in the shop in spite of the shock of finding Hazelwood there.

Her thoughts settled on the distracted moments on the steps outside the little shop, and she took the time apart, moment by moment—Hazelwood wrapping her in his great coat, shielding her from some object that had hurtled past them shattering glass, assisting her into the barouche. She had been lifting her skirts, watching her footing, and trying to attend to her cousins' reproaches. That was the moment he'd done it.

It was not enough for him to steal a kiss. He had to steal her book, too. She had not cursed him in days, but now a curse rose to her lips.

She sent it into the air. She wished him clumsy and awkward and confused. She wished him ragged and tattered and muddied. She wished him stuttering and tongue-tied and speechless, and she wished that whenever he tried to kiss a maiden, toads would fall from his mouth.

Her voice rang in the entry. Her grandmother's butler listened in silence until she stopped.

"Are you ready to ascend now, Miss?" he asked.

She begged his pardon, and he unbent so far as to acknowledge that he suspected she was seriously vexed. She followed him up to her grandmother's drawing room.

She remembered how she'd felt in Hazelwood's carriage, how eagerly she had returned his kiss, how he must have known how lost she was in his embrace, how she had relished his strength, his arms tightening around her as if he, too, were helpless to do anything less than surrender to that kiss. Now it occurred to her that the kiss was a pretense from start to finish. It was nothing but an attempt to steal her book.

She slowed her steps and lifted a hand to her burning cheeks. She had come to her grandmother's house to escape him, but she did not have to worry. She would probably never see him again now that he had the book.

The thought led to a still more lowering realization. She had considered herself above the common reader of the book. She did not need the writer's advice. She could be amused by its passages on bonnets and balls. Her only use for the book had been to further her search for her father. And yet she had failed to heed its wisdom and suffered for it like the least sensible ninny whoever hunted a husband.

She was guilty of folly, deceived into thinking a man sincere, not by succumbing to his words, which she could easily dismiss, but succumbing to the flattery of his attention. And, if she were wholly honest with herself, flaming cheeks honest, to the flattery of a man's body pressed eagerly to hers. He had probably deceived Miranda, the shopgirl, in just the same way. The girl had been jealous, needlessly so, but jealous nonetheless.

It was not just Hazelwood's perfidy fueling her frustration. Her cousins, too, had foiled her. She had wished to linger discreetly nearby the shop to follow the big man when he emerged, but she had been unable to even broach the matter with her cousins. She could not pursue the big man at the moment, but she could get her book back.

She found her grandmother dozing in the overheated room while her companion read aloud. Jane offered her grandmother the lemony soap and persuaded her to take a drive in spite of the cold that afflicted London. As soon as they were settled in the carriage, her grandmother confessed. "You rescued me, miss, and I know you know it. I could not have endured another chapter of that dreadful Raby novel Margaret is reading."

Jane laughed. "Then perhaps I may ask for a favor, grandmother."

Her grandmother frowned.

"Nothing grand. I need to send some messages without Hazelwood's notice. Could I employ one of your footmen?"

"Hah! Escaped your keeper's leash, have you?"

"For now."

Upon their return to the house, Jane set to work to craft a message she hoped would persuade Miss Miranda Kirby to help her.

\* \* \* \*

The shop was colder than ever when Nate slipped in from the back with a hammer and nails and some thin strips of wood. Even for a man who'd grown up on Bread Street with thin coats and no coal, the cold felt unusually bitter.

Miranda sat huddled on her stool and didn't look up. The glow of the lamp picked out the fiery strands of her hair.

"I'll board up that window now."

"I thought Papa was going to do it."

It wasn't Nate's usual work, but of course, he'd volunteered to do it just to see her. "He's finishing an evening coat for Lord Hazelwood. He takes Miss Fawkener to a ball tonight."

"Oh that. It's not a *ball*," she corrected him, "it's a party. I'll be surprised if Lord Hazelwood does take her."

"What do you know about it?" Nate leaned the strips of board against the wall and dropped a fistful of nails on one end of the counter.

"They met right here in the shop today."

He couldn't help but turn, and saw his mistake at once. Miranda's eyes were lit up with whatever secret knowledge she possessed. He turned back to position the first of the wooden strips across the broken window. "She knows about this place? Does she know about the club?"

"Of course not. She came to buy French soap, about which she knows nothing."

"How did her buying soap put them at odds?" He hammered in the first nail.

"You'd like to know, wouldn't you?" Miranda really was a frustrating female.

"You want to tell me, so, I expect, I'll find out." He hammered three more nails in place. He was positioning the second strip of wood when she spoke again.

"Do you think she's pretty, Miss Fawkener, I mean?"

He knew how a smart man would answer that one. "Not like you."

He had time to nail in the second board before she responded.

"What does that mean—*not like me*—is she pretty in some other way?"

"Most girls are pretty in some way. They all have eyes and cheeks and curls and…" He could see from her frown that he was not making things better. He gave up trying to convey the nuances of male appreciation for female beauty. "You are pretty in all ways."

He lifted the third board into place, and cut off the chill wind.

"Well, I'll tell you what put them at odds. He let her see his attachment to me, and she didn't like it one bit."

If Nate didn't know better, he'd think that Miranda had been smoking a pipe in the opium dens of Wapping. He finished his hammering before he turned to her. She would get her heart broken dreaming Lord Hazelwood would marry her.

"Miranda, Lord Hazelwood never suggested that he and you had any kind of attachment. He's a viscount, and you're—" He paused. He couldn't bring himself to say that she was nobody. He knew all about being a nobody, but he couldn't let her deceive herself in such a serious matter.

She had come off her stool, her eyes big, ready to battle for her illusions when the shop bell jingled.

A footman in dark green livery entered, carrying an envelope in his gloved hand. He stopped cold when he saw her. "Miss Miranda Kirby?" he asked.

Miranda nodded and held out her hand for the envelope. She broke the seal, unfolded the pressed paper, and turned away to her lamp to read.

"Can Miss give me an answer?" the footman asked.

"One minute." She disappeared through the curtain. The footman cast a dismissive glance over Nate with his hammer and nails.

Miranda returned with a skip in her step and a look that told Nate she would not reveal the contents of her letter.

"Here's my reply to your mistress." Miranda handed the footman the folded paper again and a tip for his service like the haughtiest London lady, and the fellow took off.

"Miranda, what are you about?"

"Wouldn't you like to know." She lifted her chin in her best fine-lady imitation. Nate felt his heart sink. It was pointless to tell his proud, stubborn love that she would suffer if she did not mind her place in the world.

*The best remedy for the inevitable disappointments and embarrassments of the Husband Hunter's misjudgment in one case is a return to the fray. One ball, one rout party, one excursion to the park or to a museum, or one evening at the theatre is inevitably followed by another. A certain stamina for pleasure is a necessary quality of the serious Husband Hunter. She must be willing, even after severe disappointment to dry her tears, don her best raiment, and go forth to give and receive pleasure in the company of others. A willingness to let go of the anticipated pleasures denied her and to look with favor on the pleasures immediately available marks her as a woman worthy of the happiness that will ultimately be hers.*

—*The Husband Hunter's Guide to London*

# Chapter Seventeen

When Jane returned to the hotel, she discovered that Hazelwood had been there and left her a message. There was an evening to be got through, and then she would put her plan in motion.

It was plain that Hazelwood was not strictly a protocol officer. He was a tool of the government. He had stuck to her side and flattered her and even made love to her simply to obtain her father's hard won information while doing nothing to find her father.

She would get her book back and move out of Hazelwood's reach. She would be safe from him in her cousins' house. Once there, she would take the first opportunity to find the hidden map. As long as she, not Hazelwood, possessed the information for which her father had risked his life, she would be in a position to bargain with the Foreign Office.

Mrs. Lowndes listened without comment to Jane's plan of moving to her cousins' house and began to help direct Nell in packing Jane's things. Jane offered her a hug, and the good lady waved away Jane's thanks. Jane set to work immediately sending messages. Activity kept her mind as fully occupied as she could wish right up until the moment that Hazelwood called to collect them for the evening's engagement.

In the carriage no one remarked on anything other than the weather. Hazelwood and Mrs. Lowndes agreed they'd not experienced a colder January. Jane said nothing about mountain caves and passes in that part of the world where her father might be held captive through the winter because the British government refused to come to his aid and instead set a protocol officer to spy on his daughter.

Outside the grand house, where the party was to be held, they waited in a long string of carriages, growing colder by the moment, until it was their turn to alight and enter the heated rooms of their hosts. The requirements of politeness, the noise of guests greeting their hostess, and the tide of movement made conversation impossible for nearly half an hour as they ascended a grand staircase and passed into a vast glittering salon. The press of the crowd did not permit Hazelwood to offer both ladies an arm, so Jane insisted he give his arm to Mrs. Lowndes while she walked behind them. The ladies around them looked so lightly clad they might have been in the disrobing room of the women's baths of Halab. Beside them, Jane felt invisible.

As they finally entered the salon, Hazelwood grasped her arm firmly above the elbow, arresting her movement. He spoke directly into her right ear. "Shall we argue?"

"Later," she said, shaking off his hold and smiling to see Lady Violet present. Violet at once introduced Jane to a gentleman of her acquaintance. Jane accepted the arm he offered and followed him into a room arranged for dancing. Jane's partner led her to a place in the set that was forming, and she set herself to concentrate on the pattern of the unfamiliar dance. Her partner was handsome, young, rich, and mad for politics. And Jane discovered how difficult it was to attend to an eligible partner when invisible gossamer strings bound one to another person in the room.

In spite of a warm welcome from Lady Violet and the dignity of Mrs. Lowndes on his arm, most of the guests, as they recognized Hazelwood, turned away. Jane tried to give her partner her smiles and her attention, but against her will, her gaze kept returning to Hazelwood as he crossed the salon speaking lightly as in jest to Mrs. Lowndes, apparently indifferent to the shoulders and heads that turned away from him. When he had settled Mrs. Lowndes among the chaperones, he did something Jane now knew him to be an expert at. He made himself invisible.

She told herself that he deserved such slights if he had done to others the sort of thing he had done to her, if he made girls love him with no intention of loving them back. He had probably made some ladies among the guests tonight love him, and now they punished him for having rejected them.

By the end of the first set, she could no longer find him, and she accepted her partner's offer to accompany her to the refreshment room. From there it was easy to find her way back to the dancing with a new partner. She expected to wear away her slippers with dancing until it was time to collect their cloaks and gloves and step back into the carriage. The musicians upset her plan by taking break. Her partner of a moment before was distracted by an acquaintance. Jane turned and found Mrs. Lowndes beside her.

"My dear, I am going to accompany Lady Violet home. Can you manage on your own with Hazelwood?"

Jane nodded. She could. She was undeceived now about his character. One short carriage ride more, and she would be free of him.

He was there to meet her just beyond the blaze of torches that lighted a path to the waiting vehicles of the guests. Hazelwood hauled her into their coach beside him with a firm grip on her arm. "Let's have that argument now," he said.

"All right then." She twisted on the bench and leveled a fierce gaze at him. "You stole my book."

"You exposed yourself to unnecessary danger."

"You mean, rather, that I exposed the book to danger, that had I been felled by that brick or stone or whatever it was that smashed the shop window, the book you wanted would now be in someone else's hands."

"The hands of an enemy with the will and means to destroy your father and his friends."

"Like a certain large, redheaded man who entered Kirby & Sons shop? Are you not in league with him against my father?"

"What makes you think that?"

"Do you deny that you know the man?"

"I work for him."

She gasped and backed as far away from him as the narrow bench permitted. "From the moment we met you have attempted to charm me into giving up that book. The only motive for such a campaign of deception has to be your belief that the book contains information your employer wants."

"In that we agree. It's no accident that your father gave you a 'guide' with a sequence of initials in the margins of its pages. You and I both heard your uncle describe your father's long habit of using family names to identify places on maps. And you and I both suspect that the painting of Nelson above the staircase in what was once your father's house conceals a map that is the key to unraveling your father's journey and identifying England's friends in the East. Have I left anything out?"

"You admit it all. You are no protocol officer. You were sent to spy on me."

"I was."

If she expected remorse, she heard none. His voice was hard and flat. "Then you and I must have no further connection."

His gaze searched her face. "Ah, you think the big red-haired man betrayed him."

"You know his name?"

"Goldsworthy. I've worked for him for a year. He's as loyal a man as there is, as secret as the grave, and an enemy to all of England's enemies. Don't mistake him for your father's real enemies."

She turned her face straight ahead. There was no more to say. She could not credit his assertion of the big man's honesty.

She did not quarrel with him about seeing her to the door or speaking with the guard. As she opened her door, he caught her by the arm one more time and spoke in a low voice.

"Before you go, there is one last thing you must allow me to tell you."

"Must I?" She kept her gaze on her hand on the doorknob. She would not look again at the handsome face so near her own.

"Yes, because it concerns another to whom you would not wish to be unjust."

"Very well." She waited.

"Miranda Kirby, a girl of seventeen, is not my mistress. She is not under my protection. She is a husband hunter, like yourself, and she will, in time, make sure of her man before she offers up her person to him."

"And you have not led her to believe that you will offer her marriage some day?"

"Far from it. I have proclaimed my unworthiness as a husband many a time."

\* \* \* \*

At the appointed hour of the morning when by some persons' reckoning it was still night, Jane, a shivering Nell by her side, knocked on the chemist's shop door. Along the street a few lights gleamed in windows from which came the noise of reveling, but there was no one to observe the two cloaked women.

The door opened, and they hurried inside. Miranda faced them, cloaked and gloved herself. A candle on the counter cast a dim glow over the dark shelves.

Jane nerved herself to deal with the girl. "Did you bring the book?"

Miranda shook her head.

"You agreed to meet me with the book," Jane protested.

"First, you must promise to give up Lord Hazelwood."

"He is not mine to keep or to give, but I will cut my connection with him directly. You know where the book is? Where he lodges?"

Miranda nodded. "I deserve him, you know. I am kind to him when no one else is. I keep him fine. Everyone thinks ill of him, but I know the truth of his...character."

"Then we are agreed." Jane stuck out her hand in the English way, and after a brief hesitation, the girl took it.

"Come then," she invited. "Be quick, say nothing, and mind your steps on the path. It's icy."

They left Nell in the shop with a second candle. Jane gave Nell's hand a squeeze, and told her not to worry.

Miranda took a candle and led Jane through the curtains, along a hallway and out a door into cold so sharp her chest ached when she drew breath. She concentrated on her steps over a patch of icy grass that crunched under foot. They reached another set of steps at the back of a larger building. Miranda opened a door and they descended into the basement of the house, where Jane could hear servants stirring in the kitchen. She could smell bread baking.

They turned and began to ascend the servants' stairs. Miranda moved quickly and surely, and Jane stayed right at her heels. At the top of a third flight of stairs, Miranda opened a door into a carpeted hallway lighted with sconces. She led Jane to a door on the left and nodded. She mouthed the word, *here.*

Jane mouthed back, *locked?*

Miranda shook her head. She turned and headed back for the stairs.

Jane let Miranda's footsteps die away. She listened carefully at the door, and when she heard no sound from within, she put her hand to the knob and turned.

\* \* \* \*

Hazelwood woke on his back in the darkness in a state familiar from his Cambridge days, his body ready for female companionship of the most intimate sort. *Jane.* He recalled no dream of her that had stirred him, so he could only blame his present discomfort on the folly of kissing her the night before. He lay staring at the invisible ceiling, waiting for his brain to take over his thinking processes.

He became aware that his feet were cold, colder than the rest of him. He must have kicked the counterpane aside in whatever unremembered dream he'd been having. In the next moment he realized that he wasn't alone in his room. Even as he had the thought, he steadied his breathing, wondered how the club's defenses had been breached, and weighed the chances that the book still lay on the table beside his bed.

"Shall we have some light, so that I may see you?" he asked the invisible presence. He tried to guess the time and whether anyone would be stirring yet. He had no weapon, but Clare was sleeping just down the hall. A shout would bring him.

"No need." Jane's voice answered. "I have what I came for."

His body had an instant and enthusiastic response to her presence in his room. His mind applauded her boldness. "Have you?"

She must be cold. He could hear it in the little quaver in her voice. He could warm her. A rapid succession of images passed through his mind of taking her hand, drawing her to the bed, pulling her down, removing her cloak and gloves, opening the covers, and letting her slip in beside him. Her clothes would be cold against his skin, but he would remove those too. All the veils would fall away. They could sleep skin to skin.

He tried to push upright and discovered that his feet were bound together and to the end of the bed to judge from the pull on them.

"I'm just leaving now. Do not trouble yourself to rise."

"You took pains apparently that I should not." She had been touching his naked feet. No wonder he'd awakened as he had. It occurred to him that Jane was the sort of intrepid girl he'd dreamed of as a boy, not a sleeping princess to be kissed awake after all, but a girl who would pick up a dropped sword and face the dragon.

"I'm afraid I've ruined one of your cravats, but you have others, I'm sure."

He tried to shift his feet to see how much give there was in the binding and found none. "You could stay, you know. We could work out the book's code together."

He couldn't see her in the dark, but he imagined her shaking her head.

"I've left the hotel. I will remain with my cousins until the investiture." Her voice sounded sad. It was a farewell she was offering.

*An open carriage such as a Landau or a Barouche is
essential to the Husband Hunter's quest. In fine weather, and
any day without rain must be considered fine, such a vehicle
is the velvet box in which the Husband Hunter appears as a
rich jewel. The open vehicle allows her to make the best use
of her time in the public parks, for while she might appear to
advantage on a horse or in a curricle, each has its peculiar
disadvantages. On horseback, she risks drawing attention to the
horse itself and must be an accomplished rider to show herself
to advantage. In a curricle, she will inevitably be perceived
as fast, in that either she is driving, and thus vying with her
potential husband in one of the manly arts, or she is riding in
such close intimacy with one gentleman as to discourage the
attentions of any others. Therefore, this guide recommends that
the Husband Hunter contrive to appear in the park in the front-
facing seat of a Landau or Barouche.*

*—The Husband Hunter's Guide to London*

# Chapter Eighteen

Jane allowed her cousin Clive to help her into the waiting barouche with
the firm intention of making the most of this attempt to connect with her
cousins. For one afternoon at least their interests and concerns would be
her interests and concerns. She would try to see London as they saw it,
and learn its customs from them. She would banish Hazelwood's mocking
voice from her mind. They were her cousins, and she would honor the
family connection, no matter the size of Allegra's hat. They were going
to see a man attempt a rare feat—driving a loaded wagon over a frozen
lake in the middle of Hyde Park. From the way her cousins talked nearly
everyone in London would be there.

"So, who *is* this man who proposes to race his van and horses over the
Serpentine?" she asked Clive as they pulled away from the hotel.

"He's quite the popular hero. Hunt, or rather Hunt the younger. His father
is a famous radical orator, jailed more than once for his attacks on the king."

"Attacks?" Jane had not heard of the king being attacked.

"In print only."

"He's hardly a hero," Allegra said. "Though he is a notable whip. That's why fashionable people come to see him."

In the intense cold, the horses wore blankets, and the coachman was invisible in his greatcoat and gloves, a long brown woolen scarf wrapped around his face, so that only his eyes showed beneath his hat. They entered one of the northern gates of the park, and its vast sloping expanse stretched before them.

Pock-marked mounds of glittering snow with dirty edges like yellowed lace dotted the bare brown hillsides. Carriage wheels made dark tracks in the drive. Distant trees arched in charcoal smudges against the low gray clouds. Jane tried to get her bearings, but she hardly recognized the icy landscape as the place where her father had taken her fishing on the Serpentine in the rain.

She did not see the lake of her childhood, like a finger crooked in summons. Instead a huge crowd had gathered at the base of the slope, restlessly moving about in a tide of dark cloaks and coats in which bright bits of blue, yellow, and red bobbed like flotsam on the muddy Thames. As the carriage drew closer, Jane realized that the crowd stood and skated on the ice of the lake itself. Clumps of brown reeds and bare, black-limbed trees marked the edge of the water. Across the breadth of the long, narrow lake was a swath of ice empty of spectators. Other fashionable carriages like theirs converged on the slope above the lake. Gentlemen called greetings and ladies waved at her cousins. Clive directed their driver to the right along the brow of the hill above the crowd.

Allegra immediately protested. "Clive, we must be nearer." She spoke directly to the coachman, telling him to drive to the water's edge.

The coachman appeared not to hear her.

"Clive, tell him."

"Allegra, show some sense. We'll be mobbed when the ice goes if we come too close."

"You think the ice will collapse?" Jane asked. The lake was perhaps a hundred yards wide and fifteen feet or more in depth. She had no idea how thick or sturdy the ice would be.

"Oh pooh," said Allegra. "Clive just wishes to remain aloof. He's not much of a sportsman, our Clive. He rarely wagers on anything."

Jane smiled at Clive. "Sounds sensible to me."

"All true gentlemen wager," Allegra declared with a toss of her head that shook the ribbons on her bonnet.

\* \* \* \*

Hazelwood might not like Clive Walhouse, but he approved of his good sense in choosing a spot on the northeast slope from which to view the Radical Race, as the print shops and papers were calling Hunt's proposed dash across the width of the lake. Allegra's elaborate bonnet made the open barouche easy to spot in a loose circle of fashionable vehicles. Coachmen in their greatcoats had gathered together to smoke their pipes and no doubt to share their own opinions of the exploit about to be attempted.

Hazelwood was willing to admit that his year of spying might have impaired his ability to judge danger rationally. England, London, and Hyde Park might have their share of rogues and footpads, but enemy agents were rare, and not likely to join in the amusements of the king's ordinary and loyal subjects. A public kidnaping at a fashionable gathering in front of hundreds of people was unlikely, but if not a kidnapping, what? In the fortnight she'd been in England, Jane Fawkener had been followed, had her hotel room invaded, been nearly pulled from a carriage, and had a stone chucked at her head. Whoever had orchestrated those earlier attacks on her would not likely let an opportunity pass. And through Hazelwood's blunders she was no longer in his care.

The carriages on the slope, occupied by people he knew or had known, offered some protection for Jane, but a challenge for him. His eye had to discern between the ordinary and familiar and the unexpected and out of place. The real danger, he decided, was in the restless movement of men on foot. A hired fist, dressed as a coachman or a hawker, could move among the carriages without anyone's notice.

Hazelwood glanced back at Nate and Miranda in his own vehicle and set off across the slope, crunching through the frozen grass, to position himself closer to Jane. He picked a vantage point from which he could see the girl, the carriage, and the surrounding turf and tried to shake off his unease. A quick downhill sprint would bring him to her side if anyone suspicious approached her. He thought again that maybe he was crazy to imagine enemies in the midst of such a crowd. Jane's family might be as vain and obsessed with rank as most of their circle, but they weren't going to let Jane be kidnapped.

Once he had his spot, he widened his gaze to take in the larger scene. Touts circulated, taking side bets from several men he once counted as friends. An enterprising pie man worked the crowd with his wares. Young gentlemen hung about the open Walhouse barouche, plainly vying for Allegra's attention, and Hazelwood swore to himself when one of them opened the door and let down the steps. Without meaning to, the man had made it easier for the enemy to reach Jane Fawkener. His sense of unease increased when he spotted Lord and Lady Ravenhurst with their good friend Count Malikov. The position of the Ravenhurst carriage above and to the east of the Walhouse barouche was no accident. Count Malikov would have Jane directly in his sight as he watched the race below. The thought of Jane in the hands of the enemy lodged like a stone in the pit of Hazelwood's stomach.

* * * *

Jane studied Allegra. Whatever was happening on the ice below, Jane could learn the most by watching Allegra manage her admirers. Several young men had gathered to lean against the vehicle looking up at her. Jane had met some of them at her cousin Phoebe's musical evening. Now each gave her a polite summary glance, rating her attractions, and an equally quick dismissal. By turns Allegra invited a favored man to step up into the carriage until she dismissed him to give one of his rivals a place in the seat of privilege. Hazelwood had warned Jane that she might lose her head when she, too, found admirers, if she ever did, but Jane could see that Allegra was not losing her head, at least not in the way Hazelwood meant. But she was not using it, either. Allegra's method did not give her more knowledge or understanding of the young men vying for her attention, instead it reminded Jane of looking in a mirror at oneself to see which angle flattered.

Clive, too, Jane observed, did his share of looking about. The trick with both of her cousins seemed to be to take notice of others without letting anyone see you do it. It was something her father could do quite well, and she wondered if he had learned the trick in London society rather than in the palaces and courts of the East. Clive was taking particular care not to notice a striking group in a nearby carriage above them. His studied disinterest made it seem to Jane, as if an invisible string connected him to a golden-haired lady in lavender silk and dark furs who sat with two gentlemen in another open carriage. The one gentleman, fair and relaxed, shared the back seat with the lady, and made occasional comments that drew her laughter, while the other gentleman, dark-haired and restless, talked a great deal to two boys with him in the other seat, pointing out elements of the great scene. The second gentleman never looked at the lady. The lady herself seemed an expert in taking no notice of others, but Jane suspected that she knew Clive watched her.

She was on the point of asking Clive about them when Eversley, standing below the carriage, asked Jane how she felt about the race. A quick glance at Allegra showed that she was occupied with her other suitors. She did not greet Eversley, who hung on the edge of the group, looking on. It was not an overt declaration of indifference, but Jane felt she might take a chance on talking to the shy gentleman.

"How are your dogs?" She turned to him. She had not thought of dogs in years. Dogs in Halab lived on scraps, slunk around the edges of town, and figured in curses and insults hurled between enemies. Eversley's round, ruddy face had an open, trusting look, as if any unkindness toward dogs might wound his feelings deeply. "Are the new puppies getting on?"

"They are," he said. "I'll be looking out for homes for them soon. I think people in general underestimate dogs. My Ajax understands hundreds of words."

"Words? Do you speak with him then?" Jane had not thought dogs knew words. They knew scents and gestures and tones of voice, but did they recognize words. She smiled at Eversley to encourage him.

A roar went up from the crowd on the ice, and they both turned to see a green van drawn by four bay horses appear through the trees on the other side of the lake. The driver, dressed in a white coat and hat with a dotted neckerchief, waved at the crowd. Two servants in green livery to match the van, clung to the rear, and waved in their turn. Huge lettering on the side of the van proclaimed, MATCHLESS BLACKING.

"Now that's a rig," said her companion. "Big as a gypsy's wagon, and those bays are no lightweights. Prize horseflesh. Hunt's got some nerve to try this stunt."

The horses were beautiful, and Jane wondered whether the driver felt any compunction about risking them on the ice. He took obvious pride in his driving skills. For the next several minutes while the crowd buzzed with excitement, he tooled his rig up and down the far bank. He halted his wagon and lifted his white hat aloft with his cane, twirling the hat about on the end of the cane to the crowd's joy. Then he tossed the reins to one of the two servants, jumped down from the box, and with businesslike energy strode across the Serpentine, looking at the ice. The crowd shouted and cheered. Having crossed, Hunt shook hands with a group of gentlemen. At Jane's side, Clive drew her attention from Eversley to point out the judges and the man betting against Hunt. Then with another tip of his hat to the crowd, Hunt strode back across the ice. He vaulted up onto the driver's box, and started his horses in motion, turning them back along the carriageway a distance from the lake. It was all done in high spirits with reckless disregard for any danger. *Like Hazelwood*, Jane thought. As the appointed time drew near, the crowd surged forward toward the open space on the ice, packed densely in a dark line along either side of the ice path. The noise subsided to a low rumble as Hunt turned his van around, facing the lake again. Allegra squealed as her favorite of the moment pulled her to her feet, and Jane stood, too. In a moment everyone was standing in the carriages around them.

\* \* \* \*

Now that the appointed hour had arrived, Hazelwood tried to judge Hunt's chances. Ice on the Serpentine was usually no more than a few inches thick and apt to break into hundreds of jagged fragments under the influence of London's changing weather. It was a testament to the past fortnight of severe cold that with all those bodies on the lake's surface no cracks had appeared. It occurred to Hazelwood that Hunt had used the gathered spectators to test the ice for him. Had their number and weight caused a collapse, the whole race would have been called off. No wonder Hunt appeared so unconcerned. The Matchless Blacking van with its four horses was a feather compared to the mass of Londoners watching. A prudent man would clear the crowd from the ice, but then a prudent man wouldn't attempt the thing at all. Hazelwood himself had never been a prudent man.

He swung his gaze back to Jane. Now that the carriage occupants were standing, he shifted his position slightly. Allegra's ridiculous bonnet was still visible, but Jane, at her side, was just a hint of a blue brim. He moved to keep her in sight. If anyone planned to strike against her, it would likely be when Hunt reached the ice and drew all eyes his way. Hazelwood scanned the carriages around the Walhouse barouche again. Nothing seemed out of the ordinary or alarming. Everyone was standing, all eyes fixed on Hunt's van. Even Malikov appeared to be absorbed by the spectacle. He might have a wager on the outcome after all.

Hunt halted his horses above the short, steep southern embankment. Their nostrils streamed vapor into the frigid air. The crowd on the ice grew quiet. Hunt's man blew his horn from the back of the van like the guard on a mail coach. On the north bank the man holding the hundred-guinea purse looked on unmoved by the show. Beside him another gentleman raised a white neckerchief, which fluttered in the stiff breeze. The handkerchief dropped, and Hunt's horses sprang forward smartly, negotiated the bank, and trotted briskly onto the ice. The crowd cheered. A thousand watching gentlemen lifted their hats in tribute.

Hazelwood shifted his gaze back to Jane. She stood with her companions, intent on the drama below. Then the lifted hats obscured Hazelwood's view. As he tried for a better angle of vision, a man in a coachman's greatcoat rolled from under the carriage and scrambled to his feet. As the man trotted off, the carriage lurched down the slope to bump against the horses' hindquarters. Clive and Jane wobbled on their feet, and Jane grabbed for the side panel. Allegra tumbled backward onto the rear seat with sharp cry. Clive twisted and threw a leg up over the front seat, attempting to crawl forward onto the coachman's box. Hazelwood swore and sprang forward.

As he ran, a loud roar erupted from the crowd on the ice. The startled horses, with no one at their heads and a heavy vehicle pressing against their hindquarters, sidled and lunged farther down the hill. One of Allegra's suitors, the one who'd been speaking with Jane, was knocked off his feet by the swinging carriage door. He pushed himself up and stood looking after the moving carriage.

Hazelwood hurtled downhill, sliding on the slick grass, straining to close the distance. He couldn't see how the coach had been disabled, but the horses with the wagon bumping against their hindquarters, veered sharply to the right, and the vehicle swayed on the uneven ground, its uphill wheels losing contact with the slope. Allegra screamed as the tilt of the vehicle threatened to dump the passengers onto the slope where they might be crushed by the carriage body. Clive clung to the sloping box, unable to loose his hold to grab the reins. Hazelwood sprinted the last few yards and flung himself for the rear of the carriage. He caught the curved iron footman's handhold, and clung, hanging low, using his boot heels to plow into the frozen grass. His hat tumbled from his head. Over the rim of the rear seat he looked up into Jane's startled face.

"Hold on," he advised through clenched teeth. He wanted to make a joke, but none came to mind. When her gaze met his, she stared at him as if she were seeing him, really seeing him, with all his disguises stripped away.

The floundering carriage swung right across the hill, and the wheels hit grass again. The jarring impact rattled his teeth, made his knees bend, and bounced Jane loose. She was airborne, and he felt everything slow down, even his heart as if the pause between beats would go on indefinitely. She landed on the forward seat and righted herself. The seams of his new jacket gave way at the shoulder, but he held on.

He leaned his head around the body of the carriage and saw a clump of bare elms straight ahead and a pair of coachmen running for the horses' heads. Before the runaways reached the elms, they plunged into a patch of old snow, and the coach came to a shuddering stop. The impact shook Hazelwood loose. He picked himself up and backed away with the exaggerated care of a man in his cups. He would rather his knees did not buckle just now.

The Walhouse coachman checked his horses. Another driver held up the left trace, which had become disconnected from the front axle. Allegra's admirers converged on the carriage. Allegra sat sobbing under her hat with Clive's arm around her heaving shoulders. Jane Fawkener sprang up unnoticed in the throng of concerned gentlemen and looked around methodically, as if her surroundings could offer some explanation of what had happened. It was what he should be doing, but the fellow who'd rolled from under her carriage was long gone, merged in the great crowd of Londoners. Hazelwood stepped behind another vehicle and stood for a moment catching his breath.

He watched Malikov step forward from the crowd and extend a hand up to Jane. "Make room for the ladies to descend, gentlemen," he said.

Hazelwood took a step forward before he recollected himself. There was no direct link between Malikov and the runaway coach. There was no law that said a man got to keep a fair maiden he'd rescued. He'd learned that as a boy, and Goldsworthy had reminded him of it the previous spring. Thudding footfalls behind him made him turn.

"Sir, are you hurt?" Nate Wilde came to a panting stop at his side. "Sorry, I didn't move faster."

Hazelwood shook his head. "Knocked about is all."

"And muddied, sir." Wilde grinned. "What happened?"

Hazelwood looked at his ruined boots. "Someone tampered with the carriage."

Below he could see the huge blacking van roll up the opposite bank of the Serpentine, and Hunt engulfed by the cheering crowd in a hero's welcome.

*Every Husband Hunter must acknowledge that she
has rivals. If a gentleman is handsome and possessed of
a reasonable estate, or if he is extraordinarily rich and
possessed of even modest personal attractions, he will draw
his share of female admirers, and more to the point, mothers
of daughters will know to a precise degree how to rate his
worth as a potential marital partner. The less scrupulous of
Husband Hunters and their mothers may stoop to calculations
and tactics, which the Husband Hunter disdains to employ. In
refusing to use such ploys, the Husband Hunter may fear that
she is ceding the advantage to one or more of her rivals. She
may, indeed, see a partner for whom she has an inclination,
whisked down the set by an enterprising young lady who, seeing
him approach, threw herself in the man's way. She may, at
another time, observe her chosen one, ensnared by a bosom,
amply displayed.*

—The Husband Hunter's Guide to London

# Chapter Nineteen

Nate knew Miranda was itching to box his ears or comb his hair with a rake, but he quelled her with a sharp glance. He would give her a chance to pitch into him later. His job was to help Lord Hazelwood solve cases, and he knew better than she did what the viscount needed at the moment.

In the club foyer under the scaffolding, Nate helped Hazelwood shed his muddied greatcoat and boots.

"Oh, Lord Hazelwood, your poor jacket!" Miranda cried.

Hazelwood managed a wan smile. "Will your father be very angry that I've ruined his handiwork again?"

Miranda shook her head. She reached up like a seasoned valet to help him. Hazelwood winced at the movement required to shed the jacket. Miranda folded it over her arms. "We'll have you looking fine again in no time. The mud will brush right out, and if it doesn't, we'll see that you have a new coat," she said.

"Thanks, Miranda." Hazelwood cast a look up the stairs and then started to climb them with less than his usual jauntiness. Nate followed behind. He knew Hazelwood's bruises and scrapes would be making themselves known, and Nate wanted to get the viscount some coffee and a hot bath away from Miranda. A hovering sympathetic woman was not what Hazelwood wanted.

In the coffee room, Hazelwood lowered himself gingerly onto his favorite couch. He didn't stretch out as he usually did, rather he stared unseeing at the table where he'd been studying their copy of the little guidebook. Nate went right to work to produce a steaming cup of coffee and put it in the viscount's hands.

"What are you thinking, sir?" Nate asked.

"Why didn't they try to snatch her? Why try to kill her and anyone who happened to be in the way? Unless they meant to attack the Walhouses, too."

"Looks more accidental that way, sir."

"True, but it's definitely an escalation, isn't it? We have to get her back before they kill somebody."

"We will, sir."

"Do you have a plan, Wilde?"

"Kidnap her ourselves, sir?"

"I like the way you think, but I have a different idea. Are you willing to play the footman again?"

"The Walhouse cook took a liking to me, sir. I'm sure I can get back in the house."

"Good."

Miranda was waiting for Nate in the shop when he brought Hazelwood's greatcoat for repairs.

She didn't look up from her needlework when he came through the curtain in the back of the shop.

"He's going to be okay. Bruised is all. Nothing broken."

"Papa says his jacket can't be saved."

"I'm sure your father can make him a new one."

She looked up then, her eyes flashing angrily. "He spent nearly a year wearing soiled, stinking linen and ill-fitting coats, and now when he gets to dress like the gentleman he is, you let him ruin his clothes."

"If you want to blame anyone, blame yourself. You wanted to see Hunt drive his van over the Serpentine."

She jumped up off her stool, shaking now. "Like half of London. It's not my fault. If you could drive, this wouldn't have happened. You could have taken me to see the race, and Lord Hazelwood would never have been hurt. You're supposed to be the muscle, aren't you? Haven't they hired you to get your thick head broken, while they do the clever work?"

"That's not exactly the way it is. Besides, you misunderstand Hazelwood, if you think he doesn't like danger." He didn't want to tell her the real reason Hazelwood had dashed down that hillside and flung himself onto that carriage, but he would if she pushed him too far.

"You should have stopped him."

Nate shook his head. "You can't stop a man from rushing to the aid of the woman he loves."

Her head snapped up, her eyes big with awareness of the truth of it. She, too, had seen the viscount's mad dash to save Jane Fawkener. "He doesn't love her. She's just a case, and he would never let a case go wrong."

"You, Miranda, need to go back to *The Husband Hunter's Guide.* You need to read the chapter on getting above yourself. He's not for you, and the sooner you accept the truth, the better for you."

"I hate you, Nate Wilde. You just want to put me down. I'm much prettier than Jane Fawkener. And she promised—"

"What?"

"Never mind. She doesn't know Lord Hazelwood's worth like I do."

Nate came right up to her, close enough to feel her breath huffing out in her anger. "Miranda, when did she promise you anything?"

Miranda stuck out her stubborn chin. "I'm not saying anything. She left him, didn't she? Went to stay with her cousins."

"That doesn't change anything. He'd pretty much die for her."

"No." She stared at him in horror.

Nate stepped away. "He would. He's that kind of man, and he's that in love."

\* \* \* \*

Clive kept himself under rigid control in the Ravenhurst carriage on the journey home. He had his arm around Allegra, who leaned against him, her eyes closed in pain. Jane had helped her remove her ruined hat. He found it difficult to appreciate Malikov's light tone, and he felt deeply grateful for the glances Pamela gave him, indicating her sympathy. Later they would meet in their usual way. He held on to that thought through the scene of his mother's distress, the summoning of the doctor, his father's usual unhelpful confusion and concern for his horses, his younger siblings' shocked curiosity. He tried, as well, not to resent Jane's quiet competence.

Malikov waited for him in his mother's drawing room. "No serious harm done, apparently."

Clive saw that Malikov had helped himself to a drink. He poured himself a short measure of his father's brandy to avoid saying something intemperate, like—*Are you mad? You could have killed us all.* It seemed to him that to acknowledge the extent of the danger would put him at a disadvantage in whatever game he and the count were playing.

"I'm beginning to think that you like courting danger, Walhouse." Malikov spoke from one of the two gilded chaise longues his mother had purchased when she'd redecorated the room. The low, backless sofas with their bold black and gold striped pattern dominated the pale blue room.

"Whatever gives you that impression?"

Malikov dangled his glass from his fingertips over the scroll arm of the sofa. "First the affair with the ripe and delicious Pamela and then your unwillingness to protect yourself from the danger your cousin represents."

Clive forced himself to laugh as he took a seat opposite the count. "Oh, really? Surely the danger from Ravenhurst is nothing. He will never notice his wife's affair, or know what to do if he does. And what has Jane Fawkener done? I think she's trying to learn from Allegra how to snare a husband."

Malikov shook his head. "You trust the girl not to act against you? Don't let yourself be fooled."

Clive shrugged. "Jane? I think you exaggerate her ability to move the English government."

"She may look meek, but, remember, Walhouse, the girl can destroy your family's comfort, and your family is most attached to their comforts. Your sister won't thank you for ruining her chances for an advantageous match."

"She won't thank me for a broken neck."

"There you exaggerate the danger. The barouche rolled down a little slope. The ladies were jostled a bit. You have driven faster and more dangerously yourself."

"Nevertheless, leave Allegra out of this."

It seemed to Clive that he waited a long time for Malikov's reply.

"Happily, if you will let me deal with your cousin. You've no attachment there, have you?"

"None." Clive liked Jane well enough. If she didn't stand in the way of the Walhouse family fortune, he would have nothing against her.

"You go to the Langford ball, don't you?" Malikov asked.

"Yes, if Allegra recovers."

"She will. Make sure your cousin goes to the ball, and leave the rest to me."

Clive could not have heard properly. "My cousin is scheduled for an investiture ceremony with the king. The authorities will miss her."

"Who? The king? He'll never notice one less trinket to hand out. Chartwell? When has Chartwell done more than a lot of hand-wringing?"

Clive studied his near-empty glass, a thin amber veil of drink covered the bottom. He didn't like Malikov's attitude, but Clive had worked under Chartwell long enough to know the muddle his office made of most affairs. He could let his cousin go to whatever fate Malikov had in mind for her, or he could see his family slip back into their old situation. His sister would lose all chance of a decent match. His mother would have to give up her parties. His father could no longer have his dogs and horses. And he would have to give up Pamela.

He considered his family's capacity for such sacrifice and found it wanting. He knew from the state of his own heart, that giving up one's comforts and even worse, one's claims on the notice of the world, was not to be borne.

Clive looked up from the liquid in his glass to meet Malikov's gaze. His mother's beautiful drawing room surrounded them. Her taste, her care had furnished the house as the house of a gentleman should be furnished. Jane Fawkener was nobody. She was nothing to any of them, a cousin from nowhere, with nothing to offer in exchange for such losses. She was lucky to have lived so long considering the risks her own father took. Really, Fawkener was the one who had endangered her by taking her abroad and doing the work that he did.

Clive stood and strolled back to the sideboard where the drinks tray had been left. "We will be at the ball with Jane."

Malikov was on his feet in an instant and at Clive's side, clapping him on the shoulder in that friendly, avuncular way of his, like a slightly older, wiser friend. "You've made the smart decision, you know. You must not imagine that anyone will mistreat the girl. I simply do what I must to improve things in St. Petersburg. Ah, to go home with some useful information, to return to my family." Malikov set his own empty glass next to Clive's.

And just like that, Clive knew Malikov was lying, that there was no lost career in St. Petersburg, no faithful sweetheart at home for whom Malikov worked, only a desire to work his will on others.

"You'll see the fair Pamela tonight?" Malikov asked.

"Yes." Clive swallowed the bad taste in his mouth. He was doing what was necessary for his family. Once their future was secure, he would end his association with Malikov for good.

\* \* \* \*

Jane stayed with Allegra until the soothing draught given to her by the family doctor sent her off to sleep. Then she stayed on in a plump armchair in Allegra's room as the early dark of a winter's day settled over London. It was the least she could do after she had involved her cousin in danger. Allegra might be shallow and vain and sometimes annoying, but none of those character flaws deserved a death sentence. It was a hard truth, but a truth nonetheless, that in removing herself from Hazelwood's care, Jane had brought the danger that followed her into her cousins' household.

She needed time to reflect on what had happened, away from anyone else. She did not want to meet her cousin Clive until she'd had a chance to sort through the jumbled images in her mind. She suspected that he would minimize the danger. The brief wild ride could not have lasted two minutes from the first lurch of the carriage under her feet to its collision with a mound of snow. At first the image of Hazelwood's face over the back of the carriage persisted in her mind, so sharp and clear that other details of those perilous moments were obscure. But it was those other moments that she needed to recall in order to understand what had truly happened.

In the Ravenhurst carriage that brought them home, Clive had been strangely silent about the accident, while his friend Count Malikov teased him about having a team of such high-spirited animals that they wanted to join the race on the ice. Jane had heard enough of the talk around her after the barouche came to a stop to know that someone had tampered with it. Hazelwood's presence confirmed her sense that the runaway carriage had been no accident. He had been watching, anticipating danger, and he'd acted when it came. She wanted to talk with him about it, but by misunderstanding him earlier, she had made seeing him again nearly impossible.

And yet, for those few mad moments when he'd had nowhere else to look, no joke to make, no disguise for the naked expression in his eyes, he was not a spy but a man who didn't want to lose her. She mattered to him. It was not, after all, about his job, about the information she possessed, about the friends of England along her father's route across the East, or about what she might know of Russian plans for the region. In that moment, it was about the lost connection between them, about wanting her to go on in the world even without him. That look had held her there in the wildly tilting coach more than her grip on the side panel. Then she'd been jolted loose, and when she'd landed, he'd been gone. She had looked, carefully, as her father had taught her to look at a scene, breaking the vast panorama of the park into discreet sections, but Hazelwood had vanished in the crowd.

Really, if she'd found him, she likely would have leaped from the carriage and whacked him over the head with whatever weapon came to hand. What had he been thinking to fall in love with her and to make her glad for his love?

The jolting carriage ride had reversed her understanding of where the danger lay. To protect her precious guidebook from Hazelwood, she'd accepted her cousins' hospitality, and, now, she needed to figure out how to protect her cousins as well from the people who wanted her father's information.

A low moan came from Allegra, and Jane left the chair.

"Is my hat ruined?" Allegra stirred, then sank back against her pillows.

Jane went to her cousin's side with a glass of water. "Your hat can be saved. How's your head?"

"Terrible." Allegra's eyes closed in her ashen face. "It's dark in here."

"Are you ready for a candle? The doctor warned against too much light."

"Where's Mama?"

"She's dressing for the evening." Lady Strayde had told Jane that she felt the importance of keeping her evening engagements, that way she could reassure people that Allegra had taken no serious hurt. Jane lit a candle on the mantel and brought it to the bedside table.

Allegra blinked and held a hand up over her eyes. "So, you're here with me?"

"I am. Water?"

"Yes. Please." Allegra's voice was a croak. She accepted the glass Jane offered, and with a shaking hand, brought it to her lips. She took a sip and nearly let the glass slip from her grasp. Jane caught it, and Allegra's hand fell back against the coverlet.

"How long am I going to feel like this? I can't miss the Langford ball."

"The doctor said you are to rest. He's left a draught for the headache, and he wants to know what else you're feeling."

Allegra's hand plucked at the coverlet. "It's unfair. Caroline DeVere will go to that ball. She'll dance with my beaux. She'll make everyone forget me, as if I'd never existed."

Jane took her seat in the armchair again. "You'll just have to be a sensation when you return, like Sleeping Beauty, after her long nap."

"But everyone will talk about what a stupid, pitiful girl I am to fall and miss the Radical Race."

"By the time you return, there will be something quite different to talk about."

"How can you be so sure? You know nothing about London."

"Haven't you been trying to teach me? And I've been reading my *Husband Hunter's Guide to London*."

"You're joking. I've never heard of such a thing."

"You have your mother to advise you. I have none."

"So how did you come upon this guide?"

"It was given to me when I arrived by someone who realized I'd need sound advice."

"What does it say?"

"That rest is essential for the young woman who wants to shine at a ball."

A knock on the door made Allegra turn. "Yes? Who's there?"

Clive answered, and Allegra invited him in. "Does everyone think I'm a stupid fool for getting knocked down?"

"I haven't heard from everyone yet." Clive crossed the room, but stood in the shadows beyond the soft candle beams. He spoke gently, but he wore a grim expression. "Your admirers' flowery tributes and notes will arrive soon."

"Everyone will just forget me."

Clive shook his head. "I hope you still want to attend the Langford ball?"

"Oh yes. I must. It's the first real ball of the year."

"Then we must see that you recover." Clive glanced at Jane. "Jane, you'll stay with us until the ball?"

"Of course."

*One of the more serious errors of perception the Husband Hunter must avoid is the failure to distinguish between the general and the particular in the attentions of a gentleman. A young woman may be drawn to a man who shows kindness to her. She is grateful for his attention when seeing her overlooked, he draws her into a conversation, or seeing her fatigued, he procures her a chair or a place in a carriage, or seeing her slighted by other partners, he restores her to dignity by soliciting her hand for a set. Such a man deserves the Husband Hunter's careful attention. She will want to note whether he is as kind in general and thoughtful of other ladies, no matter their age or condition in life, as he has been to her. If he is, if she discovers that his disposition is to be kind to all women, she will then have to exercise the most dispassionate judgment to determine whether there is in his kindness to her any element of particular interest. And here, the Husband Hunter may err from wanting it to be so.*

—*The Husband Hunter's Guide to London*

# Chapter Twenty

On the third day after the accident, when Dr. Lions declared Allegra recovered enough to join the family for a meal, and when the stream of messages and floral tributes had dwindled to a trickle, Jane helped Allegra descend the two flights of stairs from her bedroom to the breakfast room. It still troubled Allegra to look down, and her peach silk wrapper trailing long pale green ribbons brushed the floor, so she clung to Jane's arm and the banister.

In the breakfast room, the family sat around the table with the exception of Clive. Four golden heads lifted and turned to Allegra and Jane when they entered. Phoebe at the foot of the table cast a critical eye over Allegra, and raised a brow indicating that Annabel should move her seat.

"Papa, do I have to give up my seat for her if she's better?" Annabel demanded. Teddy winked at her over the top of his newspaper, but nodded his head toward the lower seat.

"Does your head still hurt?" Philip demanded at a headache-inducing volume.

Allegra winced, but took Annabel's seat, arranging her silk and lace and accepting a shawl from Jane. Jane offered to fill a plate for her from the sideboard.

"Just toast and jam, please, Jane."

Annabel and Philip questioned Allegra as Jane stood at the sideboard, sensing something different and wondering what it was. The same platters of eggs, bacon, toast, and ham lined the sideboard. She handed Allegra the plate of toast and jam, and turned back, reaching to pour herself some coffee when she realized that the coffee had changed. The smell was rich and earthy with a lingering hint of caramel, brought out from the roasting. Even in the large English cup, even without the distinctive *crema* of coffee in Halab, the taste was unmistakable.

*Hazelwood*. The association was instant. Briefly she imagined him on the other side of the breakfast room door, holding his flannel-wrapped flask.

"Jane," Allegra said, "are you going to eat?"

All the golden heads were turned her way, reminding her of not being one of them. "Of course, I was just enjoying the coffee."

"Oh," said Phoebe, "The coffee is different? Allegra, dear, don't slump. Hold your head up."

Annabel spoke up from her seat next to Jane. "It's the new footman. He's Nick or Nate or something. He's taught cook his way."

Phoebe cast her youngest daughter a sharp glance of disapproval for consorting with the servants.

Jane dropped her gaze to her cup. Whoever the new footman was, there could only be one explanation for his being there. Hazelwood had sent him. In the three days she'd spent with Allegra since the accident, there had been no further attempt to harm her cousins or herself, but that did not mean that the danger had ended. And Hazelwood apparently didn't think so either. He'd managed to place someone he trusted in the household. The coffee was a message. The trick would be for Jane to find this new footman and speak to him privately.

She looked up from her coffee to find Phoebe studying Allegra. "I don't like your color, dear. We have to restore some bloom to your cheeks."

Philip glanced up from his eggs. "You look like a trout belly, Al," he told her.

Allegra stopped tearing her toast apart and glared at him.

Bolton, the butler, who had been looking on, went to answer a knock at the breakfast room door.

In the opening stood a footman, who announced that a gift had arrived for Miss Walhouse. Annabel leaned toward Jane and whispered, "That's him. That's the new footman." Jane caught just a glimpse, enough to know the young man had prominent ears and white, white teeth. She would have to think of some way to excuse herself from the group to speak with him.

Allegra lifted her head at the promise of a gift. "May I see, Papa?" she asked.

"Just the thing to put color in your cheeks, girl," said Teddy from behind his newspaper. He nodded to Bolton.

"What can it be?" Allegra wondered.

"Who is it from? Do we know, Bolton?" asked Phoebe.

"I believe we're about to discover, my lady," Bolton replied. He opened the door to another knock, and there stood, Eversley, wearing an expression of hope and earnest longing, and holding a large red box tied with an enormous black velvet bow.

"Oh, it's you." Allegra's face fell.

Her father grinned and put aside his paper. He left his seat and held out his hand to the newcomer. "Eversley, my boy, come in. Brought a gift for my girl, have you?"

"Yes, sir." The young man's face colored brightly. He tucked the box under his left arm as he extended his right hand to greet his host. The box tilted and emitted a sound like mice in the woodwork. "I thought of just the right thing for Miss Walhouse, sir. Annabel put me on to it."

Allegra shot Annabel a hard look, but Annabel was beaming at Eversley and bouncing in her seat. Jane thought there could not be two people who understood Allegra less.

"Let's get to it, then," said Teddy. "You can see how done in Allegra is. Needs a bit of cheering up. Three days in the house and all."

"Papa!" Allegra protested.

Eversley looked at Allegra sitting at the table and seemed to doubt the wisdom of his gift briefly.

"I'll open it, if she won't," Annabel offered.

"Annabel, hush," said Phoebe.

Annabel turned to her sister. "Allegra, push your chair back, so Eversley can put the box in your lap."

Allegra looked momentarily helpless as if shifting in her chair were impossible, but Jane stood and offered her arm, and with a little maneuvering, the chair was scooted back, and Allegra received the box onto her lap.

She looked up in immediate surprise. "It's warm."

The box wobbled on her knees, and Allegra pulled the bow loose. The box lid popped open without her touch.

A black-muzzled puppy with floppy gray ears sprang from the box, thin tail wagging, and planted large gray puppy paws on Allegra's chest.

Allegra looked at Eversley in horror. Annabel bounced in her seat. Philip let out a snort of laughter.

The puppy gave Allegra's chin a lick, sank his sharp, white teeth into the lace of her wrapper and tore. She shrieked and let go of the box. The lace in the puppy's jaws gave, and puppy and box tumbled to the floor. The puppy trotted off with his lace prize between his teeth and settled on the carpet in a corner of the room, growling and tugging at the lace anchored between his paws.

Eversley watched the pup with obvious pride, ignoring Allegra. "He's eight weeks old out of Hector and Countess, the pick of the litter, and he's got the perfect disposition to be a lady's dog."

"Mama, he's torn my lace," Allegra wailed, pressing her damaged wrapper to her chest.

"Just a bit of puppy teething. He'll get over that in no time." Eversley tried to pat Allegra on the shoulder, but she cringed.

The puppy trotted around the room, snarling over his prize, until he came to the sideboard, where he dropped the lace and stood up with his legs, his nose sniffing the breakfast above him.

"One of your mastiffs, eh, Eversley?" Teddy left his seat to watch the dog. "He's a fine specimen, top of the line, pet," he told Allegra.

"Papa," Allegra wailed. "What do I want with such a creature? He'll ruin everything. Mama"—she turned to her mother—"everyone's forgotten me."

Eversley's reddened further. "I only meant..."

"Can I have him, if you don't want him, Al?" Annabel asked, sliding from her seat, and offering the puppy a bit of bacon from her plate. He wagged his tail and went right to her as if they were old friends, snapped up the bacon, and buried his head in Annabel's skirts.

"If he should belong to anybody, he should be mine," Philip declared. "I'm old enough to have my own dogs now."

Cousin Phoebe rose from her chair, her gaze steely. "Children, you forget yourselves. Annabel, unhand that dog, and wait for me in your room. Allegra, pull yourself together and thank Eversley for his gift. Strayde, see Eversley to the door. Philip prepare yourself for your tutor."

When her gaze came to Jane, she faltered, as if trying to determine in what way Jane was to blame for the poor showing the family made before a guest and potential suitor. Eversley might love dogs, but he did have thousands of acres in Wiltshire. "Jane..."

Jane seized the moment. "Shall I take the *gift* to one of the footmen, cousin Phoebe? Perhaps a place can be found in the stables until you decide what to do with it?"

"Yes." Phoebe turned back to the rest. "Now, go, everyone. Allegra, come with me."

\* \* \* \*

Jane found her footman lurking in the back of the foyer. He stepped out of the shadows without speaking and reached for the squirming puppy in her arms. As Jane surrendered her burden, she could hear Phoebe admonishing Allegra on the stairs above them. She looked at the earnest young man all ears and teeth, and it occurred to her how awkward it was going to be to convey the message she wished to convey to her love through the medium of the sturdy young man in front of her. Then he spoke.

"Miss, Lord Hazelwood says we must get you out of here. He has a plan." He spoke in a low, serious voice for her alone.

*Out of here?* "Of course he does," she said. *So much for a deep exchange of sentiment with Hazelwood.* "Help me take the puppy to the stable, will you?" she said in a carrying voice.

"Yes, Miss. Follow me, Miss." They passed through a concealed door in the wall into a narrow hallway. The puppy looked at Jane over the footman's shoulder and licked the young man's ear. Jane tried to see the danger in her situation. Allegra's bedroom, the bedroom of a baron's favored daughter, had to be one of the safest places in London. Jane had detected no signs of followers or intruders there. Her enemies had not been able to reach her in days. She had read her guide to Allegra, handed her cousin a glass of water, or helped her arrange the cards and flowers of admirers in her room. No one came to Jane's own room except Nell, who helped her dress and undress, and the young maid who did the fires. If there was danger in her cousins' house, she did not know where it lay.

When they reached the stable, the young footman looked around. The grooms and coachman were not about. "Lord Hazelwood can't protect you here."

"But I'm with my family," she explained. She could not see Teddy or Philip as stout defenders, but surely Phoebe or Clive would stand up to an attacker. "Don't my cousins need protection, too? Allegra was hurt when someone tampered with the carriage."

The puppy pulled on the young man's ear. "Please, Miss. Lord Hazelwood wants you to go shopping today. You can take me to carry the packages. And we'll get you to a place where he can keep you safe."

"I promised to stay with Allegra until after the Langford ball."

"He won't like that, Miss."

Jane raised her brows. She looked around for someplace where the wriggling puppy could be contained and opened an empty horse stall.

"You're watched, Miss. There are two of them. They trade off. They know your window." The footman let the puppy down, and he trotted into a corner and relieved himself.

"But it's Allegra's window that I look out of, not my own. They can't be very smart."

The young man snorted. "They're not paid to be smart, Miss."

"I mean, we ought to be able to outsmart them. Tell Hazelwood I can leave from the ball." Jane watched the puppy poke his nose into the straw and sneeze.

"He won't like it, Miss," he repeated, shaking his head.

"Tell him...tell him, I know. I understand."

*Unless one is a duchess, the experience of taking one's place in the great world of London society requires the enduring of slights. Inevitably, the Husband Hunter will meet people whose sense of their own superiority is so keen that they will look down on her as from a great height, as if she were an insect on a leaf, to be trod underfoot. These persons are conscious of every distinction of rank, particularly rankings of their devising. One person may be a snob in the matter of personal appearance and think everyone else deficient in handsomeness. Another person may be a snob in matters of accomplishment and may disdain your modest achievements with a musical instrument. Still others, many indeed, are snobs in matters of taste. These latter will see inferiority in every preference of yours that does not conform to their refined aesthetic sense.*

*What is the Husband Hunter to do in the face of such slights? Surely, she should laugh.*

—*The Husband Hunter's Guide to London*

# Chapter Twenty-one

Hazelwood swore quietly as he removed his evening pumps at the top of the servants' stair. His love was inconveniently principled. He understood that a promise was a promise, but he regretted that she'd given hers to a vain beauty from a family of idle, self-indulgent twits, who hadn't the wit to avoid a present danger. Jane's promise was keeping her where Malikov and his thugs could get at her.

The night had gone three. The watcher across the way had retreated to someplace where he wouldn't be turned to a block of ice by morning, and Wilde had admitted Hazelwood to the house through the kitchen and directed him up the servants' stair to the floor where she had a bedroom. He found his way to her door, which was locked, used the key Wilde had procured and let himself in. She breathed softly in sleep, on her side, turned toward the window. He didn't risk a light, but crossed to the bed and placed his hand over her mouth. "Jane, it's Hazelwood," he whispered.

She started and her teeth sank into his fingers. He held on, repeating his earlier words. She let go with her teeth and shook her head free of his hand, and he heard her push herself upright in the bed.

"What are you doing here?" she whispered hoarsely.

What was he doing there? Momentarily, he was a man drawn to the temptation of a warm woman newly roused from sleep. In the cold room, her warmth was as palpable as the embers of a banked fire waiting to be stirred to life. He was perfectly willing to do the stirring, to tend and stoke that fire till it blazed.

Of course, he was a spy, and his mission was to remove this girl with her valuable information from the path of the enemy. They were closing in. He only hoped they did not know how much she knew.

"I believe you started this particular game."

"Ah, so I did."

"I don't think you fully understood the message I sent through Wilde."

"I promised I'd stay with Allegra through the Langford ball."

"Because she's so sweet and charming and attached to you?"

"Because Clive asked me to, and because whoever tampered with that carriage, did it to get at me, but caused Allegra real harm."

"How is she?"

"Improving."

"Clive didn't ask you to stay longer than the ball?"

"No."

Hazelwood let her think about that. The best possible outcome would be for her to descend with him now through the sleeping house and let him take her to the room above Kirby's shop prepared for her. She need only take her guidebook. The government could replace anything she left behind. She would be safe. He held himself still while she thought, though his toes were growing decidedly cold.

She let out a breath. "Surely, Clive doesn't want the information I have. He's not a spy."

"But his friend Malikov most likely is."

She went back to her thinking, and he tucked his cold hands under his arms. "So Malikov might exert some pressure on Clive to..." Her voice trailed off, puzzled.

"To get information from you." He didn't want to admit to his deeper fear that Malikov was planning to abduct her.

The bedclothes rustled around her. "And this is what you came here in the night to my room, against all protocol and decorum and sense, to tell me?"

He felt off-balance. There was no point in admitting anything else. His feelings about her had changed, had grown into a fitting punishment for a man who had in his youth disdained propriety and who now was well-served in loving a woman he could not wed without involving her in his own ruin and disgrace. Such selfish love did not deserve to be called love at all.

"Hazelwood, think," she said.

He was trying to. "Leave with me now, and I will get you to secure place, where the enemy can't reach you."

"And help me prove that my father is alive?"

Was her father alive? Hazelwood doubted it, but if the proof was in that guidebook, he would gladly help her uncover it. Goldsworthy would ask him to betray her again, but Hazelwood could not lose her more than she was already lost to him. The thought cleared his head.

"Of course."

"Liar. You don't believe he's alive." She spoke without anger or resentment, a reasonable woman stating a fact.

"Alive or dead, your father would want you safe." That was a truth he could agree on.

"My father would want me to finish the mission. He would want the information he gathered to get into the right hands."

Hazelwood heard the bedclothes rustle again. A draft of warm air full of the scent of her washed over him. More silken noise, and she struck a light on the bedside table. The glow illuminated her hands and the lace cuffs of her night rail. Her toes peeked from under the hem of the modest gown. The sheet and coverlet had been flung back on the bed exposing the slight depression where her hips had lain. The narrow bed called to him and he turned from it.

She faced him with the book in her hand. "You took it before. Now, I'm giving it to you."

Extravagant declarations rose to his lips. The book didn't matter. Goldsworthy didn't matter. England didn't matter. The Russians could have the book. They could have the whole of the East for all he cared, its vast deserts, its towering mountains, and its passes to India, if she would come with him.

He steadied himself and swallowed the words clamoring inside him. She would smack him in the head for such sentiment.

"Kiss me," he said.

She shook the book at him. "Take it."

"Kiss me first," he amended. "Put it down, and kiss me."

"A kiss won't change my mind."

"If you're so sure, you have nothing to lose."

She gave him a measuring look, a weighing of an adversary's strength. He'd kissed her before, but not as he meant to kiss her now. Apparently she decided she could meet the challenge.

"Remember," she said. "It's all about the family." She put the book back on the bedside table and stood waiting for him to make the first move. He reached out and drew her into his arms and settled her against his chest. She leaned back immediately to look up into his face, a smile playing on her lips.

"You're cold."

*Not all of me.* "Only my toes, but you don't have to kiss my toes."

She shivered in his arms, and he pressed her closer, sliding his hands around her. Without stays, there was just the natural shape of her, the straight back, the bend of her waist, and the flare of her hips. She lifted her face to his, the smile gone, replaced by a look he recognized all too well.

He tried to keep his head, to remember that he was the one seducing her, making her forget her determination to stay with her cousins, but she stirred the forgotten longings of his boyhood, when he'd dreamed of being a knight and rescuing a fair damsel and earning her love as a reward for his noble deeds. He had dreamed then of being worthy of the prize. So he let himself kiss her as he wanted to kiss her.

He pulled her close, as close as their clothes permitted, locking his arms around her, lifting her off her feet so that her weight, which was nothing, rested against him, so that she had only him to hold her up. Her kisses rained down on him, melting his indifference to fate, washing away the slights he had endured for so long that they seemed a part of him. He had perfected his own form of self-mockery in defense, but there was no defense against her love.

When, minutes later, he set her lightly down, she rested her head against his chest.

"What was that?" she demanded.

"That was an argument," he said, breathing unevenly. "That was the whole of Aristotle, all the grammar, rhetoric, and logic I ever learned. It was a speech in the Lords. Are you going to come with me?"

She shook her head. "It was very persuasive. I was moved. But I made a promise."

"I can't protect you here."

"But you can protect my information. Take the book." The solemn expression had returned to her face. She slipped from his arms, took up the book, and held it out to him. He slid it into his jacket. She turned him around and gave him a shove toward her door, and he went because though he was a man in love, he was also a spy.

His hand on the doorknob, he turned to have one last glimpse of her over his shoulder. She came up on her tiptoes and kissed his cheek.

He swallowed. "I will come for you. Do not leave that ball with anyone other than me."

"I promise."

* * * *

Miranda held the note in her hand. She had only to knock at the servants' entrance to be admitted. She had promised to deliver the note directly into the hands of Miss Fawkener this morning, but she knew she would be asked to wait in a dark hall on a narrow bench or in some shabby, out-of-the-way room where the housekeeper dealt with tradespeople.

Though Lord Hazelwood had sent her in one of the club's closed carriages with a driver and a footman, the lofty butler had turned her away from the front door with its brass knocker. And now, standing below the street with the iron railing above, the smell of the coal cellar around her, and the mean little door in front of her, Miranda felt her grievances fully.

Jane Fawkener had gone back on her promise to keep away from Lord Hazelwood. She had contrived somehow to ensnare him when it was Miranda who had loved him best and longest. She knew that Lord Hazelwood could love her with the proper encouragement. He had thanked her for her willingness to contribute to his last case. He had squeezed her hand with the note in it and said he owed her a great deal because she had believed him when no one else did.

And Jane Fawkener had exposed Miranda to Nate Wilde's mockery. And worse, his pity. Nate Wilde, who came from nowhere and who was nobody in spite of his fashionable coats and his big words. Nate Wilde, who had been a pickpocket and a spy before better men had taken notice of him. Nate Wilde, who thought she, Miranda, should pick him, when she'd had a mother who'd been born a lady in France. What did his fine shoulders and his sweet kiss matter when he could never make Miranda a lady?

A swirl of cold, gritty air eddied around her, and she turned away from the door. She tucked the little note into her bodice and held her cloak close about her. Her gentlemen spies did not need Jane Fawkener to crack the code and save those Englishmen abroad in heathen places. Lord Hazelwood had figured out most of it himself. No doubt he would solve the case by himself. Miranda would help him.

Jane Fawkener didn't love Lord Hazelwood. She had been willing to toss him aside, and now she was going to a great ball where there would be dozens of gentlemen. Let Jane Fawkener take one of them. Miranda would not help her to take the one gentleman that rightfully belonged to Miranda.

*A ball is thrilling. Whatever the intentions of the host and hostess, whatever the motives of the individual guests, a ball promotes courtship, that form of intercourse between a lady and a gentleman that leads to love. In a ballroom a gentleman and a lady, though strangers, may progress rapidly through the stages of growing intimacy from first glances to direct gazes to conversation to an electric meeting of hands, and beyond to a striking degree of intimacy where the dance permits—the touch of a gentleman's hand to a lady's waist or her hand to his shoulder.*

*The ballroom itself is an altered space that delights the senses. Under the dazzling lights of the chandeliers, warmed by the exertions of the dance, breathing the perfume of banks of flowers, and feeling the pulse of the music in her very soul, the Husband Hunter feels exhilarated. Once singled out from among the ladies present to receive a charming gentleman's particular attention, she must be hardheaded indeed not to be misled into believing instantly that she has found the husband she seeks.*

—*The Husband Hunter's Guide to London*

# Chapter Twenty-two

Until Jane entered the Langford ballroom, she had forgotten how her appearance marked her as a husband hunter of the common English variety. In little more than a fortnight of following her guide, she had acquired an appropriate look and manner and sufficient acquaintance to insure invitations to dance a set or two. Now all that remained was to complete the conquest of some available manly heart and choose a life for the years granted to her. Around her were gentlemen from the most humble who could offer a comfortable establishment to the most exalted. In choosing one man she might be called to be a political hostess. In choosing another she might be mistress of a vast estate and involve herself in the health and happiness of its staff and tenants and in the stewardship of its great treasures. She laughed at the idea. Allegra would choose one of those lives, not Jane.

Jane was not free to choose any gentleman unless she could unravel the skein of choices that made her someone quite different from the husband hunter she appeared to be. And really, she realized, as she looked in vain for the one face that would not appear, it was only one choice after all that she could not unravel—falling in love with Hazelwood.

She had had no word from him since the night she had given him the book, neither had she seen Nate, the footman, in two days, but she supposed there was a plan, and that she would hear of it soon. She was ready to leave the Langford ball on her own two slipper-clad feet if she had to. She knew where Hazelwood's club was and how to enter through the chemist's shop on Old Bond Street.

In the hours ahead, it was her duty to help Allegra make a triumphant return to society. Allegra, much recovered from her injury, still whimpered at bearing any weight on her head and grew easily fatigued. Instead of feathers and yards of ribbon, she had accepted Jane's idea of threading a single strand of pearls among her curls. The arrangement made her look less like her mother and more like Annabel. Allegra had been all smiles at the effect until a comment from Philip as they left the house that she looked like a pirate's treasure chest had knocked the confidence out of her.

Now, the slow mounting of the Langford's stairs on Clive's arm left her fretful and shaken on the ballroom threshold as their party was announced. For a terrible moment after they entered the room, it seemed that no notice would be taken of Allegra's return. No heads turned their way. No smiles greeted them. Clive turned a worried face to Jane as he led Allegra to a seat at the edge of the room, usually reserved for chaperones.

"You'll keep a close eye on her, won't you, Jane?" he asked. His care for his sister since her injury had won Jane's approval.

"Of course."

"If she becomes faint or fatigued, send for me. We can leave any time."

Allegra clutched her fan, her hands in her lap, her head down.

Phoebe snapped her fan open and said, "This night will be a disaster if she can't even stand up."

"Mother," said Clive, "come with me to the card room, and let Jane help Allegra." Clive gave Jane one last pleading glance as he led his mother away.

Jane sat beside Allegra, talking softly, until one of Allegra's beaux glanced their way. He saw Jane first and looked as if he couldn't quite recognize her, but the next instant he spotted Allegra and crossed the room to ask whether she had recovered sufficiently to grant him the favor of a dance. A smile of genuine pleasure lit Allegra's face and the young man blinked as if he'd stepped into bright sunlight. He pulled up a chair and began speaking in a low earnest voice, making every effort to coax another smile out of her. In minutes Allegra's old court of admirers had gathered around them. As the first set of the evening began to form, Allegra turned to Jane and gave her hand a squeeze.

"We *are* grateful to you, you know, for coming to us. You've been kind to me when I did not deserve it. I'm sure Clive is most grateful because his situation was so hopeless before..." She shrugged. "He had to work for that tedious Lord Chartwell, and he hated it so. But everything is better now. So thank you. I have told all my beaux they must dance with you tonight, so you will never be without a partner."

Jane did not immediately recover from Allegra's disclosure. Clive had worked for Lord Chartwell, in the very office through which information about her father's journeys passed. Clive had been in a position to know in advance where her father traveled. And Clive had benefitted from her father's disappearance. She was rethinking Clive's actions when Eversley appeared and abruptly solicited her hand.

She hardly knew what she did as they went down the set. She quickly lost sight of Allegra, but could see no sign of Hazelwood or his footman accomplice. She wanted to know whether Hazelwood saw Clive as a danger. Clive with his sister had called on her, introduced her to his friends, and taken her driving and shopping. There was nothing in these acts to rouse her suspicion, yet Allegra's remark made her doubt her cousin.

There appeared to be a conspiracy to keep her dancing, but she could detect no danger in Eversley's telling her of his puppies' progress, or Allegra's suitor, Ainsworth, who was of a mathematical turn of mind, showing her a trick for remembering the pattern of a dance. Once or twice she caught sight of Allegra, her cheeks flushed with excitement and as yet no signs of fatigue. An hour or more passed quickly with no sign of Hazelwood. It occurred to her that perhaps he would send for her at the interval when the guests would be moving from the ballroom to the rooms where supper would be provided. She resolved to be alert for any messenger he might choose to send.

At the end of the fourth set, the movement of the dance carried her to the far end of the room, and her partner, momentarily distracted by other acquaintance, left her. As she looked about for Allegra, she saw Count Malikov approach, his face grave and his manner earnest.

"Miss Fawkener, I don't mean to alarm you, but I've been sent to bring you to Allegra. She feels rather faint and is calling for you."

Jane felt at once that she'd been remiss. "And her mother?"

"Clive is looking for her in the card room. They've taken Allegra out of the noise and confusion. I'll lead you to her, if I may."

"Of course."

The count offered his arm, and Jane gathered up her skirts in a motion that had become familiar. She chided herself for losing sight of Allegra and hoped her cousin had not wholly undone her recovery with the exertions of the dance. The count deftly threaded a way around the crowd at the entrance to the supper room. At the great stairway, he led her down. In the entry, a footman stepped forward with her cloak and gloves as if her coming had been expected.

"Oh," said the count, "I see they've moved Allegra to the carriage already."

Outside in the dark, he took her arm and led the way to a waiting coach. When it opened, he motioned Jane to step inside.

Jane halted. It was not the Walhouse coach. She realized she'd been duped.

She backed away and collided with the count. Instantly, a cloth came down in front of her face and was pulled tight across her mouth. She tried to twist free, but was lifted and shoved stumbling into the coach. Her hands and knees hit the floor. Inside a rough man reeking of spirits and onions hauled her up and bound her wrists. He tossed her onto the backward facing seat, pulled a pistol from his belt, and aimed it at her with a steady hand.

Jane froze.

The count poked his head inside the coach. "I will see you shortly, Miss Fawkener."

* * * *

Hazelwood waited in the shadows of the balcony of Langford House. Listening to the fiddlers, looking out over the dark gardens at the rear of the house, he let himself imagine for a moment dancing a waltz with Jane in full view of London. It was an idle fancy. Perhaps she loved him. He thought she did, but he could not, in good conscience, marry her. Marrying him would be social ruin. He had to keep that thought fixed firmly in mind.

The musicians left off. Footmen threw open the balcony doors to cool the ballroom. Hazelwood pushed away from the balustrade, watching for his moment to slip in amongst the guests passing freely in and out. He saw his opportunity and stepped inside. Most of the crowd moved toward the great doors of the ballroom headed for the supper room.

Once Jane was safe, he could report on what they had learned from her copy of *The Husband Hunter's Guide to London*. Her father had mapped not only England's friends, but also Russia's, those caliphs and satraps who would support the Czar. The proposed Russian rail lines would pass through friendly territories along a river he suspected was the Oxus. But Jane could confirm that. He had asked her in his note to bring the map hidden in the Nelson painting. If she could not, they would piece together from her memory, each place her father had visited a friend and where he had identified an enemy. Jane's memory was as valuable as any piece of paper the government possessed. No more than two minutes had passed when he slipped into the appointed room.

* * * *

Clive watched from the landing as Malikov returned. He glanced up the staircase once and nodded at Clive. The deed was done. As the count had predicted, there was no trouble in removing Jane from the ball. The ruse of Allegra's feeling faint had worked. Still Clive felt unsettled as if he had eaten a bit of bad beef. The affair connected him too closely with Malikov. The Russian was not, after all, a charming émigré with a longing for home. He was a man capable of using and casting aside anyone who stood in his way. Malikov knew ways in which Clive could be hurt. The situation was untenable. Clive needed to rid himself of his false friend. Some way to do it would come to him he felt sure. The more immediate problem was what to tell Allegra and his mother in the next few minutes when they inquired about Jane.

* * * *

The chiming of the hour by the mantel clock did not bring Jane. Hazelwood knew he could not have missed her earlier. He left the anteroom and made his way back to the grand staircase where guests leaving the supper room would pass. This time he looked for Allegra. With her golden hair she would be easy to spot, and presumably Jane would be close by. He glanced from one elaborate coiffure to another, but did not see Allegra or Jane.

He saw Clive Walhouse opposite also watching the flow of guests.

As the crowd bunched up at the supper room entrance, Hazelwood attempted to slip by. A hand on his shoulder stopped him abruptly, and he turned to see an old school friend.

"Hullo, man. It's Thorndike. Haven't seen you in a proper ballroom in years. Are you back in your father's good graces?"

"Thorndike." Hazelwood shook the man's hand. "Still out of favor, I'm afraid, but not with the ladies, you see." Guests streamed by, casting curious glances their way.Hazelwood looked for Jane.

"Ah, wrangled an invitation, did you? Brilliant. Found that lady who fancies herself the mother of the next Earl of Vange?"

"Exactly. But must keep it quiet, you know, 'til the deal's done." What Hazelwood didn't need was to be spotted by anyone who might take exception to his being there.

His friend offered another hearty handshake. "Let me know when congratulations are in order."

Hazelwood nodded. Just then Clive caught sight of him and started.

"Where's Jane?" Hazelwood asked.

"Allegra was feeling faint, and Jane is attending her." His glance at the supper room door gave away the lie.

"Try again, Walhouse."

Allegra chose that moment to pass by on the arm of Ainsworth. "Clive?" She looked from him to Hazelwood and back. "Have you seen Jane? She did not come in to supper."

Clive met Hazelwood's stare. "Do not alarm my sister." He turned to Allegra.

"Let's look for her. It's not like her to desert you unless she's stolen one of your beaux."

\* \* \* \*

Clive could feel Hazelwood's gaze on his back, but the man was powerless here. He could not provoke a scene in Langford House. Clive thought he had rid himself of Jane Fawkener, but she was proving inconvenient. She had been so from the first. It was her return to London that had set Malikov off. Clive had not bothered to think why, but now he tried to sort it out. What the count wanted was information, so it was reasonable to assume that Jane had information, and it must be valuable information at that, nothing like the letters and papers that Clive had handed over to the Russian in years past.

Hazelwood was a further complication. His actions would make the count unhappy. Clive really needed a plan to eliminate the two of them. It occurred to him that he knew how to do it. First he would ask Pamela to forgive him for not keeping their engagement tonight. Then he would see his mother and sister home, and finally he would find Lord Chartwell at the man's club. It was time to confess to his former employer that he had stumbled on a plot by the disgraced Viscount Hazelwood to betray British secrets to a subject of the Czar.

*There are two antidotes for the dizzying effects of a ball. The
first is immediately to seek a genuinely thrilling experience. If
a balloon ascension is not an available option, it is advisable
to take a fast gallop over open fields and set one's horse at a
high fence. At the very least, the Husband Hunter should ascend
Primrose Hill (see the map inset) and consider the sweeping
panorama before her. The second antidote is to contrive a
meeting with this paragon of gentlemanly excellence in the most
prosaic of circumstances. You must visit him when he is felled
with a cold, or observe how he handles a session with his man
of business. Observe him shopping with his mother at the linen
draper's, or instructing his nephew in flying a kite. If he is as
charming in the harsh light of day in the company of his family
as he was in the ballroom, then you may permit yourself to like
him.*

—The Husband Hunter's Guide to London

# Chapter Twenty-three

Hazelwood strode into the club, Wilde at his heels. They'd lost her.
The count had her. Hazelwood needed a convenient heath or moor, a vast
wasteland where he could howl out his rage and loss, not the coffee room
of a gentleman's club.

It was his fault, of course. He'd been playing at being a spy. Already
an outcast in London, it had cost him nothing to spend his nights in the
lowest pits of sin and villainy. It had cost nothing to live in comfortable
rooms, well-fed, well-dressed, and flattered. What had he sacrificed but
the sponging house and the duns who'd dogged his every step before he'd
accepted Goldsworthy's offer? He'd liked the spying life so much that he'd
made no preparation for leaving the club at the end of his term of service.

Then, unexpectedly, when his time of playing the game was nearly done,
Goldsworthy had dangled before him a prize he actually wanted. To have
it, he now saw, he would have to lose at the spying game.

Such a simple thing she seemed to be, Jane Fawkener, a thing that had
eluded him before his disgrace. But to have her, to get her back from the
enemy, he would have to give up the club, his friends, and his future. The
thing that Malikov wanted was the map. And he wanted it not because it

revealed those eastern caliphs and satraps friendly to England, but because it revealed England's false friends, those who pretended loyalty but who would side with the Czar in return for power over their neighbors.

The coffee room had never looked more welcoming with its lamps lit, a fire burning, the tray of punch and cups set out for the last drinks of the evening. Blackstone and Clare looked up from a document spread out across a leather ottoman.

"Did you get her?" Clare asked.

"She didn't make the meeting. She left the ball about midnight, about the time Wilde saw Malikov gag a woman and send her off in a coach. Jane's cousins didn't know where she was."

"Walhouse?"

"Lied." He did not trust himself to say more about Clive.

"So, do we have any idea where Malikov's taken her?" Blackstone asked, getting to his feet.

"Yes." Hazelwood saw at once that he'd erred by stopping at the coffee room entrance. His friends stood ready to help him recover Jane. But he could not accept their help, as he was about to betray the British government. "Wilde followed one of her watchers to where the fellow's been living on the sly. He can lead us."

"And if she's not there?" Clare asked. He, too, was standing, with an air of impatience for action.

"We find Malikov and apply pressure. Arm yourselves."

"Is there a plan?" Blackstone asked, sensible fellow that he was.

"I'll tell you on the way. Let me get my pistols." He turned away and started for the stairs.

Blackstone called up after him. "Do you want to send Wilde to rouse a coach for us?"

"No need. Coachman's waiting," he called down. He hoped he had not given himself away. They trusted him. It was his case. They would wait for him. He would have perhaps a quarter of an hour's lead.

\* \* \* \*

By the light of a single lantern on a white stone hearth, Jane watched the smaller of her two captors prod the embers of a dull fire. He didn't speak. He merely pointed his pistol her way to indicate his wishes. The scrape and clank of iron echoed in the empty room until he put aside the poker and applied a wheezing bellows. The hearth emitted a cloud of soot that made him cough and draw his wool muffler tighter around his face.

Jane stood where she'd been ordered to stand, quietly clenching and unclenching her bound hands to keep some circulation in them. The gag that bound her mouth cut into her cheeks and dried her tongue. She found it hard to breathe steadily through her nose and impossible to swallow. Her scraped knees stung.

They had not traveled far from Langford House. Jane had counted six turns of the unhurried coach, which had led them south and east to this apparently deserted house. A change in the sound of the carriage wheels told her they had entered a short, graveled drive. Then her captor had hustled her through a portico into the dark house at pistol point.

He faced the feeble fire, his hands extended toward it as it started to burn. Its glow illuminated more of the room, which wasn't as deserted as she'd first supposed. For the moment his pistol lay on a green baize table such as one would see in a card room but littered with papers. On the floor by the table was a traveler's satchel. Around the table at the edge of the lamp's dim light lay mounds of bedding as if someone had kicked apart a nest of blankets and cushions. On the blackened fender sat an iron pan and an object she had not thought to see in London, a small, long-handled coffeepot like the one she'd left behind in Halab. The smell of coffee lingered in the room mixed with smells of mold and rodents. She guessed that the heavily curtained chamber must have been the reception room of some lord's mansion before its abandonment and ruin. Without turning her head, she tried to judge the distance to the nearest door. A quick calculation told her that her guard could grab his pistol long before she reached the door.

She assumed that no one knew where she was, at least no one who would help her. Hazelwood's plan to come for her had failed. Allegra and Phoebe might worry about her, but she now knew that Clive would lie to them as he had been lying to her. They would go to bed imagining her somewhere safe, perhaps with her grandmother, or with Mrs. Lowndes. It was a lonely thought to think of her friends ignorant of her situation curling up in their beds as if she too were as warm and safe as they were. She ached suddenly for her father and the loneliness he must feel. Of course, he would be strong and clever. He would make his captors laugh. He would keep his mind keen and always look for an escape. She straightened her spine. Her captor picked up his pistol again as a door opened and footsteps echoed across the bare floor.

Count Malikov strode up to Jane and looked her over, coolly. He reached up and pulled away the gag. Jane swallowed and worked her aching jaw. Instantly, her teeth started clicking with the cold.

Malikov crossed to the fire and gave his henchman a clout on the ear.
"Is that the best you can do? It's colder than St. Petersburg in here."

She did not catch the man's mumbled reply. It was the first speech she'd
heard from him, and it was not English. She had assumed the man was
a London ruffian hired for his muscle, but now she realized he might be
something else. His features were hidden under his hat and the muffler
around his face.

Malikov settled in the chair at the green baize table. She supposed he
must be thought handsome with his fair looks and blue eyes. Until this
evening, she had only seen him as an older version of the young men around
Allegra. Now the smooth, languid manner was gone. The dropping of the
pretense of civility sent a different sort of shiver through her. "Come here,
girl. You have questions to answer."

Jane stepped forward. At least she would be closer to the fire.

"Where's your father?" Malikov demanded.

The unexpected question made her blink. "According to the B-B-British
government, he's dead."

Malikov shook his head. "But you don't believe that, do you?"

"He may be alive and held captive in the East. K-k-kidnapping merchants
for ransom is not uncommon there."

"But he's no merchant, and there's been no ransom demand, has
there? Why is that? One must wonder, and one imagines that instead
there was a plan."

Again he puzzled her. She had assumed that her father's enemies knew
where he was. "I do not understand you."

"Oh, I think you do. A year ago your father smuggled a stolen map out
of Khiva. He sent you to London to retrieve that map, didn't he?"

She shook her head. She tried to keep her gaze uncomprehending, but it
was one of those moments when a different explanation of the facts appears
and causes one to rearrange the details. The puzzle pieces suddenly fit
together. The scrambled ivory letters make a word. Her father's enemies
did not have him. "The government brought me here when he disappeared."

"Miss Fawkener, I do not think you understand the gravity of your
situation. The Russian government does not take kindly to the theft of
vital information."

Jane wished she had a curse to banish quaking limbs and chattering
teeth. The count was not, after all, a bandit, with whom one could bargain
for safe passage. "Count Malkov, you overestimate m-m-me. No one in
government entrusts a young woman with imp-p-portant information."

"It is not through the government, however, that you received a message from your father, but rather through his bankers."

In spite of herself Jane could not conceal a small start. Malikov watched her narrowly.

"You see, Miss Fawkener, I know a great deal about your movements since you arrived in England."

There was little chance then that she could convince him he was mistaken, that she was just a girl enjoying the Season. She could deny him the information she possessed. She could delay him, and hope that Hazelwood had a way of finding her. "The only information my father's bankers imparted to me was the meagerness of my fortune. By restricting my funds until such time as I marry, my father encouraged me to become a husband hunter."

"Yet you are seen everywhere with the disgraced Viscount Hazelwood."

"I was. Until my cousins explained the danger of such a connection. I have not seen the viscount since the Walhouses took me in."

"So, you claim that you have no information to give me."

"N-n-none." She doubted he believed her.

"An unfortunate answer, Miss Fawkener. If you have no information, we will have to find another use for you."

*There is inevitably in the Husband Hunter's search for her partner in life a moment when it appears that she will fail in the quest. It may be that a heart she believed to be turning her way is captured by another. It may be that she has smiled and danced and listened and attended and worn her loveliest gowns in vain for no one has singled her out as worthy of his special notice. She is liked. She is admired. She is not loved. The end of the Season approaches, and happier girls confide in her the professions of love they have received, while she alone imagines a future of wearing lace caps and tending the sickbeds of nieces and nephews with no one to observe her tender ministrations or share her anxieties. If she is wise, the Husband Hunter will immediately cease to imagine her bleak future, offer her friends her heartiest wishes for their health and happiness, and consult her dressmaker for how best to appear at each of the weddings she will soon attend.*

—*The Husband Hunter's Guide to London*

# Chapter Twenty-Four

Nate did not like the way things were going. Hazelwood had shared no plan with him. The clocks in the coffee room ticked forward indifferent to Nate's dilemma. The quarter hour would chime, and the two men in front of him would turn to him. He would have to decide where to lead them.

Harry Clare had armed himself in his customary way with a pair of Land Pattern pistols and a Mameluke sabre, the British cavalry's preferred sword. As he donned his greatcoat, he glanced pointedly at Blackstone.

"Shall I see what's keeping our friend?" Blackstone asked.

He returned grim-faced in less time than Nate expected. "The fool's gone off on his own, Clare."

Clare turned to Wilde. "Well, whelp, do you know his plan?"

"No, sir." Nate squared his shoulders." The thing is, sir, Hazelwood's a man in love."

"That explains it, then," said Blackstone with a dry laugh, and Clare winced. "Let's hope we're not too late to stop him from sacrificing himself."

"And England," Clare added under his breath.

The quarter hour chimes sounded, and Nate steeled himself to lead the way when below them the club doors opened, and the sound of angry voices and tramping boots rose up to meet them. The three men appeared, blocking the coffee room entry, Goldsworthy, Chartwell, and a third man Nate had never seen before. Clare and Blackstone exchanged a look. They had a problem.

Round-faced, bespectacled Chartwell was the smallest of the three men, dwarfed by Goldsworthy's great bulk, but he immediately took charge. "Gentlemen, where's Hazelwood?"

Blackstone looked around the coffee room as if his friend might be lying on one of its sofas or lounging in one of its chairs. "He's not here. May we help?"

"Of course, you can lads," Goldsworthy said. "Just tell us where he's gone."

"Upstairs?" Blackstone shrugged. Nate appreciated the man's cool. "You don't mind if Clare and I take off, do you, Chartwell? We were on the point of leaving." He made it sound as if they meant to go around to a club or a pleasure house.

"Upstairs! What sort of answer is that? I do mind." Chartwell seemed to puff up under his coat. His pointed gaze took in Blackstone's pistol and Clare's sword. He turned and signaled behind him, and a troop of red-coated Horse Guards filed into the club. Chartwell pointed to the stairs, and the captain led his men up them. The tramp of boots filled the club.

"Lads," Goldsworthy said, frowning severely, "no use trying to disguise the thing. Hazelwood's gone off on his own, I expect."

"And you've brought a unit of the Horse Guards to back him up?" Blackstone asked. He could be as pointed as anyone.

Goldsworthy looked grim, and Chartwell, furious. The third man, a bearded fellow, who looked to Nate as if he belonged in the Canadian wilds, watched the proceedings with a curious, detached expression. "A precaution merely," said Chartwell.

The troops came tramping back down the stairs, and the captain reported that there was no sign of Hazelwood.

Chartwell spun on Goldsworthy. "By God, man, he's selling secrets to that Russian scoundrel. I'll have him hanged, and I'll have this damned club shut down!"

Goldsworthy looked as if he might bat Chartwell away like an annoying insect. "Lads," the big man said, "time to finish the mission. Where are we headed?"

Clare and Blackstone exchanged another look, and Nate felt better. Whatever Lord Hazelwood had got himself into; his friends would not let him down. Still Nate's stomach clenched when Clare turned to him. "Well, whelp, lead on."

\* \* \* \*

Hazelwood stood at the gate of the deserted house, where Nate Wilde had earlier seen the watcher enter and leave. He had walked by the place for years without giving it any notice. Now he saw that one of the iron gates was no longer chained shut. With a little shove the gate moved enough to admit his entry. A pitted gravel drive made a short arc from gate to gate past the portico. To his left a horse nickered softly where a carriage waited in the deeper gloom under some trees. Oddly, a pair of lamps sat on the front step, as if Malikov expected visitors. And a large figure waited there in a hat and greatcoat, and no doubt, armed.

In his swift passage up the club stairs to his room and out again through the chemist's shop, Hazelwood had considered and rejected a half dozen schemes for recovering his love. He had quickly decided that his pistols had no part in the plan forming in his head. Instead, he returned to his old claret-stained waistcoat and cravat. Only one part of the plan mattered, after all, the rest he would contrive as he went along. He would rely on his wits. And his friends. They would arrive with plenty of firepower, he was sure.

Malikov's henchman reacted with swift and brutal efficiency to the sound of Hazelwood's footfalls on the gravel drive. Hazelwood was searched for weapons and brought before Malikov as rapidly as he could wish. It took considerable self-control to refrain from expressing his feelings at the sight of his love bound and shivering. A second henchman, smaller than the first, but equally concealed by a greatcoat and muffler, stood by the hearth holding a pistol pointed directly at her.

"You!" Malikov did not conceal his obvious surprise.

"You were expecting someone else?" Hazelwood wondered for whom the lamps had been lit. The fellow with the pistol at his back reported that he'd found Hazelwood lurking outside.

"Not lurking, surely. I came right up the drive." He took his first look at Jane, trying to judge how cold she was by now. He could see her breath in the frigid air.

Malikov had his guard up again. "Hazelwood, you interrupt my business with Miss Fawkener."

"My mistake, Malikov, I heard you were hosting a card game." He looked at the green baize table. "You know I've never been able to resist deep play."

"Ah, but when your pockets are to let, you can hardly expect to join the game."

"My pockets are not entirely empty. I have something you want."

"What could you have that I could possibly want?" Malikov's usual affability was strained.

Hazelwood looked into the man's smooth countenance. At the moment the curled lip, the flared nostrils, and the fingers drumming on the arm of his chair suggested that Malikov was thinking of how to rid himself of an irritation. He saw the old Hazelwood, the sot, the wastrel dismissed as a bird-witted thrall to drink and gaming. Hazelwood was about to open the man's eyes. Of course, he would betray his friends when he did it.

"A map."

Malikov's manner changed instantly. He sat up very straight in the chair. Hazelwood knew that look, the look of a man being undeceived, seeing for the first time what he had overlooked or underestimated. Malikov did not quite believe what he was seeing, but he reached for his henchman's pistol and signaled for the man to search Hazelwood. The fellow stripped off Hazelwood's greatcoat and made a rude and thorough search of his person. The man stepped back and shook his head at Malikov. The pistol changed hands again.

"Hazelwood, I am in no humor for games."

"Did I mention that I have a condition for sharing this map with you?" Hazelwood said. He risked a second glance at Jane. Her eyes were watchful even as her body shook with the cold. Her cheeks bore two red streaks like burn marks where something had pressed against them. A gag, he realized.

"A condition?" Malikov's voice was contemptuous. "I think you misunderstand your position."

"Do I? I'm the only man in London who can lead you to the map you've been seeking."

"Have I been seeking a map?"

Hazelwood nodded. Without his coat, he could feel the warmth leaving him. "I know where this map is."

Jane made an odd strangled protest in her throat. She was shivering hard now. Hazelwood did not imagine she could talk.

Malikov did not even glance at the girl. "What an odd thing for an English gentleman to propose—to give a map to a subject of the Czar. I wonder what moves you to make such an offer."

"Money, of course. Treasonous of me, isn't it?" Hazelwood shrugged, at least he hoped it looked like a shrug. The careless pose was difficult to manage with a pistol still pointed at Jane. "As you pointed out, I'm a man with pockets to let. Humor me."

"What is this condition you mention?"

Hazelwood looked briefly at the floor. Malikov had taken the bait. "A thousand pounds would suit me."

Malikov laughed. "Really, Hazelwood, you do not understand the situation here."

"No ready cash available? Suppose we settle on something else. Jane Fawkener leaves your company now. When her friends report that she's safely among them, I take you to the map."

There was a silence in which Hazelwood thought he could hear the coals hissing in the grate before Malikov laughed, a hollow unpleasant sound. He stood. "I fail to see the advantage of your offer, Hazelwood, but you do give a man ideas." He nodded to his henchman, who steadied the pistol in his hand, and left the room.

                                    *  *  *  *

As soon as Malikov's footsteps retreated, Hazelwood crossed to Jane's side and pulled her to him. Their guard reacted with a snarl of unintelligible words and a threatening wave of the pistol.

"I don't think he speaks English," Jane told him. "Turkic, perhaps."

"Interesting. I noted the coffeepot. Let me warm your hands," Hazelwood suggested, ignoring another outburst from the guard. He began to chafe her hands, keeping her gaze on him, trying with his fingers to determine whether he could loosen her bonds at all.

"H-H-Hazelwood, don't provoke him. He'll shoot us."

Hazelwood glanced at their guard. "He won't shoot without orders. Malikov wants the map, so he still needs us. Let me warm you, love, before Malikov returns."

"You don't believe M-M-Malikov will let us go in exchange for the m-m-map, do you?"

"Sadly, not at all. He can't risk either of us talking. But I've made him think. We may get out of this yet." He didn't know how long Blackstone and Clare would delay. So far he had avoided involving them in treason.

"H-h-hurts," she said, as he warmed her hands.

"I imagine." He kissed the top of her head. The imperfect moment was of a piece with the way his life usually went. Something he very much wanted was his briefly under threat of being snatched away.

"Hazelwood, Malikov betrayed my father, didn't he?" her voice was a low shaky whisper.

"With help from someone inside Chartwell's office."

"Clive." She said it sadly. "He worked there. He knew my father's plans. He gained from my father's death."

"Clive is a proper scoundrel. You didn't suspect him before tonight, did you?"

"No. But at the ball Allegra said something. I hardly had time to think about it before Count Malikov came to tell me she needed me."

"You didn't get my message?" There was a mystery there, but he would think about that later, if there was a later.

"No," she said. He could feel her spirits reviving. "I don't want Malikov to get away with betraying my father."

"I share the sentiment, but unless we catch him dealing in secrets with something in his possession that more rightfully belongs to the government, he walks."

"Like our map? But you don't have our map."

"Malikov doesn't know that." Hazelwood felt her hands begin to warm.

Jane was shaking her head. "Malikov will be looking for a specific map. He will spot a fake or a copy."

"True. The plan has some flaws. But it should work well enough for you to get away. My friends are coming. They'll create a distraction. Promise me you'll leave."

She shook her head.

"There is an unguarded back door," he said gently. "Use it when the time comes. You can go your grandmother or to the chemist's shop." He hated to confess that the whole of his plan was to save the one thing that mattered to him, even if she would never be his.

"What if," she said, "Malikov were to be holding the map in his hands when your friends arrive?"

"That would be brilliant." There was a flaw in her plan, but he would not mention that now. "If you are determined not to leave, can you faint on command?"

"I can drop to the ground."

"Good. I suspect that our guard may lose his head and fire at some point."

"What's to be my cue?" she asked.

He did not get to answer as the door opened at the far end of the room, and Malikov came striding back. Their guard began to speak in rapid angry bursts of words, gesturing at the two of them.

Malikov glanced at them as he dropped a satchel on the baize table. "What have you two been hatching that causes the fellow such distress?"

Hazelwood shrugged and stepped away from Jane. "Malikov, what brings you to Crannock House in the middle of the night if not cards?"

Malikov looked at him, a man still deciding how to solve an unexpected problem. "Crannock is a friend of mine. He suspected that someone was abusing his hospitality and making a home for himself here. He asked me to look into it."

"Did you find the interloper?"

"I fear your presence here tonight may have frightened him off."

"I had no idea. Perhaps the evening will not go to waste if you acquire the map."

"Hazelwood, you grow tiresome. I have not seen this map you offer me. A quarter of an hour ago, you claimed you could lead me to it. Now, you claim to have it."

"Would you care to see it, to verify that it is the map you seek? My condition this time will cost you nothing." Hazelwood angled toward Malikov, crossing between Jane and the man by the fire. He stopped a few feet from the baize table.

"What is it?"

"Simply that your man put his pistol in the corner."

Malikov looked at the jumble of papers on the baize table. The disorder reminded Hazelwood of Goldsworthy's desk. The truth of it struck him. Malikov was Russia's Goldsworthy in London. He dispatched spies and collected information from them to send home, and he was about to pack his satchel with a treasure trove. And still he wanted that map. He motioned to the man on the hearth to put the pistol in the corner.

Hazelwood lifted his right foot and reached into his shoe for a piece of paper. Jane gave a smothered cry.

Malikov's gaze stayed on the paper. "It's a folded piece of paper."

"As is a bank note, yet most men find it valuable. Are you ready to hear my condition?" Hazelwood began to unfold the paper.

\* \* \* \*

In spite of the cold Nate found himself sweating as he led his party through the back of the darkened house to the very door of the room where they could hear Hazelwood and Malikov in conversation. He would never have guessed that a man as large as Goldsworthy or one as stiff-rumped as Chartwell could move so stealthily. The third man created no sound at all. All but two of the horse guard troops were to wait in place on the Piccadilly side of the house, ready to intercept anyone who tried to bolt out the front.

Clare had his ear to the door from which the faint voices came. He turned the handle, and pushed the door ajar enough to hear Hazelwood offer Malikov a map. Chartwell stiffened in the dark. Clare raised his arm to give the signal.

Clare's arm dropped and they burst through the doors, fanning out across the bare floor, Blackstone and Clare at the center, Goldsworthy and Chartwell to the left, and Nate and the third man to the right, boots smacking the floor and weapons jingling. Behind them the Horse Guards.

Malikov's hand swept up a paper from the table in front of him, crumpling it in his fist and pivoting toward the fire. Hazelwood's left fist shot out and caught Malikov squarely in the face, knocking him back, and making his nose gush blood. A dark figure from the hearth dashed for the corner and spun, wielding a pistol.

The shooter in the corner looked wildly at the firepower arrayed against him, and coldly took aim at the stranger beside Nate.

Hazelwood called out to Miss Fawkener, "Jane, your stays are too tight."

The girl collapsed, and the man at Nate's side dropped to his knees on the floor at her side as the dark fellow on the hearth fired. His shot whistled over the kneeling man's head, past Nate's sleeve, and into the woodwork at the dark end of the room.

The shooter turned to flee, but a bullet from Clare's pistol brought him moaning to the ground clutching his leg. The room rang with echoes of shots fired and stank of burnt powder. Blackstone hauled Malikov to his feet and secured the crumpled paper he'd attempted to discard. Malikov pressed his ruined cravat to his streaming nose.

Clare moved to stand next to Hazelwood. They all looked to Goldsworthy, but it was Chartwell who strode up to Malikov and Hazelwood. "Arrest them both," he said.

"No," the girl shouted, her gaze on Hazelwood. She attempted to stand, but stumbled, her feet caught in her skirts and the folds of her cloak. The man at her side reached to help, and when she took his hand and turned to him, she cried out, "Papa?"

The stranger took her in his embrace, and Nate did not hear what they said. She was sobbing and laughing and beating the man with her fists.

The Horse Guards marched forward to seize and bind Malikov and Hazelwood. Manacles clanked as they were applied. It was wrong. It was mad. Nate glanced at Blackstone and Clare. Their faces had turned to stone. The girl, caught in her father's embrace, did not see Hazelwood marched off.

As Chartwell passed out the door behind the manacled men, he turned to Goldsworthy, and under the noise and confusion of shouted orders and jingling metal, Nate heard him say, "I'm shutting your club down, man. Your unorthodox methods are a formula for catastrophe. No more."

*The Husband Hunter, of course, wishes for the blessings of her friends and family when she has found that man above all others that she can truly love. While she hopes that they may see her delight and his merits, not having her knowledge of his character, they doubt his worthiness from worldly standards. She will now hear from all and sundry the flaws in his manner, his education, his politics, and the size of his income. Now that her success as a Husband Hunter is assured, her relations will predict the unhappiness and failure of the very enterprise they have been insisting she embark upon. They now wish to prevent her ever becoming a wife, for what is her success, but the breakup of the family in which she had lived these eighteen or twenty years. The Husband Hunter must be prepared, indeed, to defend her love.*

*—The Husband Hunter's Guide to London*

# Chapter Twenty-five

For once on the morning of her father's return Jane did not mind the overheated drawing room in her grandmother's house. An unexpected shudder shook her body now and then, rattling her cup against the saucer, as she and her father drank coffee together. Margaret had found a faded blue wool gown for Jane to wear until her clothes could be retrieved from her cousins. Her father wore a coat of his from before their time in Halab. It made a striking contrast—the old-fashioned English coat and the full beard and swarthy looks of a man of Halab. She could not stop looking at him.

"You look very English," he told her, putting down his cup. It was a signal to begin the real talk they had not yet had.

"How long have you been in London?" she asked him. He had brought her pistachios and almonds. Margaret put them in a dish on the little table that held the coffee tray.

"I arrived just days after your own arrival. I had to remain dead until we could find out for certain who was betraying our people in the East."

"Clive?"

"Clive and others who have been passing secrets to Malikov. We suspected him, but were never able to prove anything."

"We?"

"Goldsworthy and I."

She put down her cup as well. "Why?" She wanted him to tell the story, to explain why he'd let her think him dead, and why she'd been shipped to London, and told she must become someone she was not.

The question seemed to stump him. He stood and walked away to the window, looking out into the street. She did not know whether he found London familiar or unfamiliar.

"I'd been compromised. Our friends were in danger. One of them died getting me that map. I knew I could no longer do the work I'd been doing. I knew I had to get you out of Halab before anyone decided to use you against me. And I had to find out who had compromised our network. It had to be someone in London."

"But you could not tell me any of this, any of your plans? You had to let me imagine you captured or dead?" Jane's throat ached. He was explaining the spy's reasons for doing what he'd done. Not the father's reasons. "I did not mind, you know, that we lived in Halab surrounded by families, by markets full of *tetas* and *ammis* and *kaitis*. We were only two, but I was *Rana*, and you were *Abu Rana*, Rana's father. It was enough for me. I did not miss family, but when you were no more, what was I to feel?"

He turned back to her from the window, his expression changed. "Ah, I see you are ahead of me. It wasn't until I went to Barker, the English Consul, to arrange your return to England, that I saw the error of my ways as a father."

He came back to the sofa and sat facing her, his clasped hands hanging between his knees, his head down. She waited for him to go on.

"Barker gave me a piece of his mind when he realized how we had been living. He made me understand that I'd deprived you of the English life you were meant to have, of all the things I had taken for granted because I had had them as a boy and because they no longer mattered to me when your mother died. You were supposed to be an English girl."

"And you thought giving me a book would make me an English girl?" She said it gently, but she could not help but think of that black moment in the bank when the Hammersleys had first put the book in her hands, and she had cursed it.

He looked up then, his eyes bleak with loss. "It was your mother's book. I thought… I wanted you to have it no matter what happened to me. Can you forgive me?"

"Oh, Papa, I forgive you. How could I not?" Jane crossed the room and knelt and took his clasped hands in hers, searching his face. How could she blame him when she had failed to recognize the love behind his gift. "I thought I'd lost you when you were the only family I had." Then she stood, pulling him up with her and offering him a grin she knew was every bit as cheeky as a Hazelwood grin. "But I have to get my book back, Papa, and there's only one way."

Her Papa held her hands and looked into her face, the bleakness in his eyes replaced by a wary questioning look. "You don't have the book?" She shook her head. That was the spy in him still. "It's quite safe."

"Who has it?"

"Lord Hazelwood." Her papa looked shocked. "You see, Papa, I did become a husband hunter, and I've found the husband I want."

He freed his hands from hers abruptly, looking shocked. "You can't be serious. Not Hazelwood? Do you know that man's past, his history, his—" He bit off further details.

Jane smiled. Her father's objections were just what she expected. "I'm going to marry him just as soon as you get him out of jail. Today, would be good."

"I can't do that. He gave the map to Malikov."

Jane shook her head. "No. He didn't. He used your notes in the book to make a map to deceive Malikov. I have the real map, and I will return it to you when I marry Lord Hazelwood."

"You really want to marry this man?"

"I do. Just as soon as you secure his release from prison and clear him of the charge of treason." He was her father, and he loved her in his way, but he had loved his spying more for a very long time. Hazelwood, who had nothing to gain and everything to lose, had tossed aside his spying when it was the only thing he had, just for her. "And, Papa," she said, "you will arrange our marriage today like a good papa in Halab."

*The Husband Hunter's wedding whether it is celebrated
in the conventional way on a Sunday morning followed by
a breakfast and cake, or in some way suitable to the parties
themselves, either elaborate or simple among few or many
guests, is merely the outward sign of an inward joy. The bride
and her groom appear to be figures in a larger design. The
world will note its surprise or its satisfaction in their union. The
guests, and even the papers, will comment on her gown and his
handsomeness, but the unveiling of their true selves, one to the
other, will happen only when they come together as husband
and wife in that extraordinarily private place, the marriage bed.*

—*The Husband Hunter's Guide to London*

# Chapter Twenty-six

Jane Fawkener married Edmund Dalby, Viscount Hazelwood, in her grandmother's drawing room on a rainy afternoon as London began at last to thaw from its great freeze. She married him in the Halab way. Her father and the groom both signed the *aqd,* the marriage contract, and she and Hazelwood declared the free will of two partners to join in love.

The wedding did not take place quite as soon as Jane had wished. She had had to endure an endless day of interviews with Lord Chartwell over the map. To all questions she had stubbornly repeated that she would make a gift of the map to her husband when he was free to be her husband and when all charges against him had been dropped. She pointed out to Lord Chartwell that considering his unwillingness to help her in the matter of her father's disappearance, she was being extraordinarily helpful to the government in its current dilemma.

While the matter remained unresolved, and while the government collected her possessions from her cousins and made a thorough search of them, she sent for the dress made for her for the investiture ceremony. The ceremony took place on the second day of Lord Hazelwood's incarceration with her father receiving the silver cross of the Order of St. Michael and St. George in person. He and the king had exchanged a few words when the king saw him.

"Thought you was dead, Fawkener," said the king.

"Clerical error, your majesty. Still very much alive and at your service," her father replied.

On the third day of Hazelwood's incarceration, while Jane's newly knighted father worked to gain his release, Jane paid a visit to Lady Vange. It was a brief call, well within the limits prescribed for such visits. Jane merely went to acquaint the countess with her intention to marry Lord Hazelwood in the English way on the first Sunday morning after the banns were called. Across a few feet of rich carpet the countess's green eyes were strikingly like her son's but without the laughter that habitually lighted his. Jane refused to be daunted by her future mother-in-law's grave elegance, but she thought it wise to refrain from praising her love to his mother just yet. The countess would see for herself in time the man Hazelwood had become if once Jane could bring them together. She thought she knew the perfect way.

What was a mother-in-law after all but a *teta*-in-waiting?

A small wedding party of Jane's grandmother, her companion Margaret, Hazelwood's friends Captain Clare, and Lord Blackstone and his lady, and Jane's Uncle Thaddeus dined on tea and cake after the brief exchange of vows in the drawing room. After toasts and embraces all around, the newly married couple left for her Uncle Thaddeus's cottage in Hampstead.

The bedroom on the upper floor of the cottage was as light and airy as the lower floor was dark and closed in. The roof sloped upward high above them. Two windows cut deep in its slant admitted light and offered a view of heath and sky. The rough white walls were bare, but the four-poster bed was covered in a blue quilt and a vase of early hyacinth sat on the mantel. A cheering fire burned on the grate with a bucket of water and a kettle at hand.

They stood and faced each other before the fire and listened to the whisper of the rain on the thatch and the rattle of it in a drainpipe while the steps of Uncle Thaddeus's man retreated down the wooden steps to the floor below.

"Are you sure you want this?" her new husband asked. "Because I can think of a score of reasons why you should not marry me." He set their two small bags on the floor at the foot of the bed.

"Such as?" she asked, looking around for a place to hang her damp cloak.

He sighed and ran a hand through his hair, disordering it, just as she longed to do. Today it reminded her of the dark gleam of coffee beans roasted in the Halab way. He squared his shoulders in a most un-Hazelwood way. She tried not to smile.

"The Season is just about to begin. Your father is recovered. You could be a proper husband hunter now. I have your book in my bag. You could begin again."

"Hmm? And go to balls and routs and be seen in the park and at the theatre and wear those gowns we ordered together?"

"Precisely. And I can name ten men better than I"—he swallowed— "worthier than I to be your husband."

Jane undid the ties at her throat and slipped out of her damp cloak. She wore the white gown from that day at Madame Celeste's, without the panniers. He really was going to resist happiness all the way. But happiness had its ways, like sand from the desert, of slipping through the cracks of barred windows and doors. "Ten men? Hmm. I think it's too late for that. I don't want a better man than you. Do you have any other objections I should consider?" She tilted her head, considering the shade of green in his eyes. They were still shadowed.

He swallowed. "Your father does not like me. Did you know that he insisted on a clause in that contract that allows you to divorce me?"

"An *esma* it's called. It allows a woman to divorce a man, a rare thing." She folded her cloak over the back of a light chair under the nearest window and faced him again.

"What did you do to get him to agree to our marriage?"

"I told him what my wedding gift to you would be. Now, do you have any last objection to my decision to marry you?" She turned to the hearth and picked up the kettle. It was full, and she placed it on the hob.

"It's a bad bargain for you. I come to you about as rich as Adam was when he got himself tossed out of Eden. I will not bore you with the details, but in failing my mission for Goldsworthy I end my brief spying career in considerable debt."

"Had I been seeking a very wealthy husband or one at the center of London society, no doubt I would agree with you, but I always had a different set of criteria."

"Did you?"

"I did." She crossed the room and opened a small cabinet that sat against the wall between the two windows.

"What are you looking for?"

"This." She held up a large china bowl. "There's a protocol, you may not know, for the way in which a bridegroom in Halab approaches his bride."

"Is there? Tell me." He took the bowl from her. And she saw in his gaze that at last his resistance was melting. If his eyes did not yet have the dancing lights she liked so well, at least the shadows were fading.

"First, he removes her shoes and bathes her feet."

"Ah." He went right to work then, taking the bowl from her and placing it on the hearth, and leading her to one of the chairs and seating her. He was a man of action, after all. He stood before her and shrugged out of his greatcoat, which he draped over her cloak. He stripped off his jacket, undid his cravat, and rolled up his sleeves. Then he knelt and lifted her skirts and folded them back over her knees.

He sat back on his heels and ran his warm palms up her stocking-clad legs. He let his hands drift down again to her ankles and rested his head in her lap. She touched his hair, tangling her fingers in the dark silky strands.

When he lifted his head, his eyes had darkened again with what she recognized as desire. She knew it because she felt it, too.

He bent and concentrated on unlacing and removing her slippers. Then he reached up under her skirts along her thighs for the garters that held her stockings in place. He released them and rolled first one and then the other of her stockings down her legs, baring them to his gaze. He kissed each of her scraped knees.

The kettle whistled, and he rose to pull it off the hob and fill the bowl. With a cup from the cabinet he added cold water from the bucket to the steaming bowl. He found a pair of towels, one to lay under the bowl, and one he draped over his shoulder.

"Should I have jasmine petals to perfume the water?"

"Not required."

He lifted each foot into the warm bath and cupped the water in his hands to pour over her legs, sliding his hands along her slick, wet skin. Jane's eyes drifted shut as the sensation of his hands on her feet warmed her everywhere.

He surged up, leaning forward on the chair arms, kissing her. She reached up to draw him closer, and he pulled her to her feet. Her skirts dropped into the bowl of water, and he lifted her up, his arms around her back, the kiss unbroken, until he swung her around away from the bowl of cooling water, and set her down on the carpet by the hearth. She lay her head against his chest, feeling the rough rhythm of his breathing and beating of his heart. He kissed the top of her head.

"My love, we are wearing entirely too many clothes, for a bride and her groom. Do wish me to leave and give you a moment alone?"

She shook her head. "I wish you to help me with my fastenings and stays." It was time for her to give him his gift. She turned her back and smiled over her shoulder to encourage him.

\* \* \* \*

Hazelwood's hands closed and unclosed at her side. He undid the first of the tiny buttons up her back so that the closure of her dress gaped. His fingers felt suddenly clumsy, but he kept going, until he'd exposed the crossed laces of her stays. Her corset was plain, but far from the ugly one she'd been wearing that first day in the bank. He kissed her back between her shoulder blades. He wanted her hair down.

She reached up, as if she read his thoughts, and began to pull the pins from her hair.

He undid the laces at her waist and spread the sides of her corset when it crackled. She dropped her hands to her side and shook her hair loose and turned to smile at him over her shoulder.

"Your gift?" His fingers made contact with the edge of a folded piece of paper, sticking out of her corset casing. "This bit of paper?" He managed to take hold of the paper between his thumb and forefinger and gave a tug. "The map?"

"Yes." He felt her sigh of relief. "I took it from the back of the painting my first night with my cousins."

A few more tugs, and he had the map in his hand. He turned her to face him. He had a confession to make. "I thought Malikov would take you from me. I could not let him do it whatever the cost."

"I know." She reached up and put her hand to his lips to silence him. Then she smiled and shrugged, and the light gown fell to the floor.

She turned to face him then. He took his time unveiling her person the way he'd first imagined when he'd been set to spy on her. Laces gave and silk slipped away until she stood straight and sure, facing him in her own shining skin as boldly as she'd faced danger. With a knowing smile she reached for him in turn. Speechlessly, she worked at buttons and closures, undoing his wedding finery as she had undone all his disguises. He let her look, and touch with trembling fingers, laughing away the layers between them. As he stepped free of the last of his garments, the frank wonder in her eyes made him new, a second self, not the idealistic youth whose honor and reputation he had squandered, but the man he'd become by loving her and being loved.

"You like what you see?" he asked.

She nodded, sliding a hand down his chest, her palm coming to rest flat against his belly. "But then," she said, "I've known for some time that I would."

He laughed for sheer joy and took her by the hand and led her to the bed he'd never thought to enter, his marriage bed. And though he felt the wonder of it, he was at heart a cheeky fellow, and so, once he had her in his bed, he did not hesitate to kiss and touch and rouse and stir until his love took his face in her hands, looking up at him, damp and disheveled and breathing as unevenly as he was, and said, "Get on with it, love." And he did.

*Stumbles and missteps are an inevitable consequence
of taking one's place in a new circle of acquaintance. The
Husband Hunter cannot say or do exactly what she ought to say
or do on every occasion. The very qualities of spirit, curiosity,
and independence that are so much a part of any young
person's charm are apt to betray her into conduct that may
produce unpleasant reflections. The blush that stains her cheek
in such moments of self-scrutiny will recall her to a sense of
what she ought to be doing. Should any actions of hers lead to
a persistent sense of discomfort, or to a sense that some amends
must be made, she should seek the counsel of a wise mentor.*

—The Husband Hunter's Guide to London

# Epilogue

The proper church wedding was over. Her viscount had married another. Twice. They had come down the aisle together sharing a look of joy so bright that Miranda had put her gloved hands over her mouth to keep from crying out. No one saw. Now she was alone, or almost alone.

Above her in the choir loft the organist rustled papers, putting away his music, by the sound of it. The white-haired sexton called up to him to remind him of a coming concert, then he, too, shuffled off toward the little office at the side of the sanctuary. No one noted her.

She had chosen to sit in the very back pew of the church for the ceremony. The people there seemed to know one another, but they had made room for her, and nodded and smiled. Miranda had worn her best fir-trimmed cloak and the pale blue silk bonnet that always made gentlemen notice her eyes and turn their heads her way. The back bench group included two gentlemen and four ladies, two of whom appeared to be twins, and one of them quite young and pretty. They had been among the last to leave the church, standing in the corner, talking and laughing, and trading books, even the men. The pretty girl was especially pleased to receive a book. And her pleasure had given Miranda an idea. She had thought to confess to someone what she had done, but now she knew she never would. Instead she would make a sacrifice. That sacrifice would be her atonement for the wrong she had done.

The club was closed. No one blamed her. No one knew what she had done, but it was her fault. If she had delivered the note to Jane Fawkener, the woman would not have been abducted from the ball and Lord Hazelwood would not have gotten himself arrested and the club would not have been shut down. It was true that the spy Malikov had been unmasked, and that Clive Walhouse had fled England, but the club remained closed, nevertheless.

Now there would be no more spies coming to be fitted and measured in the back room of her father's shop. Her father would return to the counter, and she would return to their rooms, doing for him, cooking and cleaning and mending for him. She would not have her time in the shop to tell her mother's story to gentlemen customers. She had listened as her father sighed over the story of where all the fine lords had gone. Only big old Mr. Goldsworthy was left to rattle around in the empty club. Lord Blackstone had gone with his wife into the country for the birth of their child. Captain Clare had moved into an inn on the south edge of town, and Nate Wilde had gone to live with his grand friends.

If there was one good thing that came out of the whole trouble, it was that. Nate Wilde could not come strolling through the back of the shop to tell her how wrong she'd been to love Lord Hazelwood. He could not remind her that he'd been right all along that she had set her sights too high. Nate Wilde must never know what she had done or how she felt. She would hold her head as high as ever.

She would forget fine lords with laughing eyes. There were other gentlemen in London, and she would judge better now. She opened her bag and drew out the little book, *The Husband Hunter's Guide to London*. It had failed her. She laid it on the bench for some other girl to find, a girl with better luck than Miranda Kirby.

*Dear Reader,*

*The slim blue volume with gold lettering, entitled* **The Husband Hunter's Guide to London,** *next falls into the hands of Lucy Holbrook, who is on the verge of losing her inn...*

*Read on for a preview of Kate Moore's next Husband Hunter's Guide Romance, available in summer 2017.*

*Most readers of this slim volume are, no doubt, young women whose families have made some provision for them however modest. Now we must consider two special cases from the ranks of Husband Hunters—the woman of property and the woman who possesses nothing but her shift. A woman who inherits a house, an income, or an estate may wrongly assume that she need not follow the practices outlined in this guide because she has suitors aplenty. Such thinking will be fatal to her happiness. Indeed, the woman of property must actively engage in husband hunting lest she mistake the ardor of her many suitors as desire to possess her rather than that most common of male desires—the desire to possess a pretty piece of property.*

—*The Husband Hunter's Guide to London*

The Tooth and Nail Inn
London, 1826

# Chapter One

At the crunch of carriage wheels on gravel, Lucy Holbrook stuck a last branch of golden forsythia in a black jug on the sideboard of the Tooth and Nail's only private dining room. By placing the forsythia just so, she concealed a spot where the edge of the ivy wallpaper curled away from the wall. To Lucy the inn's flaws were as dear as its comforts, but she didn't want her home to appear shabby or rustic in her friends' eyes, and worse she didn't want them to blame Papa for the inn's defects. She knew her father had meant to get to the wallpaper, and she was sure he had given her a childhood as golden as the flowers in the jug. She took a quick look around the dining room, prayed that its faults would be overlooked in the pleasure of the company, and descended to meet her guests.

The usual crowd of neighborhood men, who came for their daily pint and a smoke, had ceased their talk to gawk at the visitors on the landing as if the curtain had opened on a wonder at the St Botolph's Fair sideshow.

The ladies, for their part, took no notice of the bench sitters. The twins, Cassandra and Cordelia Fawkener, in matching dark green, fur-lined cloaks, concentrated on removing blue kid gloves and black bonnets. The sisters were used to being remarked upon from their habit of dressing in matching outfits since their come out some twenty years earlier.

Only Margaret Leach turned to Lucy with a broad smile and opened her arms. Lucy stepped without hesitation into her friend's embrace. A brief flood of memories washed over her. So many times at school when the subject of a girl's connections had arisen, Margaret had offered kindness and wisdom. Lucy had come to appreciate the distinctly feminine nature of such comfort. While he was alive, Papa had patted her shoulder and told her she would be a lady someday. And old Adam had mutely squeezed her hand when he sensed her distress. But her friend Margaret knew when to hold her. Enfolded in that familiar embrace against a silken scented bosom, Lucy felt yet unshed tears threaten. She pulled back. Tears could wait.

"Dear Lucy," Cassandra began, turning her back on the public room, "we've been so worried."

Lucy smiled at that. "Surely not, though I expect you've been eager for me to return that third volume of Mrs. Raby's romance."

"To think of you here, alone, child," Cassandra added, draping her cloak on the growing stack in her footman's arms.

"Which, you see I am not."

"Lucy," Cordelia thrust a brown paper wrapped package at her, "we've brought you a gift. You must open it."

"Don't rush the girl, Cordelia," Cassandra advised.

Lucy thanked Cordelia and took the package. "I've a private room ready for our luncheon." The ladies exchanged a glance of obvious relief as they turned their backs on the common room. As they climbed the stairs, Lucy took a moment to summon Hannah to help the footman with the cloaks, and tell him that he might make himself at home in the taproom or the stables.

In the little room that she and Hannah and Ariel had done their best to smarten up, the ladies studied the cold collation Mrs. Vell, the inn cook, had consented to serve on a Sunday. Pigeon pie, sliced tongue, pickled eggs, and a glistening apricot pudding filled the inn's best plates arranged on a clean white linen cloth with shining silver serving spoons. While the ladies filled their plates, Lucy poured glasses of a raspberry cordial she had persuaded Mrs. Vell to uncork.

"We have not put you to any trouble, I hope," Margaret said, looking up from the sideboard. Lucy saw where Margaret's glance caught a yellowing water stain like a lace fringe above the bow window.

"None," Lucy insisted, unless one counted persuading Mrs. Vell to alter her time-honored patterns. "It's a cold collation, as our cook has strong feelings about Sunday cooking."

The ladies settled themselves at the table and gingerly picked at the food.

"We've missed you at services, dear. Our little readers group is not complete without you," Margaret said. Their group called itself the Back Bench Lending Library from their habit of exchanging novels after services each week at the chapel in South Audley Street. Lucy had not joined them since her father's death a fortnight past.

"But we've brought you a book," Cordelia added, breaking off at a look from her sister. "Well, Cassandra, really, Lucy, can see without unwrapping it that it is in fact a book, and what else, pray, would we be bringing?"

Most people could not tell the fashionable dark-haired twins apart until they spoke. Then Cassandra's forcefulness of personality made one notice the sharper arch of her brows and jut of her chin. And Cordelia's eagerness to please made one conscious of the softness about her mouth and eyes.

"Nevertheless, Cordelia," Cassandra said turning to Lucy. "Before we get to the book, we must talk about your situation, dear girl."

"My *situation*?" Lucy held her fork suspended above a pickled egg. It was a careful word, a word that meant there was a problem to be dealt with, something that could be fixed or altered or improved, the way one cleaned a chimney that smoked or moved one's seat away from a draft.

The three ladies nodded in vigorous unity. Cassandra looked to the other two and clearly received some signal to proceed. "You do see that you must leave the inn."

Lucy put down her fork and slid her hand into her lap. She did not want her friends to see that hand tremble. She should not be surprised that they judged the inn as an unacceptable setting for a lady of their acquaintance.

"Yes, now that your dear father is gone," Cordelia added, "you may not stay in a common inn."

"But the inn is my home. It's where I live."

"It is what you've been accustomed to, to be sure," said Cordelia, "while your father was alive. However, a gentlewoman does not stay in a public house without a male relation on the premises and indeed without a female companion."

"Surely, my case is different, as I am now the innkeeper." Lucy watched Margaret for any sign that her dearest friend was on her side in the matter, but Margaret seemed intent on cutting a piece of tongue into the smallest possible bites. Margaret had been an instructor at Mrs. Thwayte's Seminary for Young Ladies in Hammersmith until she left to become the companion of the twins' elderly mother, Lady Eliza Fawkener. It was Margaret who had introduced Lucy to the twins and the Back Bench Lending Library group.

Cassandra pushed her untouched plate aside. "What you are, Lucy, is a woman of . . . property. You'll sell the inn of course," she announced.

"Sell the . . . inn?" Lucy had almost said *sell my home,* but she could see that her friends would be deaf to the claims of such a home with its noise and bustle, its rustic furnishings and humble hospitality.

"Once you've sold, you may convert the profits of the sale into the funds," Cassandra continued.

Lucy looked at the three solemn faces, alike in their expressions of certainty. Behind them the forsythia branch hid the wallpaper. They, too, had a plan for hiding any flaws Lucy might possess as she entered their world, such as being the daughter of a former pugilist who kept an inn.

At school, a girl named Amelia Fox had been the self-proclaimed expert on origins. "Your origins are your destiny," she would say, as she rated each girl's family ties. In Lucy's case Amelia had proclaimed that nothing could be done about her father, and it was just as well that nothing was known about Lucy's mother, because surely nothing good could be known. Now Lucy's friends invited her to shed her questionable birth forever with a simple economic transaction. As an heiress with her money in the funds, Lucy could slip into their world as if there'd never been a Papa, a Tom Holbrook, who'd once been Iron Tom in a bout against the champion. It was a tidy plan.

"Lucy, dear," Cordelia urged, "do open our gift. We found it in our pew, just where you usually sit and knew at once that it was a sign." Cordelia gave the package a shove across the table toward Lucy.

"Not yet, Cordelia," Cassandra admonished. "Everyone should eat. I recommend this pudding. You may compliment your cook, Lucy."

\* \* \* \*

Captain Harry Clare, late of the First Royal Dragoons, opened the door of the Tooth and Nail, a south London inn from which coaches and travelers set out for Dover and the continent. He let in a gust of cold March air that caused the men on two long benches to glance his way and holler greetings. He had not encouraged the familiarity, but they greeted him as if he were one of their own.

He slipped out of his wet coat and hat and tossed them on a hook by the door. He had been lodging at the inn since the debacle that closed the Pantheon Club. The club, a front for a group of handpicked spies in England's great game against her former ally, Russia, had been Harry's home for nearly a year as he and his fellow spies had tracked down enemy agents operating in London.

The club's unexpected closing had come just as Harry was about to complete his final assignment and receive the promised reward for his year and a day of service. Instead, he'd been cast out to shift for himself. He was an old hand at such shifts, having joined the army at seventeen and seen action from Spain to Waterloo. He could make a billet anywhere from a muddy mountainside to the ruins of a shelled castle. And he was a man who never failed to complete an assignment, even one as puzzling as the one he'd been assigned—to find a blind man who was the only witness to a murder.

He'd found his unlikely murder witness at the Tooth and Nail, where the old man sat on a bench near the kitchen door, doing odd bits of handwork. The man, Adam Pickersgill, was simple-minded and easily agitated. A stray bit of conversation from the bench sitters could rouse Adam to a frenzy of waving fists and shouted words until his voice failed. Harry had seen similar cases of sudden starts in men who'd been subjected to the shock of war. Getting information out of him to solve a crime would not be easy.

The old man's daily pattern revolved around Lucy Holbrook, the innkeeper's daughter. She was a distracting female. The eye wanted to follow her, all golden hair and fair skin, but Harry was generally good at ignoring distractions when he had a job to do.

Then Tom Holbrook, the innkeeper, had died. "Iron Tom" as he'd been known in his youthful days in the ring, had been buried the previous Sunday, and his golden-haired daughter had become a woman of property. The Tooth and Nail looked just as it had the week before, but its usual customers had taken to combing their hair and replacing stained waistcoats and worn jackets with Sunday finery. It was plain that, as the inn's new owner, Lucy Holbrook had become a sought-after prize. Harry was not a betting man, but he'd wager that the girl had other plans than marrying one of her neighbors.

From the entry Harry stepped down the three wide steps that led to the common room. The inn's oak wainscoting was as brown as beef and ale. Its walls were gold as mustard or onions. Its hearths were black with a century's worth of soot.

Under the old mullioned windows facing the yard were the long tables where coach passengers could get a quick meal. A slate menu read *Lamb. Pork. Beef.* A great stone inglenook fireplace divided the room between the front tables for travelers and the lowly benches where the inn's daily customers had their pints and smoked their pipes, dipping the stems in their ale.

The place was a bit of England for which the long war with France had been fought, but the men who sat on its benches knew war only as plunging or rising prices, changing governments, and distant battles that faded into history faster than the local champion's fame in the ring. They were civilians, and even after ten years of peace Harry did not know how to be one of them.

A thin layer of bluish smoke hung in the taproom air. The long-case clock ticked, the fire crackled, and outside rain clattered in the drainpipes. The regular bench-sitters slumped over their pint pots. Harry guessed the reason for their dejection—the innkeeper's golden-haired daughter was nowhere to be seen.

Will Wittering, a blacksmith with a nearby forge, called out, "Captain, come wet yer throat w' us this sad day."

Harry strolled their way, and the group shifted to make room for him on the bench.

"A bit of news for you, Captain," Will offered.

"What's that?" asked Harry. He nodded at Frank Blodget, the tapman, to draw him a pint. With the spy club closed, Harry no longer had to stick by its rule of no spirits.

"One of Sir Geoffrey Radcliffe's Rockets was stopped by a gang of highwaymen last night."

Harry took his first swallow of ale and listened as the tale poured out from several tellers. He took a moment to glance at the blind man, alone on his bench without his usual work. Queenie, the inn's orange and white cat, lay curled in Adam's lap between the big man's slack hands.

"Did the robbers get much?" he asked the bench sitters. He wondered whether he could get some sense out of the old fellow while Lucy Holbrook was away.

"That's the puzzle," said Will, shaking his head. "They only took the horses."

"Not Radcliffe's gold?" Harry knew the animals on one of Radcliffe's Rockets would hardly be prize horseflesh. Radcliffe ran the kind of coaching enterprise where profits were lean, and his drivers were the kind who drove their beasts until they died in the traces somewhere between London and Dover.

The bench sitters chuckled. Geoffrey Radcliffe had been knighted for loaning staggering sums to King George when the latter was a mere prince.

The bench sitters shook their heads. "A gang, they were," Will added. "Spoke some gibberish."

"Coulda been gypsies," suggested another bench sitter.

Harry ventured a glance at the blind man. It was a rare moment when Lucy Holbrook left the old man alone. Adam Pickersgill had been Harry's objective for weeks, but finding him had only deepened the mystery. Adam was tall and gaunt with a shock of white hair above a linen band that circled his head covering his sightless eyes. Harry guessed his age to be near eighty and credited Lucy with keeping the old man clean and combed and neatly dressed.

Most days Adam sat on his bench with his brushes and blacking or a pile of silver and a pot of polish. The bench sitters knew little about him and cared less. Most of them simply considered the old man a fixture at the inn. He'd been there next to Lucy Holbrook as long as anyone remembered. Sheepishly, John Simkins, a merchant who sold water flasks, had confessed that as boys they had teased Adam and tried to provoke him whenever Lucy had led him out of the inn for a bit of sun and air. How the girl had come to be responsible for the old man no one knew.

Harry turned back to the bench sitters who were talking about roads and robberies and boasting that any one of them would have been a better match for the highwaymen than the coachman had been. It was pot valiant talk, the kind Harry had heard from raw recruits on the night before battle. As the talk grew louder and bolder, the bench sitters glanced often at the door of the inn's private dining room. Harry suspected that at least three of them were working up the courage to solicit Lucy's hand in marriage.

"Where's Lucy?" he asked when talk of the robbery lapsed.

All the heads nodded at the door on the other side of the entry, and Will spoke for the group. "Preparing a luncheon for her lady friends."

Will wiped the foam from his lip. "Here's a puzzle for you, Captain," he said. "Why did Sir Geoffrey send his gold to Hell?"

Will, a fair-haired giant of man, was the wit of the group, and his companions waited for the punch line.

Harry shrugged.

"So he'll have some when he gets there," Will said. The bench sitters laughed and slapped their thighs.

"Geoffrey ran away." Adam Pickersgill's deep voice boomed out from his corner, stilling the laughter. The men drew on their pipes. Harry nodded to them and turned to the old man.

"Geoffrey ran away," the old man repeated. His body shook the bench under him.

Harry crossed the room and put a steadying hand on the old man's shoulder, motioning Frank at the tap for a pint of small beer. When it arrived, Harry lifted the old man's big square hand and closed it around the pewter cup as he'd seen Lucy do.

Adam drank his beer in long drafts that left a foam moustache above his upper lip. He banged his cup down on the table, spilling ale. "Adam must not go. Adam must stay."

Queenie shifted her position in the old man's lap and jumped down to arch against Harry's booted calf. He leaned down to stroke the creature's head.

Adam stilled and cocked his head to the side. "You like cats very much."

"I do," Harry agreed. The old man might be blind, but he was good at detecting a person's presence and recognizing people even without their speaking. If Harry could get Adam talking, he might eventually say something useful about the case. Harry suspected that Adam's odd declarations were part of a coherent story, fragments of a narrative in which one man ran away while another stood his ground, perhaps in the face of murder.

"Geoffrey ran away," Adam repeated, this time in the volume of ordinary conversation.

Harry gave Adam's shoulder a friendly squeeze. "How's the ale today, Adam?"

Adam's face crinkled into dozens of lines around the strip of unbleached linen. He reached out his hand for Harry's and gave it two long energetic pumps, like a man working a tap handle. "Tooth and Nail ale very good. You like yer ale very dark, like coffee."

"That I do, Adam."

From the benches came another mention of the robbery of Sir Geoffrey's Rocket passenger coach. Adam stirred, his gnarled hands pulling at the cloth over his knees. Harry sat down beside him, and Queenie leapt up into Harry's lap. He stroked the cat's fur and considered how to get the truth out of the old man's muddled brain.

* * * *

The scrape of spoons against dishes sounded loud in Lucy's ears, and she realized that the conversation had died. She had no idea what her friends had been talking about the past half hour.

"Lucy, child," Margaret broke the silence. "We really can't bear to think of you here alone, so far from friends."

Lucy held her tongue. *Alone?* She wanted to laugh at the notion. When was an innkeeper ever alone?

"A suitable place must be found to be sure, and we will help you." Cassandra spoke as if the matter had been decided over plates of pudding. "But you must quit the inn as soon as possible. Within a fortnight, at the latest."

"Sell within a fortnight? Is it possible?" She was not ready. Her future as a lady had seemed quite distant only a few weeks ago.

"Of course you will not handle the sale yourself," said Cassandra. "We will recommend a solicitor to make sure the inn's assets are properly valued. With the right help, you'll be ready to begin your London Season in days."

Her friends had worked out a solution to her situation. But a dead father was not a situation. The Tooth and Nail was not a situation. And Adam was not a situation. She did not know how she could begin to explain Adam to her friends, but there were things that could not be sold with tables and chairs, plate and silver, and stables and outbuildings. Even if one could sell everything one owned, one could not really sell one's past.

Margaret rose and came around the table to take Lucy by the hands, pull her from her chair, and fold her in another embrace. "Dear child, your future has arrived in a way none of us expected. Nevertheless, it has arrived, and your father, himself, would want you to seek the best position for yourself in the world."

Lucy let herself be held. There was no denying that her father had wanted her to be a lady. When she was twelve, he had given her a painting of just the sort of lady she was meant to be. It hung in her room above the small hearth. Then he had sent her to Mrs. Thwaytes' school, and when she had finished there, he had insisted that she spend Sundays with these very friends to grow accustomed to talk and manners quite different from those of the inn. Now, unexpectedly, the moment had arrived for her to step into the life for which he had prepared her, she simply had never imagined that she would step into that life without him.

Cordelia stood and once more offered Lucy the brown paper package. "Do open it, dear."

Lucy stepped back from Margaret's hold and tugged loose the string, unfolding the brown paper. A small blue book with gold lettering appeared— *The Husband Hunter's Guide to London.* She looked up into three bright smiles of encouragement. A hiccup of laughter caught her by surprise. A month ago, two weeks ago, she would have devoured the little book eagerly, ready to learn its lessons. Now she understood that its lessons would be lessons in detaching herself from home. She wanted to toss the little book out the window and let the rain wash it away.

"You'll be brilliant, dear. We can't wait to help you enjoy a wonderful Season and a triumphant one," said Cassandra.

Lucy clasped the book hard lest she act on her first impulse. Her friends wanted the best for her even if they did not know what they asked in return—to detach herself from all that was known and loved. To adopt the ways she'd been learning in South Audley Street and to leave the ways of home behind.

A startling crash from the taproom interrupted her thoughts, followed by a man's anguished voice crying, "No, No, No."

The ladies started and looked confused. "What is that dreadful noise?" asked Cassandra.

The pained cry sounded again, louder still, full of terrible distress.

"Adam," Lucy cried. "I must go to him." She thrust the little book into Cordelia's hands and dashed for the door.

# ABOUT THE AUTHOR

**Kate Moore** is a former English teacher and three time RITA finalist, Golden Heart, and Book Buyers Best Award winner. She writes Austen inspired fiction set in nineteenth-century England or contemporary California. Her heroes are men of courage, competence, and unmistakable virility, with determination so strong it keeps their sensuality in check until they meet the right woman. Her heroines take on the world with practical good sense and kindness to bring those heroes into a circle of love and family. Sometimes there's even a dog. Kate lives north of San Francisco with her surfer husband, their yellow Lab, a Pack 'n Play for visiting grandbabies, and miles of crowded bookshelves. Kate's family and friends offer endless support and humor. Her children are her best works, and her husband is her favorite hero. Visit Kate at Facebook.com/KateMooreAuthor or contact her at kate@katemoore.com.

Printed in the United States
by Baker & Taylor Publisher Services